PRAISE FOR JE

CW01509190

"*Our Gifted Hearts* is a beaut
about grief and self-forgiveness, breathing new life and a
feminist perspective to this classic horror tale."
Sunyi Dean, author of *The Book Eaters*

"A gloriously gothic tale, yet *Our Gifted Hearts* still managed to
surprise me. Creepy, mysterious and magical. I devoured it!"
Jodie Robins, author of *The Off-Season*

"In the best gothic fairy tale tradition, Kennedy's *Our Gifted
Hearts* offers readers a sumptuous retelling, with feisty
heroine, Fortune, so much more than Bluebeard's latest
wife (and his mother is something else!) The mysteries run
dark and deep. Intriguing and compelling."
Megan Taylor, author of *The Therapist's Daughter*
and *We Wait*

"The slow, quiet horror of *Our Gifted Hearts* is so tense you'll
need to hide this book in the freezer to catch your breath
(and then get it straight out again to discover what happens
next). Beautifully written and powerfully compelling."
Dan Hanks, author of
Swashbucklers and *The Way Up is Death*

"Compulsively readable, romantic, and filled with fun and
familiar tropes of the genre, *Our Gifted Hearts* is a classic
gothic novel that nonetheless manages to offer something
new due to its witchy touch."
Johanna Van Veen, author of *Blood on Her Tongue*

Jennifer Kennedy

OUR GIFTED HEARTS

ANGRY
ROBOT

ANGRY ROBOT
An imprint of Watkins Media Ltd

Unit 11, Shepperton House
89-93 Shepperton Road
London N1 3DF
UK

angryrobotbooks.com
Beware the kindess of strangers

An Angry Robot paperback original, 2025

Edited by Dan Hanks and Dan Coxon
Cover by Glen Wilkins
Set in Meridien

ISBN 978 1 83673 019 4
Ebook ISBN 978 1 83673 020 0

Printed and bound in the United Kingdom by CPI Group (UK) Ltd, Croydon
CR0 4YY

The manufacturer's authorised representative in the EU for product safety is
eucomply OÜ - Pärnu mnt 139b-14, 11317 Tallinn, Estonia,
hello@eucompliancepartner.com; www.eucompliancepartner.com

9 8 7 6 5 4 3 2 1

For My Family

PROLOGUE

The woods offered protection. A blanket of leaves to smother the sound of the groaning, growling girl. It is midnight, the Devil's hour, as the girl pushes her secret child into the world.

The night holds its breath, the woodland animals hide and shiver in their burrows, pulling their babies close into their fur. The cries of the girl are feral, heart-breaking, bone-shattering. Only the birds gather about her. They rest on the ground, surround her at the base of the huge oak where she writhes. They watch from its old branches, their small black eyes glinting in the moonlight. They are silent and still, not a ruffle of feather or crick of the neck. Birds of all shapes and sizes. Owls next to thrushes, crows with sparrows, larks with nightingales. They gather to bear witness.

A cry that reaches further into the woods than the others puts an end to the struggle. All is silent now. The girl's breath is shallow and she is tired, so tired. But the silence is wrong. There should be noise. There should be the sound of a baby crying.

She heaves herself up to look at the babe on the mossy ground. She wipes the silent child clean with a rag. It is perfect. A button nose the size of her fingernail. A tiny plump chin beneath sweet, heart-shaped lips. Black hair sticks to the soft scalp. A fold of flesh at each wrist separates pudgy arms from tiny hands. Eyelashes form black crescent moons on smooth cheeks.

The lips are blue and the skin has the dull shine of bone china. It is a perfectly formed, intricate shell, the inhabitant of which has moved on. It is a blessing, but not from God.

The girl forces herself to action. Just one final task and she can go home and sleep. She gathers large stones and small stones, anything that will give weight. She lays the stones on a blanket and gently places the child on top. She ties the four corners into a tight knot.

She has witnessed a similar thing once before, when Farmer Fredrick drowned a sack of kittens. But that sack squirmed and meowed. This one was still, heavy with the weight of sadness. It is a blessing, she reminds herself. She carries the sack the few steps to the lake which opens up at the centre of the woods like a gaping mouth, ready to swallow all it is offered.

The moon is heavy and full. The lake is black glass, reflecting the upper world in perfect clarity. The babe will be safe in her upside-down world. She will know nothing of the cruelty of man.

The girl walks into the water. She keeps going until it covers her breasts. For a moment she considers following her child into the underworld. But she is afraid. She is cowardly. She lets go of the sack. She rubs her dress against herself, cleaning the blood and debris of childbirth from her most intimate parts. The pain is a sickening throb, but the water is soothing.

It is there, in the water, with the moonlight bathing her face and her child dead in a bundle, that the girl feels something more than physical pain. It is the sprouting of a dark seed of doubt, of anger, of hate. She mutters under her breath. A vow. "I will never let another man touch me. I will never marry. I will never bear another child," she mutters over and over. She stares at the water that has swallowed her babe. "If there truly is an underworld with a Devil ruling over, you may claim me as your own."

The water ripples in response. The night sighs.

She drags herself out of the lake and into the woods. She is tired. So tired she fears she might not reach home. Her eyes droop.

There is movement between the trees. It pulls her back to wakefulness. Something flits and starts, disappearing and reappearing. It isn't human. No human can move that fast or that deftly. The birds do not scatter. They still sit silent, filling the trees, lining her path. They are watching this scene play out. It isn't over yet.

The girl staggers onward. She is done with this night, does not have the strength for games. She wants to sleep.

Her skirts are heavy with water, they slap against her ankles and cling to her thighs. She pushes forward. Her knees buckle and she falls to the ground.

There is the movement again. Darting from tree to tree like a child playing hide and seek. The girl groans. She is so tired.

It ends the game and steps out, blocking the pathway ahead. It is a creature not of this world. The body is that of a man, but the head of a giant eagle rests on its shoulders. Ram's horns, large and powerful, jut skyward from its crown. Its long, hooked beak, sharp as a blade, shines in the moonlight. Its eyes are the colour of fire.

In silence, it glides through the veil of night towards her. She lifts her face to it. It reaches out a long, crooked finger.

The nail is cracked and mottled in decaying shades of orange and black.

I accept.

The voice comes from inside the eagle's head and the trees around her and the pungent woodland air, and deep down in the depths of her heart which has shrivelled to a blackened prune. The creature pushes the rotten nail into her forehead, scratching her skull. More pain.

She is done. Her eyes droop and she welcomes the end.

Go away, the girl thinks, *whatever you are, leave me to die in peace.*

CHAPTER ONE

Sparrows lined the rooftops that enclosed the town square. They never missed a market day. People were messy. They'd leave breadcrumbs and bits of pastry like a trail behind them as they did their morning shopping and ate breakfast while they walked. Some of the younger boys, sent out by their mothers or the cooks they worked for, would shove food in their mouths so fast that half of it would be lost down their fronts. And the sparrows were there to clean it all up. It was their favourite game. Sometimes a thoughtful person would deliberately scatter a handful of seeds or crushed burned bread, just to watch the sparrows swoop in and fight for a morsel. It was a sight. A delight for the children, and myself. The rush and noise of the marketplace agitated me, but Ma and I had to eat, and to do that I sold my eggs. The sparrows were a distraction.

I counted the remaining eggs in the pushcart. Only two dozen left. I had yet to eat my own breakfast and could hardly bear the smell of the bakery any longer. The market was slowing now, anyway. Stalls were casually being packed away. I'd made all I needed, and more, to shop for myself and Ma. It was time to go home.

I picked up my small stool and placed it in the cart, careful to not break any eggs.

"Are you sold out?"

Mr Quickly appeared before me. His large, dark frame looked out of place in the fresh March morning. His clothes were out of place too, the crisp lining of his plum jacket and feathered hat were far too smart to be stood before my pushcart.

"Almost," I said, straightening myself.

"I'll take a dozen."

"Mr Quickly, you have no need of a dozen eggs at the inn."

"Mrs Healy uses eggs from three extremely impoverished chickens in her yard, and I know that yours are the best."

"I'm not sure Mrs Healy would appreciate the insult."

"It won't be an insult. I'll say I was gifted them by a dear friend and she will be obliged to cook them for me. It will give her aged chickens a few days off. Everyone is happy." It was strange hearing Mr Quickly talk about chickens. He was usually quite formal, but today he had a lightness to him.

A dear friend, he had called me. It was surprising how the world could stay stagnant for such a long time and then a stranger arrives and throws it off kilter.

"Very well," I laughed, and held out my hand for payment. My smile stopped short when I noticed Mrs Daly talking to the butcher across the square. They were looking my way and whispering conspiratorially to one another.

It *was* something to talk about, a wealthy man like Mr Quickly making conversation with a woman like me. If they only knew that he had dined with myself and Ma on a few occasions these past months. But he was leaving soon, his business took him all over the world. It pained me to realise that I was sad to see him go, but secretly thanked providence that he was. Nothing good would come from this unlikely connection. Not for me.

He took the eggs and tipped his hat with a smile. "I'll see you very soon." I watched him leave. His large frame did not weaken his gait. He moved gracefully, as if the town and the people and myself had been put there purely for his entertainment, and he found it all enchanting.

"You got your eye on him, girl?" Mrs Daly couldn't hold her own water. She had begun shuffling over as soon as Mr Quickly left.

"I don't know what you mean," I said, hoping to sound aloof, but the words sounded childish.

Mrs Daly winked. "You can't fool me, girl. Mind you, I do feel bad for ya, ain't no way a man of his stature would marry so low." She sniffed and considered the retreating man.

"Thank you, Mrs Daly, for the wise words."

"He does seem to favour you, though."

"I think he just likes Ma's pottage."

"Tasted your ma's pottage, has he?" Mrs Daly turned her attention back to me, eyebrows raised. I flustered.

"He came to collect some embroidery."

"How is your ma?"

"She's good. Her leg troubles her some." I took the handles of the pushcart, readying to leave.

"Well, tell her I was askin'."

Mrs Daly would be spreading the gossip of Mr Quickly dining with us as soon as I turned my back. At least there couldn't be much in it, as he was leaving soon and would be forgotten. I hoped I would forget him as easily as the rest of the town, but he'd worked his way under my skin these past few months and a soft spot had formed without my knowing. It was only now, close to his departure, that I experienced a twinge of regret at his leaving, as if a tiny gap had opened in my bricked-up heart. I would seal it off again shortly. That life was not meant for me.

"Oh ay, while I remember. Could you get me a couple of doves? My youngest is getting married the week before Easter."

"I'll see what I can do."

"Thanks dear."

I made my way to the bakery before heading home. My appetite had waned somewhat, but Ma would appreciate some pastries.

A pair of young thrushes busied about me as I walked the woodland path home. It was quiet. The marketplace forgotten. I breathed a little deeper; the scent of soil and sweet chestnut relaxed my muscles and cleared my mind. The birds flitted about, chirping as they transformed from their smooth silhouettes to a blur of beating wings, like tiny perfect storms, over and over. One would land on my shoulder, the other would join it. The first would flit to the ground and the other would follow, then to the cart. A game of tag.

People don't give birds much thought, unless they're scaring them away from their plots for eating their seeds or hunting them for food. But birds are playful, intelligent creatures. Sensitive too.

A slight breeze ruffled the tops of the trees, never reaching the ground. The woods were my safe house. I was as content here as if I was sitting in the inglenook, toasting my toes before the fire. A kaleidoscope of sun rays broke through the canopy, speckling the ground with dots of light, encouraging the undergrowth to bloom once more.

The peace was disturbed with the sound of a carriage approaching. The birds fled back to the trees. I moved to the side of the path to allow it to pass safely. Just as it reached me, the nearest wheel dipped into a ditch that still held water from last night's rain. My skirt was soaked. The carriage rocked wildly, and for a moment I thought I would be crushed before it righted itself. The driver pulled the carriage to a halt and jumped down to fill in the ditch with some dirt. "You right?" he asked.

"I'm alright," I said, shaking my dress free of the water.

"What's happening?" A lady's voice echoed from inside the carriage. The window was pulled down and a head appeared: red curls and a preposterous bonnet. Amber Divine. I tried to move out of her eye line, but it was too late, she had seen me.

"Fortune! Just the person." She opened the door and the driver rushed back to help her out with the step. Her dress was a billowing yellow, so wide it had to force its way through the door frame, and so bright it appeared garish in the green and brown setting. I busied myself brushing the muddy stains from my skirt, wishing the ground would swallow her up before she reached me. But there's no escaping Amber. Her hair glowed in the speckled sunlight, adding to the cacophony of clashing colours. Her pregnant stomach protruded out so far in front of her that I was surprised she could move at all. I tried not to look at it. I tried not to think about the father.

"Fortune, are you hurt?" she said, her face an exaggerated gesture of concern.

"No." I waved away her comment.

"I'm so glad we bumped into each other, there was something I wanted to…" She paused as I aggressively hit at my skirt, where a beetle was crawling across a new patch of mud. "It's the gloves, you see," she continued, ignoring my bad manners, "they're still not quite right."

"What's wrong with them?"

"I'd like some bees sitting on top of the flowers. Wouldn't that be perfect? I saw Lady Harrison wearing a pair."

It must have been from a distance, I thought, as Amber Divine was not a lady, no matter how much she wished it.

"Could your ma change them for me? I'll have someone drop them off tomorrow. Then they'll be ready for after my lying-in." She placed her hand on top of her stomach. "But I'm planning on it being quick, so don't dawdle," she laughed.

I looked away, refusing to take part in her baby hysteria.

"Oh, have you been to market? Do you have any eggs left?"

"A dozen," I said.

"I'll take them. Yours are the best. Gerry," she called to the driver, "could you give these eggs to Cook, please?"

I handed the eggs to the driver and Amber held out some coins. "That's too much," I said.

"I insist. Take it." I took it. If Amber wanted to throw her money about then it's better in my purse.

"So, will you be attending tomorrow?" Her tone became conspiratorial.

I held back a sigh. I wasn't looking forward to the next day.

"Old Rita being a witch comes as no surprise to me," she said. "I've said for years that she should be banished from the community."

If you scratched away Amber's skin, I was certain you would find a pile of writhing worms beneath. We both remembered Amber going to Rita for a love potion only a few years earlier, but the woman had turned her away with a warning and a look of distain. Amber was mortified. But as it turned out, she didn't need the potion. Charles went to her willingly, after casting me aside like a bloody rag.

"I don't know, Ma's leg is bad, and..." I trailed off, unable to think of any excuses.

"Oh, you must attend." Amber's eyes were wide with excitement. "It is our duty to ensure the Devil is cast out."

A man's voice called from inside the carriage then. At first, I thought it was the driver, but he wouldn't dare interrupt Amber. My stomach flipped. Charles was with her! Suddenly he was on the path and the world tilted. My body lost its fixed point. I was outside of myself, looking at the three of us, wondering what I should do next. But there was nothing to do except endure.

There was a flicker, barely perceptible, of pure horror on his face when he saw me, but he seamlessly masked it with a smile.

"What a nice surprise. Good to see you, Fortune."

Charles' smooth transition to charming husband was commendable. His fake enthusiasm for me made Amber bristle. Although she didn't know the extent of the relationship Charles and I had had, she knew enough to be uncomfortable with us together.

With each step he took towards me the air grew thinner and clouded my mind with fog. He had grown a little thicker around the neck and shoulders, his eyes had developed some lines about them, but it was still Charles. The same hair I had run my fingers through, the same mouth I had kissed, the same hands that had held me. For a short while. Now all I saw was betrayal. The attributes that had once pulled me in, repulsed me. Long gone were the days when I grew hot with lust for him; now I burned with anger. After all these years it was disturbing how much I still hated him.

I tried to disguise my pain and rising bile with outward mild indifference, nodding my head in response.

"What's all this about the Devil, then?"

"I was just asking Fortune if she would be attending the hanging tomorrow."

"Ah yes, terrible thing, that. Witches in the community. Who would have thought it in this quiet place? We don't take well to scandal here, do we?" The question was rhetorical, but it was also a threat. The audacity! He didn't have to remind me to be silent. I'd never spoken of it to anyone, not even Ma.

"How are you and your mother, Fortune?" he said, changing the subject.

"Well, thank you." I gritted my teeth.

He gave a perfunctory nod, satisfied he'd completed the pleasantries, and then took Amber's arm, willing her to leave. "Dearest, we best get you home, before you give birth right here on the forest floor. In front of all these birds." He waved his hand, gesturing at the trees next to us.

I looked up and there were indeed birds all over the branches in the trees. They were also on the ground, between the trees, hopping towards me. There we were talking about witchcraft, and the birds were acting out of character. I hadn't been paying attention.

Excessive emotion seemed to draw them to me.

"Oh Charles, you are silly, it will be a few weeks yet." Amber took her husband's arm and walked back to the carriage. Her head held high, like she had won a prize. I pitied her.

"I'll send the gloves tomorrow," she called, and then stopped mid-step as she climbed into the carriage, titling her head to look back at me. "You always did have a way with the birds, Fortune. It's quite remarkable." Her features suggested she thought this more puzzling than remarkable.

Then they were gone, and I could breathe. I looked down and the pair of young thrushes had returned, sitting huddled at my feet as if they could protect me.

CHAPTER TWO

The rest of the day was unsettled. Ma was up and down, unable to concentrate, then threw herself into making enough stew to feed ten people. Caesar flew across the room every time Ma moved. He flittered back and forth between the cross beam and the mantle. Back and forth. It was very distracting.

"What's going on with you?" I asked Ma.

Caesar chirped and flew the short distance back to the beam. A blur of yellow and blue.

"Nothing. I'm cooking supper." Ma didn't look at me.

"Do you imagine we've grown extra mouths? Why are you cooking so much?"

"No reason. I felt like cooking. It's not a crime." Ma glanced at the window.

"Ma!" I snapped. "What are you not telling me?"

She continued to fuss about the kitchen.

"There was no point telling you, you'd only complain. No one will marry a woman who complains all the time, you know."

Not this again! I really thought Ma had begun to reconcile herself to the fact that I would never marry. She'd been quiet on the subject of late, and now I was beginning to understand why. She had a plan.

"Ma! Who's coming?" But I knew exactly who was coming. *I'll see you very soon*, he'd said.

"Oh, hush will you! There's nothing to worry about, it's only that kind Mr Quickly. He's leaving soon. I'm only being neighbourly."

"And does Mr Quickly know your intentions?" I glared at her.

"What intentions? I'm offering a kind man some company for his supper."

"I know exactly what you're offering and I'm not for sale."

"You make it sound so terrible. What's wrong with wanting to see my daughter with a husband? You're much better looking than that Amber. There's no reason why you can't get yourself a husband."

I knew it had been a mistake to tell Ma about running into Amber and her pregnant belly.

"And be saddled with a man to rule over me, and my belly always growing?"

"I don't see what's wrong with that." Ma laid the table and I stood close behind her, hoping she could feel my wrath. Ma was like a dog with a bone, she'd never give up on this until I was old and grey. At the centre of the table a pot of daffodils bloomed a glorious yellow. I should have guessed we were having company. They reminded me of Amber's dress. I resisted the urge to chop off the pretty daffodil heads and stamp on them.

"Why must you be so stubborn? Men aren't the Devil."

"I disagree," I muttered to myself, but Ma heard me and let out a frustrated sigh through her nose. We'd had this conversation many times before, but Ma had never had such an opportunity to see me wed as she did with Mr Quickly.

He was her last hope for me. I was approaching twenty-six. How many opportunities would come along after this? Ma would not let this pass by easily. It didn't matter how much I professed my happiness as a spinster, Ma didn't listen. The more I protested, the more determined she became.

A knock at the door made us both jump.

"Be good," Ma whispered, "for me."

I was sorry for Ma, having me as a daughter. She'd be forever disappointed.

Ma let Mr Quickly in, full of compliments and gratitude at him having accepted her invitation. His large frame filled our small sitting room. His dark hair was tied at the neck with a blue ribbon. He'd made a special effort for tonight. My stomach tightened. The fire reflected in his deep-set eyes, animal-like and black as a night, but not unattractive. They flickered and shifted as he moved, as if they were the gateways to the underworld. They sucked in the light from the room. They made me question myself and my convictions.

Caesar flew from the mantle straight to Mr Quickly's shoulder. He nipped at his hair.

Mr Quickly laughed.

"Caesar!" I scooped him up. "My apologies, he's not usually so affectionate," I laughed.

"He must be getting used to me," Mr Quickly said.

He took control of the conversation over supper, talking mostly of his travels. He was a collector of antiques and his work took him to distant lands. Ma was captivated as always by the stories and by Mr Quickly himself, who showed nothing but grace and humility in light of all his achievements. I observed him. His movements were delicate and precise, his voice deep and soothing. Soporific.

Enchanting. Perhaps there were *some* good men in the world.

He was older than me by fifteen years at least, but the lines on his face were few and added depth of character. I imagined how he might have gained each line on a different adventure. Battle scars. He was from a different world, the only thing we had in common was the air we were breathing. He broke a crust of bread, and I imagined those large hands touching me. I froze, horrified with myself. I needed him to be gone, this charade had continued long enough. Marriage was not for me, and I was sure Mr Quickly had ideas of his own about the kind of woman he would wed. Why Ma had even entertained the notion that this wealthy businessman would marry so low was beyond me. And why she didn't listen when I told her what *I* wanted was frustrating.

"Are you well?" It took a moment to realise Mr Quickly was talking to me.

Ma glared at me, sensing the change in atmosphere.

"You do look a little pale," Ma said. "Perhaps Mr Quickly would be so kind as to take a walk around the cottage with you, get some fresh air."

"I'm perfectly well," I said.

"It would be my pleasure." Mr Quickly politely ignored my protestation. Something about the soft hue of his voice cooled the angst in my belly. A walk might be good.

Outside was better. We walked in silence around the cottage. I threw some seeds into the chicken coop and stopped for a moment, watching them happily take the feed. We continued to the rickety old bench at the back of the cottage and took a seat. The sun was setting over the woods, streaking the treetops with gold. Sometimes Ma and I would sit and watch the sunset here. But he was not Ma, and his wide frame took up much of the bench. He was too close, and we were alone. What had I been thinking? I could murder Ma.

"This is a beautiful spot. I can see why you and your mother like it here. Do you like the woods?"

"They are pleasant enough." My hand instinctively slipped inside my pocket to feel the little bundle of sticks and leaves wound with a strip of twine into the shape of a human.

"There are woods where I live, too."

"Oh yes? You've told much about foreign lands but little about your home."

"It's way down south, beyond the mainland. Mine is one of a cluster of islands at the end of the world. The summers are warmer, the winters are milder. And the birds are plenty."

"There are lots of birds?"

"So many. Birds you've never seen before. They live on the cliffs and in the woods. You would like it there, I think."

I could hear the birds calling from my woods, singing their bedtime songs. I could always hear them. Occasionally one broke free from the trees, soaking up the last of the light, before disappearing beneath the canopy again.

"Caesar is a charming little creature," he said.

"He is stupid as clay," I said, and to my surprise Mr Quickly laughed, "but I do like having him around."

"Maybe you could come and see the birds on my island." He cleared his throat and I held my breath. "I'm leaving tomorrow." He paused again, allowing the importance of the moment to marinate. "I was hoping you might consider leaving with me? As my wife."

There. He had said it. I could feel his eyes on me but I

daren't glance towards him, focusing firmly on the view before us instead. "It's not the easiest life," he continued. "My island is very isolated and I'm away often. It would take a woman of strong character to make her life there."

He was flattering me. A lonely island full of birds sounded like a dream. Eventually, I turned to him. "I am very grateful for the offer, Mr Quickly, I truly am. If things were different, I may have accepted, but as things are I must decline."

He nodded his head. "You love another?"

"No, it's not that." I looked to the woods. I wanted to run to them now, but civility stopped me.

"But you have loved."

"Once," I said. "Long in the past, but it made its mark." I could hardly believe I was admitting this. Mr Quickly had a knack of disarming me. "But" – I shook my head, returning to my senses – "none of that matters now. I wish you well on your journey, and I am glad that we are friends."

"Me too," he said, smiling. He stood first and offered his hand to help me up. We walked back in a comfortable silence. It was done. He took the rejection with grace.

I stood before the cottage door and watched Mr Quickly walk back towards town.

There was something stirring in the blackened recesses of my shrunken heart. Perhaps all men were not devils, perhaps some of them were mild, with kind hearts and good intentions. Mr Quickly had been a gentleman, there was no doubt, but I knew all a union would bring was pain and suffering. It wouldn't be fair to him, or me, or Ma to accept and give false hope. At least, that is what I had always believed, but watching this man walk away now set wings flapping in my stomach. Had I made the right choice? It had been ten years since I lost her. What if something terrible wasn't to happen? What if I could live a life?

I held the poppet in my pocket. My heart and my hope lay at the bottom of the lake beside a shell wrapped in a rag, and there it would remain. Time could not change the consequences of my actions. I went inside to break the news to Ma.

"Well?" said Ma, barely containing her excitement.

"Well, what?"

"What happened when you walked out?"

"Nothing much." I poked at the fire to stir the heat and light that Mr Quickly had taken with him back into the room.

"You are keeping something from me," Ma said. She couldn't keep still. "Did he ask you anything?"

I couldn't let her suffer any longer. "I said no, Ma."

"What? Why?" She was crestfallen.

"Oh Ma, please. Why would a man, a gentleman, be wanting a wife so low as me? It doesn't make sense. And I've made it very clear I'm not going to marry. I've told you time and time again."

"So what? You're going to stay here and breed chickens and sell eggs forever?"

"Yes. I like doing that."

Her face hardened.

"You can be such a fool. And as for Mr Quickly wanting a wife like you, it is because he is wise. Some men know a good thing when they see it, not like the cads about here."

I slumped in the chair, ready for the day to be over.

Ma sidled over to me and stroked my hair, trying a new tactic. "You've always had a beautiful face, if only you'd frame it better." She pulled at my shortened locks. "You know, you try to make yourself unappealing with your short hair and dull clothes, but nothing can hide that beautiful face."

"Oh Ma," I sighed, brushing her off but offering a half-smile. What worry I caused her. But there was no choice, it was the lesser of two evils.

I held my hand out for Caesar, who obliged me by coming to rest on it. I tickled his blue crown and rubbed my nose into his tiny neck. He smelled of the woods.

"I'm sure you'll see him again tomorrow."

"Why?"

"The hanging. Have you forgotten?"

For a moment I had.

"I think I should go," Ma said.

She was no longer giddy, imagining the events to come. She removed her apron and coif, sat down and pulled the pins from her hair.

"You don't have to go, Ma."

"But people might talk."

"They won't. I'll think of something if anyone asks."

Ma nodded. "You're a good daughter. You would make a very good wife."

"Stop it."

Later that night, Ma snored softly beside me, but I couldn't sleep. The events of the day had been too much, what with bumping into Charles and Mr Quickly's proposal.

Tomorrow would be just as unusual. Frightening, even. I wasn't looking forward to it.

I slipped out of bed, making sure I tucked the covers about Ma so she didn't miss me, and headed out into the night. I went to the place that constantly called to me: the lake in the woods. I knew every step, every root that could trip me up, every burrow, every tree, and every bird that nested in them. I didn't have to think, my feet led me there without instruction, even in darkness. The night cloaked the woods in an ethereal blanket. The skitter of creatures didn't concern or scare me, they comforted me. Their lives proceeded unhindered by the outside world, unruffled by the expectations of others.

When I reached the edge of the water, I pulled the bundle of twigs from my pocket. My poppet, my reminder. The moon was full, as it had been on that terrible night ten years before, but now it sat further away. There was nothing of interest to hold the gaze of the goddess tonight.

I tugged a strand of hair from my head and wrapped it around the little doll.

Down there, in the depths of the still water, lay my lost baby. I imagined her flipping a mermaid tail in greeting to me. I knelt down and dipped my fingers in. It was icy cold, and images of my playful mermaid baby were dashed, replaced by ones that haunted me in my nightmares. The reality of what she must look like after all this time.

That was why Mr Quickly would be best to turn his attention elsewhere.

On that night, in my weakened state, where thoughts of anger and hate and sorrow and pain were amplified, and the bright light of day was so far away I feared I would never see it again; in that suffocating darkness, I signed a diabolical contract. There was no escaping it.

The birds had gathered while I sat immersed in the dreadful memory. They huddled around me, sensing my sorrow, covering the ground about me in a sea of feathers. They watched from branches, their small black eyes glinting in the moonlight. Silent and still, just as they had been that night long ago.

I looked to the moon as if her ambient glow could offer me some guidance. The birds lifted off; a great swell circled the air above me. A cacophony of beating wings rushed the air. I watched in awe, wishing, as ever, that I could fly with them. I raised my arms and closed my eyes, imagining myself circling the lake, my wings beating, feathers fanning.

A snapping sound broke my attention. A twig, a branch, a root. I wasn't sure. I dropped my arms. The birds came in to land.

I was sure the noise had been made by something other than a badger or fox. Something bigger, that tread heavily. Like a man. I held my breath, waiting to hear the sound of running feet. Something was watching me, steady and still in the darkness. Man or beast? I waited for the scrape of horns on bark, or the glint of red eyes. There was nothing there but a lingering sense of dread.

CHAPTER THREE

The birds were fretting. They had gathered on the rooftops to watch the show. Thrushes, pigeons, rooks and jays shuffled their feet and shook their feathers. An occasional cry or caw escaped them, echoing in the muffled hush. In the middle of the town square, gallows had been erected for the hanging.

People packed the square, corner to corner. There was no hustle and bustle of a usual Saturday afternoon; instead, people shifted on their feet, fidgeted with purses and belts, glanced at each other with nervous anticipation or unashamed glee. The doors of the town hall would open any moment, and *the witch* would be brought before us.

Man, woman and beast had fallen under the spell of a piece of looped rope, hanging as still as stone at the front of the square.

It had rained heavily all morning, the kind that bounces off the ground and washes the town clean. It had stopped by the late afternoon, giving us a clear window to watch these events play out, but the clouds still hung heavy above the congregation, threatening a fresh torrent.

I had arrived early, claiming a clear view of the gallows from the front of the crowd. I was glad Ma stayed home. There was something about being a part of this that made my skin itch. We would all have blood on our hands for watching Old Rita hang, and I had enough on mine already.

There was no sign of Amber and Charles. So much for duty. But towards the back of the crowd, I spotted a blue feather plume. Mr Quickly was there. His eyes met mine for a moment and he dipped his hat in acknowledgement, but I looked away, flustered by his presence and the memory of last night. In the light of day his proposal and my rejection suddenly seemed more real. I could throttle Ma for putting me in that situation.

The opening of the town hall door startled the crowd, and a gasp went up, followed by a ripple of nervous laughter. My heart quickened. Two men in black hats and cloaks towered above a mangy bundle of grey rags that they held between them.

That bundle of rags was Rita Warren, the crone who lived a solitary life on the edge of town. She must have been nearing seventy, but rumours suggested she was at least a hundred years old. She loved nothing more than her black cat, Providence, a battered and matted old thing with one eye and a stunted tail. Rita made a meagre living growing herbs and helping sickly animals and children. I'd even been to her myself on occasion, for a tonic to help with Ma's seasonal cough or her aching legs. But Rita was no physic, and therein lay the problem.

How they could hold her responsible for the death of cattle she had no connection to baffled me. Farmer Good had taken a tincture, apparently, and the next day his cattle were dead.

They were looking to cast out the Devil, but they were looking in the wrong place. The Devil is cunning and insidious, too smart to be caught out in the open like that.

Still, no one spoke up for Old Rita.

As she was dragged to the gallows, it was clear she was in no fit state. Her hair now matched her moggy's matted coat. Bruises the colour of violets bloomed across her cheeks and brow, bloody bandages loosely wrapped her hands. Her shoes were worn through, no doubt forced to walk her cell.

Poor Rita had been to hell and back.

The men led her to the gallows and up the steps that bent beneath their weight. Rita faltered but they lifted her easily. It must be hard to face death so openly. The rope was looped over her head. I was so close I could see fibres scratching the sensitive flesh of her neck.

Another man emerged from the town hall. He walked much faster than the other two, despite being shorter, and was dressed in his finery. His pointed face gave an air of superiority as he stepped up onto the gallows, a few feet from Rita. With barely a glance at the crowd, he rolled out the paper in his hands and began to read.

"Rita Warren, you have been accused of witchcraft by decimation of the cattle of Mr and Mrs Good." He read out a version of events and a list of other minor offences, but I was too focused on the small, hunched frame of Rita to hear. Her body was slumped, her eyes wandered in and out of focus.

The magistrate was coming to the end of his speech. "Through clear evidence provided within this court you have been found guilty. Punishment is death by hanging," he finished.

There was a pause. "Devil whore," someone said, loud enough to be heard by us all.

"I ain't no Devil whore!" Rita's voice was surprisingly clear above the heads of the crowd. "Though the Devil is here alright. He stands there." She raised her bound arms and pointed at the magistrate. "You mark me, I'll never let you rest when I'm dead. I'll curse your children. Mark me!" She spat as far as she could toward the magistrate. He didn't flinch.

Gasps of excitement and pious indignation rose from the crowd.

"Witch," someone shouted now.

"She's the Devil in 'er," said another.

"Murderer," cried another.

"Hangin' is too merciful, she should be burned!"

The crowd became animated, people shifted on their feet, as though they might rush the gallows and hang Rita themselves. I smelt the sour breath of the people behind as they inched forward. I didn't move.

Rita let out a sob, but only one. "You're all fools. You're all the Devil! You know me. You know me."

For a moment I thought she would beg, but a renewed verbal lashing from the crowd made her shrink back. She was a frail old woman again, beaten and bruised and defeated.

I fought the urge to vomit. Rita was harmless, but the crowd didn't care.

After allowing the mob to jostle and heckle for another minute or two, the pointy-faced magistrate nodded at the guard. In a sharp, swift motion, they pulled the rope, lifting Rita a foot into the air. A few cries went up, some men gasped. It was the quickness of it.

The air fell still. Birds and humans alike held their breath. I stared at the small space between Rita's kicking feet and the wooden platform, the air between them a silent assassin.

When her feet slowed to a steady swing, the magistrate marched back into the town hall, head held high, certain of his virtue. The two guards lowered Rita's body to the platform, where she lay curled in on herself. I looked away, up at the birds. They began to hop and ruffle their feathers. Then they took off in a mass beating of wings and flew into the distance, disgusted by what they'd seen.

The crowd followed suit, dispersing in a hushed murmur. There was no one to shout at now; a dead body wasn't as entertaining as a live one.

I couldn't move. I wished I could fly away from this town, these people. I wished I could unfurl my own wings and give the crowd another show by taking to the air before their very eyes.

People looked over their shoulders and eyed their neighbours suspiciously as they left. Accuse or be accused, they might have to pick a side when the next witch was identified. No one was safe.

I had to get back to Ma.

A fracas at the back of the square caught my attention. A group of men were huddled.

Charles was at the centre. He was bent over as though out of breath, his hand rested on the doctor's shoulder to help him stand, and then he pulled himself up again. His hair was dishevelled, as if he'd been up all night, his face full of fear. Blood stained the front of his white linen shirt.

Something terrible had happened. Inside, I already knew what it was. I remembered another night full of blood, long ago, when I'd washed myself clean in the lake. There could only be one reason why Charles would have run for the doctor himself. His mouth was moving, speaking in a rushed manner, his cheeks flushed. I couldn't hear the words. Then he looked around the square until his eyes met mine. Anger replaced the fear, his eyes narrowed, he stopped talking. He looked to the slumped body of Rita and then back to me. He raised his hand and pointed at me. I stumbled back as if he had shot an arrow. This was it. My turn.

They had seen the Devil in me. Charles would expose my crime.

A scattering of seeds was thrown on the ground between us. Mr Quickly nodded his head at me as the sparrows flooded the square. I ran.

CHAPTER FOUR

Ma was embroidering a silk glove by the fireplace. She was nervous, distracted, and unwilling to talk to me about what happened at the hanging. But there was no sweeping this black cloud beneath the rug, it hung heavy in the room. My muscles tensed, and Ma's hands shook as she threaded a needle.

Caesar flitted nervously from fireplace to window, unable to settle. Something had happened to Amber, and I hadn't stayed to find out what. I kept telling myself it had nothing to do with me, that Charles hadn't been pointing at me, and if he was, perhaps he needed my help. But I had run away. If anyone asked, I could say I hadn't noticed, I was too upset by the hanging to even see Charles. Deny any knowledge that Charles was even there.

But I couldn't lie to myself. I saw the anger in his eyes, I felt the accusation in his gesture.

They would be coming for me.

"Be still, Caesar," I snapped, and the bird let out a low chirp but didn't move again. Outside, birds lined the branches of the trees next to our cottage. They had followed me home, knowing a new story was just beginning.

Ma's needle slipped, missed the thimble and pricked her finger. She hissed as a drop of blood blossomed from the invisible wound. She put the finger to her lips quickly and sucked.

"Are you alright, Ma?"

"I'm fine, just a prick. I've suffered thousands."

"You shouldn't be working in this light. It's getting dark."

Ma sighed and was about to respond, but a rapping at the door startled us. Caesar forgot his orders and flew quickly from the window to the fireplace. "Don't answer," Ma said. "I don't like the sound of it."

I didn't intend to.

The banging came again, louder. Each knock shook my bones. Judgement was calling.

"Fortune! It's me. Come out. I know you're in there." It was Charles. It was happening. I would be held responsible for my crime. The poppet was still in my pocket. I should throw it in the fire.

A crash buckled the door and Ma yelped. Another crash sent the door flying open and we jumped from our chairs.

The crowd behind Charles was a surprise. They had gathered stealthily, all men, representing various families in the town. Some had torches. The glow turned their faces into demonic creatures, half light, half dark. Twilight flung shadows over them.

"Come outside, Fortune. We know what you are." Charles' eyes were full of hate. It emanated from him. His anger towards me had found an outlet, his secret shame would finally be put to rest.

"What is this?" Ma's voice was firm as she stepped towards Charles, using her body to shield me. Only I could recognise the edge of fear in her tone.

"What the devil are you talking about, Mr Divine?"

"Exactly that. The Devil!" The crowd behind him

muttered at the word, as if they were calling in the angels to protect themselves. "We know what she is," he said. "Now come outside and try to deny it." He sidestepped Ma, but she moved into his path again.

"She will not come out and I think you should all be off home. You've no idea what you're talking about."

I watched, paralysed.

Ma was the only thing between me and the mob. The hollow sound of footsteps on freshly built gallows haunted me. I saw a wisp of smoke as the rope burned against the wooden beam. That would be *my* neck in the rope, *my* feet kicking.

The next part happened very quickly. Ma tried to close the door; Charles reached out and grabbed her by the arm, pulling her forward, and Ma fell, letting out a cry as her knees hit the path. A few sniggers escaped the crowd. The world was spinning out of control.

"Get your hands off her!" I pushed Charles back, there wasn't an ounce of remorse on his face. I tried to help Ma up, but in an instant Charles' hands were on me. He yanked my grip from Ma and wrestled me to the centre of the gathering.

My struggles were useless against the grimy hands that pinned me. Faces full of venom surrounded me. The ale on their breath an invisible, suffocating cloud.

The light was fading. The birds shifted uneasily on their perches, letting out an occasional cry. The men weren't looking towards the woods, their eyes were fixed on me.

Only I noticed the birds. I breathed deep. I had to stay calm.

"Check her for marks," someone shouted from the back. "They all have a mark. Strip her!"

Grubby hands pulled at my apron, another pulled at the top of my bodice. I began to panic. A pounding started in my head, and I could hear Ma screaming.

Please don't make Ma watch, I thought. *Please not that.*

The birds were squalling and began leaving their branches to circle above our heads. My laces were being yanked hard enough to snap them. I could hear the chickens screaming in their coop, as if being kicked.

"Hang her."

"Forget the mark, we know what she is."

"String her up."

The crowd tightened. They grabbed at the bare flesh of my shoulder and the back of my neck. I thought I would die then, killed by unknown hands. Someone slapped the back of my head hard and laughter penetrated through the ringing in my ears. They were enjoying it. A fist collided with my ribs, the shocking pain doubled me over and I fell to my knees, instinctively covering my head. The birds screeched above the flames of the torches. They would be coming this way.

"I have her familiar," a man shouted, and the crowd about me loosened a little. A short man was holding something up to the others. Something small and yellow.

"No!" I made a break from the crowd, but they had me pinned again in a moment. "Leave him be," I cried, straining against them. I could hear Caesar calling. He was calling for me and I couldn't get to him.

"Suckle on ya, does he?" the short man shouted. "We'll have none of that."

He put his other hand over Caesar's head and yanked, breaking his tiny delicate neck. Ma cried out. The world moved in slow motion. I watched in a state of dumb silence as the man threw Caesar's small lifeless body. It hit the side of the house with a light thud and fell to the ground. There was no point in struggling, the hands that held me were strong. This was the end. I turned inward, releasing myself from my body that would have to bear more pain. Hands pushed me to kneeling. Boots kicked my ribs, my back, my thighs. I tried not to scream, to deny them the satisfaction. I sensed the mass of birds above me. A man cried out as a crow bit his ear. Another swooped and bit the back of a man's neck a moment after he had kicked me. He screeched and tried to slap the bird, but only slapped himself. His hand came away bloody. It all happened so fast. They were still jostling over me, not wanting to miss their chance of tormenting the witch. The man who had been bitten looked at me and then at the blood on his hand. He took a breath, ready to shout about this fresh evidence of witchcraft.

But another voice stopped him. It came from beyond the mob. Their hands dropped and suddenly I was free. The birds retreated to the trees.

The voice belonged to the pointy-faced magistrate, and next to him stood Mr Quickly.

"What is happening here?" The magistrate's quick, low tone demanded compliance.

"She's a witch," Charles said. "Everyone knows it."

"Have you an accusation with proof, Mr Divine?" the magistrate asked, loud enough for the whole congregation to hear.

"Aye, she is the reason my child was stillborn today."

"And the evidence?"

"We encountered Miss Blyth in the woods yesterday and it was there she cursed my wife and babe."

A burning fire of rage was threatening to engulf me. I

wanted to pounce on Charles like a cat and claw his eyes from his sockets.

"How did she do that, Mr Divine?"

"She sold Amber eggs. They made her sick. Cook broke some open this morning and there was blood in them. She killed my child. And she had birds following her. They're drawn to her. It's not natural. Look about you." He swept his arm at the tree line, hoping to show the crows that had gathered there, but they had concealed themselves deeper in the trees. The magistrate narrowed his eyes, then looked at Charles with pity.

"Mr Divine, I'm very sorry for your loss. Please go home to your wife and get some rest," he said.

"And she goes to the woods at night," Charles shouted, cutting the magistrate off, "to communicate with the Devil." He glanced at me. So it was him in the woods last night.

"I will investigate the matter," the magistrate continued, unruffled by Charles' outburst. "We have a strict process of identifying witches. You can count on me to get to the heart of it."

For a moment no one moved, so the magistrate added, "Go home," to all the men gathered. With a disappointed muttering they began to disperse.

"I'll see you hang, girl." Charles spat at my feet, and I flinched, immediately angry with myself for showing a moment of fear. But I didn't take my eyes from him as he backed away. Only when he was out of sight did I begin to tremble.

I helped Ma back into her chair by the fire. The magistrate and Mr Quickly had followed us inside.

Mr Quickly handed the magistrate a purse of coins, and he left with heavy pockets and a closed mouth.

"I have paid for a night's grace," Mr Quickly said. "But he will have pressure on him to return tomorrow, so we must act swiftly."

"What is it you would have me do?" I asked. The whole thing was confusing: the magistrate, the money. What was Mr Quickly's game? I could hardly think. My body was bruised and aching. I wished to be alone with Ma, who was sobbing quietly, and grieve my shame and the loss of my little bird.

"I would like to make a proposal, although I wish it had been in better circumstances."

He glanced at me apologetically.

"Say what you need to say, sir." Ma wiped at her face and blew her nose. My insides churned.

"I know that you have turned me down, Fortune, but if I understand correctly, it is not because of your dislike of me, or that you love another." He paused for a moment, allowing the truth of what he said to sink in. "I can offer you protection, and a good life. You would want for nothing."

The three of us stood in silence. Ma swallowed loudly.

"We would have to leave this place tonight. Time is a luxury we no longer have."

"A luxury *I* no longer have," I corrected him.

"Well, this is… this is–" Realisation dawned on Ma's face. She thought this was the answer.

"Unexpected," I cut in. "Does it not bother you, Mr Quickly, that I am branded a witch?"

"Miss Blythe, I am a man of the world. I have seen many things, and I make up my own mind about people. I can see that you are no such thing." He paused, considering his next words before continuing. "I am leaving tonight. You could come with me."

"I'm sorry, Mr Quickly, my answer must be no."

Ma stood up and gripped my arm like a vice. She smiled her fake smile and turned to Mr Quickly. "Would you be kind enough to allow us a moment alone?"

He looked from Ma to me and nodded. He stepped outside and closed the door behind him.

Ma had a serious look on her face, an expression I hadn't seen for years, not since she sat me down to tell me Pa had been killed.

"You've always been headstrong, determined. You always know exactly what you want. But sometimes you need to bend a little. You must accept the man's proposal." Ma turned me around and began fixing my laces.

"What kind of daughter do you take me for? I won't leave you here and go off to some island."

"I can fend for myself, I'm not an invalid! And he is a good man."

I pulled away from her and winced as a sharp pain ran up my arm. 'You don't know that," I said, turning back to her. "And it's not about that. I won't leave you."

"Then you would rather see me dead," Ma said quietly, as her hands fell to her sides. I was about to protest but she cut me off. "Because that is what will happen." Ma's eyes were glassy, but her voice didn't waiver. "If you stay, you will be hanged. And that I could not bear."

I couldn't think straight. My mind was a confusion of kicking feet and dirty hands.

"This is a misunderstanding; I didn't do anything wrong. I could speak to the magistrate, clear things up," I said.

Ma sighed, and I knew I was clutching at a lost hope.

"You think you can talk your way out of this? They will never let this go. They hanged Old Rita because of cattle! This is a babe you're accused of." Ma almost choked on the words. Her eyes glistened. "They almost hanged you there and then."

"But Ma," I faltered, unsure what to say, "my life is here." The words sounded pathetic.

"Not anymore," Ma said. She took my face in her hands. I let out a sob. "Don't worry about me. I'll set them on a wild goose chase as to your whereabouts, and we'll be together again in time, I promise. You have an opportunity for a life here. Take it."

I could see she was suffering terribly but I could hardly take in what was happening. Marriage? I'd made a vow already: to stay alone. I'd planned my life and was settled to those plans. "If they take you," Ma said, a determination in her eyes, "I will join you soon after." She was telling the truth and the thought of it broke me.

I opened the door. Mr Quickly was facing the trees as if lost in thought, waiting patiently. My saviour? That is how Ma saw it, but I didn't feel saved. I was bruised and beaten and torn in two. Defeated.

"Sir," I said, and he turned to face me. He knew my answer and nodded with humility, before stepping back into the cottage.

Mr Quickly was sympathetic to my plight, but he insisted we move fast. We must be married and have me on a ship by morning. In order to reach the ship, we would have to leave within the hour. He had a carriage ready to take us to the dock. He said it was the only way to protect me, and Ma agreed. The payment he'd made to the magistrate offered a small window of opportunity. Tomorrow the men would be calling for blood, and the magistrate would have an easier time making everyone forget about me if I wasn't there.

"I need half an hour," I said, "to bury Caesar."

"I'll get your things ready," Ma said.

Mr Quickly nodded his agreement.

I took a cloth and went to find Caesar. The night was calm now, quiet. Darkness was falling. I found him by the wall, nestled in the grass. I picked him up; he weighed nothing. He was a shadow of the clumsy little bird I loved. A shell only. I stroked his yellow feathers, tickled the blue crown on his head, and walked into the woods.

The world behind me disappeared, the night-time animals that rushed about in the dark slowed to a standstill in respect for the dead. They watched from behind trees and the comfort of their burrows while I made my sad journey through the woods. I kept an eye on the shadows, half expecting Charles to rush at me from the darkness, or worse, the Devil coming to collect. But all was quiet.

This would always be my home, where my daughter lay at the bottom of the lake. The water was still, shining like glass. I knelt at the edge. I didn't look into the water; I couldn't bear to see my own reflection. I closed my eyes and leaned forward, dipping my fingers into the cold blackness. I could feel her down there, my lost girl, my mermaid.

It wasn't just for Ma that I had conceded to marry Mr Quickly. My desire to survive outweighed future unseen, unfelt consequences. The thought of a noose tightening around my neck terrified me. Suffocating. Kicking. I couldn't bear it. The truth is, I was a coward. I would deal with the repercussions the best I could, but I was sorry Mr Quickly would have to suffer them too.

I looked back to Caesar. My poor bird. Another innocent casualty in my cursed life. He would be good company for my lost one. I gathered a small nest of rocks to rest him on and wrapped it all in the cloth, tying it at the top, just as I had done all those years ago. I took off my shoes and stockings, bunched up my skirts and waded in. I lowered Caesar into the water and let him go. I didn't speak, there was no need. I didn't cry. I stayed for as long as I could.

Back at the cottage, Ma had packed the only small and worn valise we owned. She was sitting in her chair; Mr Quickly stood by the fire. They both looked up as I entered. I wondered how long they had been waiting. There was no sense of words in the air, the room was still as a tomb. Mr Quickly didn't ask where I'd been or why I had taken so long, and I was grateful for that.

"We'll have to perform the rite here," he said.

The realisation of what was about to happen threatened to swallow me whole. The fire burned brighter for a moment, flashing a golden glow across the room and lighting up his deep-set eyes. I was taking too long to answer or move. My body wouldn't obey. I was trapped.

"Come, Fortune, we'll get you cleaned up."

Ma led me into our bedroom, where she had laid out her dress she wore for parish. "I can't take your dress, Ma."

"You can, and you will. You're a mess."

I changed and Ma fixed my hair as best she could.

"We could leave instead," I said.

"And go where? They would track our movements easily. We don't have the resources to protect us that Mr Quickly does. No, this is the best way. It is a blessing. He is a blessing."

I nodded. Ma's fingers in my hair sent shivers through my scalp.

"You need to see this for the miracle it is. You will have a new life, and a pleasurable one at that."

My body ached. I was tired right through to my bones.

"When you arrive at your new home, send word that you're safe and well."

"I will." My new home. It was happening too fast. I'd made a promise that I'd never marry. Rocks of dread settled in the bed of my stomach.

We returned to the sitting room. Ma lit extra candles, but the light glowed dull. Mr Quickly stepped into the centre of the room and held out his right hand.

It's your turn, I told myself, *you need to move.* I lifted my leaden feet and walked the few steps needed to position myself before Mr Quickly. I took his hand. It was much larger than mine, stronger, more powerful. But it only reminded me of the other male hands that dragged me out of the house and punched me and tore at my clothes. The base of my spine throbbed.

Ma came to our side.

Mr Quickly pulled the blue ribbon from his hair and handed it to Ma. Ma looked at me. She knew this wasn't what I wanted. I could see the pain in her eyes, but she half smiled, as if to say – what choice do we have? Ma wrapped the ribbon around our hands, binding us.

The shadows leaned towards us as though crowding for a look at this unlikely match. The light leaned away.

Mr Quickly's voice came as if from a great distance: 'I, Isaiah Quickly" – Isaiah. That was the first time I'd heard his name – "take you, Fortune Blyth, to be my wedded wife, till death us depart, and thereto I plight thee my troth."

I looked up at him. His eyes did not falter, there was not a quiver of hesitation. He had the confidence of someone who had done this before, and maybe he had. I knew nothing about his past loves.

The fire crackled. Ma breathed softly, waiting. I became aware of a rotten metallic taste in my mouth. Blood. The world was underwater, and I was drowning in a red sea.

Mr Quickly, Isaiah now, gave an encouraging closed-lipped smile. Everything would be alright, the smile said. I could be wrong about being cursed. What if my penance was already paid? I'd lived in solitude, doing the best I could for Ma. And it was so long ago, the reality of it was distorted.

Mr Quickly was here now, his presence solid, stable. It was his certainty that gave me the courage to speak. "I, Fortune Blyth, take you, Isaiah Quickly" – he smiled wider when I said his name – "to be my wedded husband, till death us depart, and thereto I plight thee my troth."

CHAPTER FIVE

We travelled like thieves, cloaked by the night. The carriage moved cautiously in the darkness. Every passing moment took me further away from the only home I'd ever known, Ma, and my mermaid. The rocks in my stomach grew heavier with each clop of hooves on the track.

Isaiah sat still and silent, watching the world pass by, allowing me time to grieve and accept what was happening. Occasionally he would glance my way, but I didn't reciprocate. There would plenty of time to talk to him later. The open fields moved in and out of silvery light as clouds obscured the quarter moon. There was no hiding in darkness. It was in the darkness that I was exposed. It was in the darkness that the horned beast would come looking for me. Charles' face, a picture of hate, travelled with me. I had known his feelings for me were difficult, but I never knew how badly he wanted me gone. The image of him pushing Ma to the ground replayed over and over. I never realised him capable of such callousness. But I should have. What kind of man left a young girl to give birth alone and suffer the loss of their child alone? The kind of man who would be capable of any despicable deed to satisfy his own power. Now he knew how it felt to lose a child. I hated myself for thinking it.

"Here, you're shivering," Isaiah said, handing me his jacket. I took it, bundled it into a pillow, and dozed off dreaming of Charles being attacked by the murder of crows that had come to my aid.

I jerked awake at the touch of Isaiah's hand on my leg, and he instantly muttered an apology. We had reached the ship. It was a large cargo ship with little room for guests. I was to be the only woman on board. And I was to travel alone.

"I'm sorry, Fortune," Isaiah said. "I need to go north to finish some business and then I'll follow you home. Two weeks at the most."

"I could come with you," I fumbled. The thought of travelling alone on the ship after what had just happened terrified me. Although I would never admit it.

"It's too dangerous for you. You must go straight to my island." He took a letter from his pocket. "Here, give this to Zena when you arrive. She's the housekeeper and will look after you."

"But I..."

"I know you must be frightened, but the captain is a good man. I trust him completely. He'll be good to you." Isaiah gestured to the captain, who had been waiting a little way off. He introduced himself as Captain Graham and shook my hand. My ribs shot with pain. I tried to hide my discomfort, but Captain Graham didn't miss it. He looked to Isaiah.

"It has been a rough night," Isaiah explained. "Mrs Quickly would be very grateful for some rest." Captain Graham held out his arm for me. "This way, ma'am."

I handled the sea leg of my journey with the grace of someone who has lived their entire life on solid ground –

vomiting into a bucket. My room was more of a cupboard, but it was joined to the captain's quarters with only one boy who attended me. I was safe. On the third night I was well enough to accept Captain Graham's invitation to dine.

"Have you been to Mr Quickly's island before?"

"No, I haven't had the pleasure yet."

"'Pleasure' may be a strong word."

"How so?"

"I'm sorry, I mean no ill will against Mr Quickly, but his island is very isolated. People can... lose one's bearings..."

"I'm sure I will do well with Mr Quickly to teach me island ways."

"Hmm." He was holding something back. "You know, I dock at the main island every year at this time. I hope that you'll come and visit me. In fact, I insist that you do!" he said, raising his glass of wine with a smile.

"Of course I will. Thank you for the invitation."

He nodded and started on his chicken, satisfied. I nibbled at the food, but it had no taste. It sat heavy in my stomach.

The next morning we docked at the island. A cool breeze washed away the sickly feeling. I breathed in deep, holding onto the rail of the main deck. I watched the harbour. A fish market was in full flow. Fishermen sold their catches, women bought them. It looked friendly, busy. It may not be so bad, living here. The women were dressed much plainer than Amber Divine. I could blend in. Start again.

A raven shrieked almost directly overhead. It glided majestically, its large wings fanned, towards the ship's figurehead: a man painted in vivid golds and greens. She landed on top of his cloaked head and cocked her head, pinning her black beady eye on me as though weighing up the newcomer. I had no misgivings about the shabbiness of my appearance. My hair was windblown and had escaped like tendrils from my hat. I was wearing a second-hand faded blue cloak, and beneath my crumpled linen dress a pair of boots held together by string. Hardly the bride of a wealthy collector. In the light of day, I wondered how the captain had treated me with such civility and not hidden me below deck. I nodded at the raven, who lifted off with a flutter and dived, sweeping low across the deck before soaring into the skies again. Sailors ducked and cursed. Some crossed themselves. Sailors had superstitions about everything. They would be glad to see the back of me, I was even more feared than the raven.

The captain informed me my transport was ready. "The first mate will take you. Now remember, every year."

He shook my hand, and I offered my heartfelt thanks. He was a kind man.

The first mate was not so forthcoming. We boarded the small boat, but instead of heading to the docks, we turned away from the market and into the open sea.

"Wait. Where are we going?"

"To the island," he grunted.

"You mean this isn't where I'm staying?"

"Nay. This is the main island. Not your one."

He sat in silence while two of his men rowed the boat. I swallowed my disappointment. Isaiah had said it was isolated, it was silly of me to think that bustling market town was my destination.

I used the last leg of my journey to consider my surroundings. Isaiah was right, the air was warmer here, even in the open sea. Unable to see land, I began to fear we would be lost in open water, but then an island emerged on the horizon ahead of us.

Soon we were skirting its edge, and the birds were a wonder! Just as Isaiah had promised. They called and cried, swooped and dived; a cacophony of shrieks and caws were carried across the sea breeze to me. We passed a flock of black-and-white birds with bright orange beaks and feet, eyes like buttons, who were gathered together on the rocks. I'd never seen birds like them in my life. Puffins, the first mate told me. Alongside the puffins, seals bathed in the sun and played on the flat rocks. The place was teeming with life, and that was some consolation. Again, as I had many times on my journey, I wished for Ma. I reached for the poppet in my pocket and rubbed the rough sticks with my thumb.

Then the cliff turned inward and the island opened up. A small beach was exposed, like a giant had taken a bite out of the island and revealed its innards. Large rocks on either side cut it off from the puffins and seals. The air settled as we entered the cove, protected by the white rock of the cliff that wrapped around the sand like a windbreak. And there, set back on the grassy crown above the cove, nestled into the island like an eagle hunkering, was the house.

It was much bigger than I expected. A stain on the beauty of the island, manmade and grey. The place gave an air of hostility, as if its many windows were watching me and did not like what they saw. Fear crept in. But I had taken vows and bound myself to a stranger, and there was no turning back now.

The first mate had pulled the boat as far up onto the beach as possible so I could remain dry, but the surf still soaked my boots and hem.

"Good luck, ma'am, and congratulations," the first mate said, and placed my valise next to me on the sand.

He looked up at the ridge, where the house lay just out of sight, and quickly crossed himself. He too must have felt those eyes staring. Before I could get my bearings, he was back in the boat and sailing away. I was completely alone, except for the birds. I watched the boat leave the cove, the last link to home severed.

CHAPTER SIX

Terrified of what awaited me in the cold house above, I closed my eyes and breathed deep. If I imagined hard enough, perhaps the beach would swallow me. Small waves lapped the shore, birds called out while circling overhead. I could have stayed there forever if my sodden shoes weren't numbing my feet.

There was nothing for it but to move. Steps carved into the cliff face led up to the house. An eerie silence descended as I began to climb, as if the cliff face muffled all sound and bounced it back to the open water transformed. My heart beat faster, but it wasn't just the climb that made it race. I was entering the unknown.

A raven flew in and landed on the rocks beside me. She hopped up the cliff face, keeping my pace.

"Come to keep me safe, have you?" The bird cocked her head this way and that, her beady eyes playful, and I couldn't help a small smile. "No matter how far I travel some things will not change," I sighed. I thought of Caesar and how I had left his little body in its watery grave, alongside another little body. But I did not want to think about that. I focused on the sleek black feathers of the much larger bird before me.

"What's your name, then?" I asked. My breath was becoming laboured as I reached the top of the steps. The bird gurgled as she hopped alongside me. "How about Purdie? Do you like that name?" A low chuckle. "Me too."

I huffed up the steps. "You know, I remember you. You were the bird on the ship earlier, weren't you? You frightened those men good." I smiled. "I thought sailors were hardened men, but old ladies have more courage. These men are scared of everything. A raven. A woman on board. I swear, if I'd pretended to curse them, they would have fallen down dead from the fear of falling down dead."

I was almost at the top of the steps.

"You best be off now. It wouldn't do to turn up with a bird at my side." Purdie looked at me and waited. We were just out of sight of the house. I stopped. "I should warn you that it doesn't bode well to be friends with me. Things always seem to get out of control." Purdie cawed a low, sympathetic acknowledgement. "Well, if you do choose to be friends, be it on your own head. I did warn you. Off you go now."

She spread her wings and took off, flapping wind in my face. It's surprising how something as fragile as feathers can hold so much power. Purdie's were of such a deep black gloss that when the sunlight hit them, they shimmered violet.

There was a slight incline up to the house from the top of the steps. It was a solid, three-storey, overly large building. The stone was weather-beaten, blasted by salty winds that had smoothed its once rough surfaces. At the centre was a large oak door.

I held my valise with both hands in front of me, as if it could offer some sort of protection. The iron knocker was heavy and cold, and I flinched as it dropped, creating a loud bang that was followed by a faint echo indoors. I waited but nobody came. Just as I raised my hand to knock again, the sound of a latch lifting made me step back. The door opened a crack, but no one appeared, only a sliver of darkness lay beyond. I waited a moment longer but still no one came, so I pushed the door open and stepped inside.

"Hello?"

The adjustment from light to dark left me temporarily blind. Slowly, the hallway revealed itself. There was clutter everywhere. The edging of the room was three feet deep in papers and trinkets. There were candelabras, jars containing unidentifiable liquids, wooden boxes, small toys. The clutter continued up the stairs and along the walls. Everything was covered in dust. The air was thick with must and an undercurrent of decomposing bodies. No doubt one or two small creatures had met their end in this chaos, and how would they ever be found? This entrance must hardly ever get used, with Isaiah away so much. The staff would use the kitchen doors, no doubt.

My heart almost stopped when I looked beneath the grand staircase. A face looked back at me, disembodied, floating mid-air. White and taut, I was unsure if it was living, but then the black, mean eyes moved and I gasped. The rest of the small woman was revealed as she stepped from the shadows into the weak light from the doorway, which was trying desperately to penetrate the gloom. The woman's clothes were all black, including her coif. She had a large bunch of keys tied to her waist. The housekeeper, then. She didn't speak. She, like the clutter about her, seemed to have moulded to this house.

"Are you the housekeeper?"

The beady black eyes swept downwards and rested on my damp skirts. There was a trail of soil and sand leading from me to the front steps. I muttered an apology. I remembered the letter and began fumbling in my pocket. My fingers brushed up against the poppet, and a needle of guilt stabbed at my heart. I'd forgotten it was there. I pulled the letter out. It was crushed from the long journey.

"Mr Quickly asked me to give you this," I said, holding it out to her, "to explain." Perhaps the old woman was hard of hearing as she still didn't respond, but then she raised her bony hand and took the letter.

The skeletal woman, who I assumed was Zena, took her time reading. I shifted from foot to foot, trying not to let her see that I was uncomfortable, but my feet were turning to ice, and I'd freeze to death if I didn't move soon.

"No," she said. Her voice was hoarse and deep, much deeper than I expected from someone who resembled bone china. She shook her head and sighed as she folded the letter.

"No? I don't know what–"

Before I could finish my sentence, the skeletal woman walked quickly towards me, grabbed my wrist with a cold bony hand, and pulled me back out the front door. Her grip was so strong I winced in pain. She stopped when we could see the cove below. She dropped my wrist and scanned the horizon. She was looking for the boat. She wanted to send me back! I had travelled so far and been through so much, and now this old woman wished to reject me. Isaiah said she would take care of me.

Zena tutted and cursed under her breath. I stood mute with shock, unsure whether to laugh or cry or scream. She eventually turned to me. Her skin in sunlight was paper thin, transparent almost. "This way," she said.

I followed her back into the house in a state of confusion. The weight of the situation was taking physical form. My limbs ached. I was cold and tired. I tried not to shiver, not wanting to show this mad old woman how beaten I was.

She led the way through the narrow passages to another set of stairs, less grand than the main entrance. Not another soul met us and there was none of the far-off bustle you would expect in a house of this size, just thick walls and dark passageways that you could get lost in.

The air inside the house was stagnant, like the stale breath of a dying animal. The stone whispered. A warm breath caressed the back of my neck. I flinched. My hair stood on end. I whipped around but there was nothing there, only the gloom. I rubbed my neck.

Zena hadn't stopped or even looked back. I moved quickly to catch up with her, suddenly afraid of being alone in these halls.

On the third floor, at the end of a row of doors which I assumed were bedrooms, Zena led me up a final few steps to a larger door, a garret. We were right at the top of the house. She opened it and stepped aside for me to enter.

This room was a breath of fresh air, spacious and bright, with huge windows cut into the thick walls allowing light to flood the space. The bottom corners of the window could be opened, which Zena did now, letting in the sea breeze, and shifting the stagnant air.

The bed loomed large, four-postered and mahogany, with red gossamer curtains hanging at the corners. I turned away from it quickly, not ready to think about why I needed such a big bed. One thing at a time. Facing the bed, on the right-hand side of the door, was a huge fireplace, cold now, with two chairs and a table between them. I looked back at her, hoping she would offer some guidance on what I should do next or where I should put my things, but the tight-lipped housekeeper was already closing the door behind her. I was alone, again.

I pulled off my soaked boots. The floor was covered in thick, luxurious rugs that felt soft on my soles. I could make this room my sanctuary, if it weren't for the bed reminding me of what was to come when Isaiah returned. I had broken the promise I made all those years ago. That Devil would be coming for me, and any children I might bear.

I sat down, crossed my arms over my stomach and cried. I cried for everything I had already lost and everything I would lose again.

A tapping at window. Purdie was on the sill.

I wiped my face. "Come in, Purdie," I said. She hopped in and began exploring, flitting from the rafters to the gold tassels holding back the heavy plum-velvet curtains. I wished I had Purdie's ignorance, it would make things a lot easier.

I looked at the empty chair to my right, where Ma should have been. Soon that chair would be occupied by a man I barely knew.

Purdie clicked at my ear from the back of my chair. I tickled beneath her chin, and she cawed. "Hush that noise or you'll have to go." She began preening her feathers, defiant in the face of the false threat.

I cried silently now, unable to stop the flow. Before me, the fireplace was framed by an enormous mantle, elaborately carved with animals frolicking in the woods: deer, foxes, badgers, wolves. There were a hundred woodland stories being told in the stone. But on closer inspection, I realised that it wasn't a joyful depiction of friendship. The animals were chasing, biting, hunting. They were tearing each other apart.

CHAPTER SEVEN

I sat for a long time, lost in thoughts of impending doom, when a knock at the door startled me. I hadn't heard anyone approach. People must creep about the place like ghosts. I shooed Purdie, who immediately flew out of the open window, but I knew she wouldn't go far. I quickly wiped my face and tried to position myself in the chair so I looked at ease, but succeeded only in being awkward.

"Come in," I said, trying to sound confident, but my voice cracked. How could I ever manage house staff when I was on the same level as them? I was an imposter here. Zena knew it and so would every other servant by now.

Bracing myself for that skeletal face, I was surprised to see that of a young man. He was of a similar age to me, late twenties at the most. Tall, but not as tall as Isaiah, light hair that kinked and curled in whatever direction it pleased, and eyes the colour of a ripe chestnut. At least, one of his eyes. The right side of his well-formed face had been burned away. His flesh had healed into a mottled red and white mess, and his right eye was milky white. His mouth and chin had been spared from the blaze.

His stony stare told me he was tired of being recoiled from and I didn't recoil, uncomfortably aware that my own face must be red and blotched from all the crying.

"I'm Mathis, ma'am. Supper is ready in the sitting room."

"Thank you." I tried to tuck my bare, damp feet beneath the chair before he noticed them.

"There are clean clothes for you in the dressing room." It seemed he noticed everything.

"Dressing room?"

"There." Mathis pointed to a door to the left of the bed that I hadn't even noticed. It had been covered in the same flock wallpaper that adorned the walls.

"Of course, yes."

"Would you prefer to change first?" Mathis asked, sensing my unease. "I can wait." He closed the door without waiting for a reply.

The door to the dressing room, of which I could now make out the edge, had no handle. A slight panic rose within me. Should I reveal my ignorance and go and ask Mathis to show me? Before stooping so low, I ran my hands over it. I found nothing. Then I pressed against it and the door opened. I breathed a sigh of relief. Disgrace averted.

Inside was a brass tub, a wash bowl and jug, and rows of women's clothes. What were they all doing there? Who had they belonged to? Perhaps Isaiah had had a previous wife. Perhaps he'd had many! There was no time to think about it. I searched for the plainest clothes possible and eventually chose a light blue taffeta dress. It was far too fine for me, and I thought about shouting through the door to Mathis that I would skip supper and spend the rest of the night here. But my empty stomach protested, and I needed to know more about this place. I put the dress on and considered myself in the full-length looking glass in the corner of the room. The clean dress looked ridiculous beneath my tangled, windswept hair and puffy eyes. I found clean boots and put them on dirty feet. There was no water in the basin.

I opened the door to Mathis.

"This way, ma'am." There was not a flicker of amusement or surprise at seeing me so finely dressed. I followed him through the gloomy house without a word, wondering what, or who, awaited me.

The sitting room was four times the size of Ma's cottage, and thankfully empty. There were various card tables, a dining table to the right and a grand piano at the window to the left, which looked out over the cliff edge to the sea. Supper was laid on the table. It was some kind of fish. I supposed I'd be eating a lot of fish now. There was also a jug of ale and a bowl of sugared almonds. My mouth watered just looking at them.

"How many staff are there here?"

"Only Zena and myself," Mathis answered.

"What? How?" I couldn't believe it. A place of this size, with no staff? "How does she keep it clean?"

Mathis glanced about him, his eyebrow raised slightly. On closer inspection of the room, I could now see there were cobwebs on the chandeliers and in the corners. Some stretched across the walls, the spiders long dead. Dust layered the mantles and antimacassars, and balls of fluff speckled the floor. And I had already witnessed the mess in the entrance hall.

"What is your role here?" I took in his casual shirt and breeches, not exactly the attire of a servant in a stately home. If that was what this place was.

"I do a bit of everything. Mostly tend the gardens. Grow food, serve food."

"There are gardens?"

"The north side houses the cottage gardens, which is the prettiest part. Behind the house is the produce, mostly."

"Do you maintain the cottage garden?"

"I do."

I wondered who had asked Mathis to maintain a flower garden when the rest of the house was so neglected. Someone here must appreciate beauty.

"Thank you for your help," I said, as I moved towards the dining table. He gave a short, sharp nod of his head and left.

The dinner for one looked lonesome on that huge table. I wondered what Ma would be eating tonight and if she had been left in peace. I hoped so. I would write to her as soon as I could.

As I gulped down the last of the ale, my belly full of fish and my eyes drooping, the sitting room door opened again. I thought Mathis had returned, but recoiled when I saw the bone-white skin and beady black eyes.

"Mrs Quickly would like to meet you," Zena said. She turned swiftly and walked away at a fast pace, expecting me to follow her. I stood stunned for a moment, and wondered if I should ask who Mrs Quickly was, as that was now my name, was it not? Isaiah had really told me nothing about this place. A bit of forewarning about who actually lived in his home might have been helpful. I decided to ask, but Zena was already way ahead, and the chill she left in her wake stopped my mouth. I'd find out soon enough. I trotted after her like a silly child obeying a strict governess. We crossed the cluttered entrance hall and entered another wing of the house. Zena carried a lamp. The light found it more difficult to enter this side of the house.

We descended a flight of stairs so steep I thought they would lead to a cellar, but instead there was a bare corridor with a single door at the end. There were no windows, and the air was thick with damp as if we were deep inside the cliff itself. The cold was biting. *This must be what it's like to live underground like a mole, or a fox,* I thought. A weak line of light flickered at the base of the door. Zena rapped on it like the person on the other side was deaf.

"Enter," said a raspy voice. Zena opened the door and stepped back, making way for me to go inside. I hesitated for a moment; unsure I had the strength to meet another unfriendly face.

Inside sat an old lady on a kind of throne. The chair was low and cushioned in velvet with elaborate gold edgings. The lady herself was dressed as though ready to attend a dance at the king's court. Her dress was big and elaborate, cream with intricate delicate floral embroidery. Folds and folds of material cascaded about her. I no longer felt overdressed. On her head was a high white wig fixed with jewelled combs. Her thin lips and bony cheeks were covered in rouge. I thought she might be mad, but when she spoke her voice was clear and her eyes glinted with the curiosity and excitement of a child receiving a gift.

"There she is! Come, sit."

I sat in a matching chair opposite. It was like sinking into a cloud.

"So, you are the dear who has stolen my son's heart."

My mother-in-law. Isaiah hadn't mentioned her. There were lots of things he hadn't mentioned, but then we'd had very little time to get to know each other.

"Zena," Mrs Quickly called as the housekeeper was closing the door, a tone of irritation in her voice. "Do make

sure you get my supper right tonight. I do not want mouldy
fish again."

Zena didn't look at her, just gripped the door knob a little
tighter as she closed it behind her. Mrs Quickly chuckled,
highly amused by the whole thing. "She is such a boring old
barnacle. Maybe she'll die soon, eh?" She winked at me and
laughed again.

"It's nice to meet you, Mrs Quickly," I said, trying to mask
my awkwardness.

"Now, you don't have to call me that, dear, Esme will do
fine."

Esme started fiddling with the china on the table before
us and I looked around the room, the old lady being but
one elaborate feature in it. Rich tapestries covered every
inch of the walls and floor. Tables were covered in trinkets,
glass figurines and brass contraptions of which I had no idea
what they did. There were cabinets, a writing desk and a
large wooden box. I couldn't figure out its purpose, either.
Candles were everywhere, illuminating the room well, and
they needed to because there were no windows in here
either. This was the womb of the house. It was suffocating.

Over my right shoulder, and directly in Esme's line
of sight, was the fireplace. Above it hung a portrait that
reached the ceiling, it was so large. In it was a beautiful
young woman with raven-black hair rolled into loops. She
had full pink lips, perfectly heart shaped. I looked back at
Esme, who was watching me with shameless glee.

"It's you," I said.

"It is! Wasn't I a beauty?" She said it with the confidence
of a woman never contradicted. "Do you drink tea, dear?"
The table before us was laid with dainty cups and a teapot
intricately decorated with butterflies and flowers. And to

my delight, a stand of sweetmeats, shaped as tiny fruits made from marzipan and sugared almonds. Even frosted rose petals.

"Take one, child, they're for you. I recommend the angelica. It's delicious."

I chewed on the stick. It was a lot better than fish. But I became aware of Esme watching me and was suddenly self-conscious. I put the sweet down and wiped the corners of my mouth.

"I'll put some sugar in your tea. It can be bitter if you're not used to it." She stirred the powdered sugar in.

"Tell me, how did you meet my son?"

"He was passing through our town, and Ma took pity on him and invited him for supper," I said, as if that explained everything.

"Your ma." She emphasised *Ma*, rolling the word around her mouth as though tasting the common dirt.

The difference between myself and this woman was like a sparrow meeting a peacock. No fancy dress could even bring me close to the life that she must have led, even if she now sat in a windowless room like a mad person. Ma always said the rich had peculiar ways. I was surprised she hadn't thrown me out of the house as unworthy of her son.

"Don't worry, child, I'm not judging you. We are all the same flesh and blood." It was as if she had read my thoughts. "Do you know what the most important thing in this lifetime is?" She waited for me to answer, her eyes twinkling. "Our bodies." Her gaze swept over me. "And I can see why my Isaiah chose you."

"Oh, I'm not sure about that," I said, picking up the teacup to distract from my burning face.

"Don't be modest. Be proud! Hold your head high." She

lifted her own chin in mock pride and chuckled, a gravelly sound that turned into a cough. "Your youth is a gift, and your jawline is a wonder." She looked to the portrait of her younger self and pulled at the stretchy skin on her neck. "So," she said, coming back to herself, "what do you do for fun?"

I immediately thought of the woods back home. I'd escape there whenever I could and surround myself with the birds. With them I was free from the world of people, and a calm would come over me as I watched them build nests, preen, dance for each other, play, sing, fight. They were nature's most precious invention, and I could *feel* them, their harmony, their peace. I could sit there for hours with them. Apart from that, everything else was work.

"I like to sew," I said.

"Hmm." She crinkled her brow, disbelieving me. "Do you smoke?" she asked. She fiddled with a box on her smaller side table and pulled out a pipe. I shook my head. Esme stuffed the tobacco in with her spindly fingers, picked up a candle and puffed until it caught flame. "You should learn, it's a true pleasure. And it protects against all kinds of disease."

The room slowly filled with blue curling smoke. It lingered, stagnant, a prisoner in the cocooned room.

"Do you paint? Draw? Play cards? I do enjoy a game, now and then. What about music? Do you play an instrument? Read books?"

"I... suppose I–"

"Forgive me, dear, I'm not used to guests. We have plenty of time to get to know each other." Esme leaned back and puffed on her pipe. The smoke wafted out on her breath then settled into slow-moving silky lines, hovering above our heads like a pit of snakes. "I'm so glad you're here. It gives me hope for the future. And you are a pretty thing to look at. Give me your hand." I placed my hand in hers. Her powdery skin was soft and delicate and very thin. "Beautiful," she said. "Such strong nails, too."

It was strange, having compliments lavished on me. I was used to staying in darkness, hiding in the background, and having the people in my town judge me for it. I suddenly felt like a fraud.

"I'm probably not what you expected, as a daughter-in-law."

"Whatever do you mean?" Esme regarded me. "Ah, because you are from common stock, is that it?" She puffed on her pipe, then let it hang from her mouth like a man would. "You are human, are you not?" The pipe shifted up and down as she talked. "You can bear children?" She removed the pipe from her lips.

And there it was. What I had feared all along. The reason why I should have let them hang me instead. I would never bear a living child.

"I think so…" I said. Not exactly a lie, but not the whole truth either.

"Then you have nothing to worry about. People with status would have you believe their blood is blue and they piss wine! Nonsense. You are just as worthy as any trained lady. Trust me." She winked and took another puff.

Esme was far too welcoming. I had no right to be in her home. Not only was I common, but I would be disappointing her when I failed to deliver grandchildren. I'd have to think of something. Was there some way to be married without getting pregnant?

I picked up the tea and sipped. The tepid bitterness, even with the sugar, made me recoil. Esme laughed out loud in her crackly way, and I smiled.

CHAPTER EIGHT

My first night was disturbed. I was woken by a scream that died the moment I sat up. But it lingered, an echo from the dream world. My mind raced in the darkness. It had sounded like a child. A recurring nightmare of mine. I shouldn't have been surprised that it had followed me here.

Immediately I knew where I was. I had closed the heavy curtains and pulled the thin bed drapes about me, creating a nest where I could sleep peacefully. But I no longer felt cocooned and safe. The cry had unsettled me. What if it hadn't been a nightmare?

I lay back down, sinking into the cotton sheets. Ma would love these. I felt guilty that she wasn't here to share these little luxuries. I had left her to fend for herself. No one would believe my innocence, no matter how much the magistrate had been paid, and I worried how this would be affecting Ma. There wasn't just guilt, there was shame. I had abandoned her. I must get a letter sent to her today. That would mean speaking to Zena.

I longed for the smaller bed I shared with Ma. I'd give anything to hear the soft snores that had often driven me mad. Soon, there would be another person lying with me. The thought churned my stomach. *You can bear children?*

I closed my eyes. In the darkness, I heard it again. A child's cry. Had they lied to me about how many people lived here? The house was so big it was possible. I left the safety of my cocoon, wrapped a shawl around me, and paused at the door. I shouldn't be getting involved.

A third cry forced me out into the hallway, which was bathed in moonlight. Nothing stirred. All the bedroom doors were closed. I crept along the hallway and down the stairs. The sitting room allowed some moonlight through its windows, enough to see that there was nobody in there either, just the spiders. It was simply my nightmares and the strangeness of being in a new place affecting me.

I stood in stillness, feeling the energy of the house around me, trying to get to know it. I didn't want to be scared here. Then a quiet tapping started up. It sounded like long nails against the stone wall. It stopped. The hairs on my arms and neck lifted, and I knew in my heart that someone was watching me. I stared at the corner furthest from the windows, black with shadow, where the sound had come from. I willed my eyes to penetrate the gloom and show me what was there. Deathly silence filled the space until I could hear my own heart beating.

The tapping started again. The shadows began to shift and change. I stepped back. Long black fingers emerged from the shadow's edge, visible in the moonlight, reaching towards me.

Slowly, without taking my eyes from the shadow, I backed into the corridor.

Before I had time to catch my breath, there was movement to the right of me down the corridor. It looked like the tail end of a skirt disappearing around the corner. I needed to stay calm. I should go back to my room, but instead I followed the skirt and soon heard the dull murmur of voices.

A door was slightly ajar. Light leaked from it. I crept closer. I could make out a thin sliver of a kitchen. Two voices began to form into recognisable words. There was the playful drawl of Esme and the clipped, harsh tones of Zena.

"...I don't know what you're fussing over, she'll do fine," Esme said. I couldn't move or breathe.

"There's nothing about her." Zena now, her voice bitter.

"Give it time, there must be something."

"What was he thinking?"

"Have you seen her close up? Not a wrinkle."

"That doesn't matter."

"Poppycock! You'll be grateful when it's done."

"I won't. And I won't be falling at her feet either, like she's queen of the castle. She's a nobody. I'm tired already."

"Then hire some more help."

"You know I won't." Zena's voice was firm.

"Such a martyr." Esme sighed. "Can't you have a little fun? Just for once?"

"All you think about is fun. Life isn't all fun."

"Oh, enlighten me, wise one. What else do we have to live for?"

Pots and pans clattered, and my heart leapt, but it was only Zena huffing and puffing, stamping about. "She shouldn't be here."

"I can't speak for you, my dear, but I for one get tired of looking at your wrinkled old skull-face day in, day out. She's a sight for bored eyes."

This wasn't what I'd expect of a lady and her housekeeper. They had been holed up in this place too long, by the sound of it. The lines had blurred. But what Zena said was true. I didn't have anything about me. I was as confused as her why Isaiah would choose me. Maybe Zena could convince

Esme to get rid of me and I'd go back to Ma. We could find a way to leave the country, set sail for the new lands. We should have done that in the first place. The attack and the proposal had all happened so fast, I hadn't had time to think.

"Besides," Esme sighed, "you'll be grateful soon enough." She paused before continuing. "Get some sleep, before the bags under your eyes get so big you disappear behind them." Her dress rustled as she moved from her seat.

"I can see a bald patch…" Zena sniped back at Esme.

I tiptoed away, terrified Esme would walk straight into me. I quietly gasped for breath when I reached the bedroom corridor. But something was wrong here, too. One of the doors was ajar. I was certain they had all been closed when I went down. And now I could hear a noise coming from the offending bedroom; someone was in there. I walked right up to it and pushed the door fully open. A figure jumped back from an open wardrobe they had been looking in.

"Mathis?"

"I'm sorry, ma'am, I didn't mean to disturb you."

"What are you doing in here?" This bedroom was very much like the rest of the house, covered in clutter. Ornaments and bowls and jars covered every surface and lined the edge of the floor. Mathis stood in the middle of a pile of linen, presumably pulled from the wardrobe he was standing at.

"I promised I would start organising the linen."

"This late?"

"I couldn't sleep." His voice was quiet, and I had difficulty making out any expression on his face as he stood in the darkness.

Something was very wrong here, besides Mathis working so late, but I couldn't put my finger on what exactly.

"I'll finish for the night, then," he said, but didn't move, waiting for me to leave first. I obliged.

Alone in my room, I stood for a moment, trying to take it all in. The adventure had left me with a stale taste in my mouth and a feeling of dread in my stomach. I opened the window and Purdie was there, waiting for me. She hopped inside. I closed the window behind her and pulled the bed drapes closed around us. I tried not to think about the shadowy creature, how it could be on the other side of the curtains right now. Zena's words played over and over as I closed my eyes: *There's nothing about her.*

Purdie nipped tenderly at my hair. The touch of another, even a bird, was comforting.

Things would look different in the morning. The house was old, my nightmares were strong. They always had been, ever since that night in the woods. Either that, or it was him. That devil. He had travelled with me and was watching me closely. Waiting for his time to strike.

I focused on Purdie. The click of her beak, the gentle tug of my hair made my scalp tingle. I began to breathe deeper, to let sleep in.

It came to me then, the thing I couldn't put my finger on – Mathis had been cleaning in the dark.

CHAPTER NINE

The days were long and rambling. I was left alone with only Purdie for company most of the time. I explored the house, constantly looking over my shoulder or listening for Zena, which was impossible as she had the stealth of a wild cat. On the odd occasion I did come across her, I would recoil in shame, blurting something about stretching my legs, and then scold myself for being so docile. She would never engage, just stare at me with her black judgemental eyes.

She had, though, given me paper and ink, and I wrote to Ma daily. I didn't tell her the details of Zena's contempt for me or that Esme lived in a dungeon. I gave her a gilded version of events, and people. I knew it would be a while before I heard anything back, but I longed each day that a letter would appear. Although, how my letters were being delivered was a mystery. Zena must have received deliveries from the mainland, but I had not seen any.

The house had many rooms. A library, snug, various sitting rooms, numerous bedrooms. I discovered another floor even higher than my bedroom at the other end of the house – attic space with servants' bedrooms, all empty. Neither Zena nor Mathis appeared to own any of these rooms.

All the rooms, every one, was covered in clutter and dust. It would take a lifetime to go through the items, clean them and store them correctly, or find out what the purpose of some these things were. In the library the shelves were lined with pots, ornaments and various unidentifiable contraptions, blocking the books behind them.

I hadn't yet dared go past the kitchen to investigate that corner of the house. That was Zena's domain, and most likely where she slept. I couldn't figure out where Esme slept, either. It seemed she existed only in that room at the bottom of the house. I never saw her taking a walk in the garden or asking for tea in the sitting room. She never dined with me, and it didn't feel right to ask. I had walked into her life unexpectedly, so the least I could do was honour her ways. Every other day or so, Zena would find me and inform me that "Mrs Quickly waits for you." That was my cue to go to Esme's room and drink bitter tea and eat sweets while she talked of far-off places that she'd visited in her youth with her husband.

The couple had passed their love of travelling on to Isaiah, who still hadn't returned home after two weeks.

I spent hours at the cove, watching the tides and listening to the birds, waiting to see how often boats would pass. I didn't see a single one. Behind the house was a thick wood. I had avoided it so far, reminding me too much of my woods at home. There was nothing else on the island, there was nowhere to go, no boats to sail off in. I was trapped. Or perhaps I was free. I was no longer in danger of being hanged, at least. And the people here were difficult, but they weren't trying to beat me to death.

I had a good understanding of Esme, endearing and slightly wild. Zena, I found unnerving. They had lived in this place for so long that they had fallen into unusual habits. A housekeeper who barely looked after the house and a mistress who didn't care. They did what they liked, they spoke to each other with bitterness. They had settled into a fractious peace.

Mathis, however, bewildered me. Why did this man work here, separated from the world? I concluded that he had found the perfect hiding place, just as I had. He wanted to hide his face from the world. From everyone, including me. He avoided me. Even if he was halfway through a task in the garden, bedding or weeding or trimming, he would gather his things and leave when he saw me. There would be no rush, he would quietly place his tools in his basket and calmly walk past me with a dip of his head. But I knew he was only leaving because I was there, as if he was afraid of me. Or he had a secret. My thoughts kept returning to the first night, when I found him "organising the linen".

I had decided to keep an eye on Mathis.

During the day, the house was still. Shafts of spring light swam with dust motes in the sitting room, like being underwater. When moving from a sunlit room to the corridor you would be blind for a moment. The light couldn't reach everywhere, no matter how hard it tried. The sound of the sea moved in and out of hearing. Sometimes I could only make out a breeze hitting the windows, other times the sound of the waves was so loud I would drown in it and could only find relief with my head beneath my pillows.

During the night, the house came alive. This was where it wanted to be, where it felt most comfortable, in the light of the moon. The darkness let the house breathe, and breathe it did. Sounds would wake me from my sleep and promptly disappear, wooden floors creaked where no foot stepped. Shadows crawled with unseen monsters. Each night when the sun set, my skin tingled. To protect my mind from madness, I would focus my thoughts on Ma, or try to. I'd imagine her smell, her fussing in the kitchen, her quiet focus on a sewing task, the weight of her sleeping next to me. But in the darkness my unsettled mind always turned to Isaiah.

Eventually he would return, and I would have to face the truth of what I'd done.

I knew my devil stalked me. Creeping footsteps with no owner would sometimes cross my door. Each night, when I blew out my candle, red eyes would gleam from the shadows. Just for a moment. But they were there. He wasn't the only thing that walked uninvited through this house. There were ghosts here. Many ghosts. And they wanted to make themselves known.

One night I woke to weeping. The gossamer curtains were drawn about my bed as usual, but I hadn't closed the thick velvet curtains at the window. Consequently, moonlight flooded the room and revealed the profile of a woman standing on the other side of the thin bed drapes. Her hair was curled and frizzy. It fell almost to her small waist. Her hands covered her face. Her shoulders shook. The smell of sour milk cloaked the room. I had to find courage. I reached out, slowly gripped the curtain, and quickly pulled it back to see… nothing. No woman, no crying. The smell evaporated. The moon watched me through the large window. I lay down, as still as I could, and focused on the moon. *There is nothing to see here*, I thought, *nothing to see*. I stayed there until dawn broke.

In the middle of the third week, Zena knocked on my bedroom door. I knew it was her by her aggressive rap. Mathis, on the odd occasion he had been sent, knocked gently. My heart hammered with every pound of her knuckles on the wood. Purdie left immediately. As usual, I opened the door to her fixed, stern gaze. She would stare at me for a few seconds before walking away without a word. I knew to follow her. I was getting tired of following her about like a scolded child and made a promise to myself that I would be in the sitting room in time for supper in future, so we could forgo this charade.

The day was drawing to a close. It had been overcast and dull. The hallways were dark. Zena carried a candle. She was in silhouette; the golden glow of the flame created a halo about her small dark head, an illusion of holiness.

Then, from beyond the sound of our footsteps and the rustle of starched skirts, music drifted towards us. The notes floated like will-o'-the-wisps through the air. It wasn't something I'd heard in the house before. Someone was in the sitting room playing the piano, and playing it very well.

"Is my husband here?" I asked, but Zena didn't offer comment, just stopped outside the sitting room door where the symphony was now much louder. My heartbeat rose to its own crescendo as I realised the moment had finally arrived. The moment I had been dreading. My husband was home. I wasn't ready. Surely there was something I should do first? Some preparation? But I had no idea what, and Zena obviously felt there was no need. I panicked. Blood rushed to my head. I closed my eyes. And then I could hear the music again clearly. It was as calming as an elixir, as if I were drinking the notes themselves and they slid down to my heart and soothed it. I opened my eyes. Zena opened the door, her face inscrutable.

I stepped inside.

Isaiah sat at the piano, back straight, fingers gliding over the keys in a blur. For a moment there was nothing else, just the entrancing music filling me with a warmth I hadn't felt in his presence before. My head was light as if I had drunk too much wine. My breath rose and fell with the intensity of the notes. Isaiah was dedicated to his task, he swayed slightly with the movement, ebbing and flowing, as though he were a part of the instrument before him.

When the song ended, he placed his hands on his lap, still looking at the keys. Then he looked up at me. His eyes glimmered in the candlelight, like tiny fires burning.

The Devil has all the best tunes.

I'd heard that somewhere, most likely Ma. He smiled and said my name, and all thoughts of the Devil disappeared. He was a man like any other.

"I'm glad you arrived safely."

I had arrived almost three weeks ago. I realised I had started to settle in the house, to get comfortable with my new surroundings. I had been distracted by the people and the ghosts of this place. But his presence changed everything. I had been granted a reprieve these few weeks, but it was time to face the consequences of the choice I had made.

"Thank you, Zena, we have everything we need for the night," he said. I hadn't realised Zena was still in the doorway watching us. She stared at Isaiah for an uncomfortably long time before leaving. Zena's icy stare was doled out to her master, too. Isaiah let out a little sigh when she was gone.

"I hope Zena hasn't been too awful. She's not the best housekeeper, but she's part of the family, been here for as long as I can remember." That explained a lot. No wonder, with so few of them in the house, she was given such leeway.

"Not at all," I lied.

He walked towards me. I willed myself not to move,

preparing myself for some awkward embrace. But he didn't touch me, he walked past and pulled out a chair at the table which had been set for the two of us.

"Shall we eat?"

I sat down, unsure if I could even swallow food right now. My throat was thick, my limbs were lead.

Isaiah was the gentlemen I remembered and seemed to sense my trepidation. He led the conversation, speaking of his work in the north and the difficult journey home. There had been a dangerous storm in the North Sea. He described the swelling sea in great detail, as if he'd happily jump aboard and do it all again. The danger excited him, I could tell.

I observed the veins in his neck protruding and disappearing depending on the turn of his head, and how his Adam's apple moved up and down as he spoke. How thick his wrists were. The sheer size of him next to me was suffocating. I never thought of myself as a small person, but beside him I felt insignificant. He could crush me with his weight, squeeze the air out of me if he wanted. Soon enough I would know the weight of him. Then I'd see who he really was. This was all just pleasantries. The room grew darker, he was projecting shadows, subduing the light. The night was drawing in. The meal was at an end. I wasn't ready.

"Would you play again?" I blurted. "You play so well." I would buy some time. He smiled, pleased with the compliment.

We moved to the piano. He pulled a chair close, so I could sit and watch him play. The music started softly, his fingers delicately pressing the keys. As the pace increased, his hands were swift and sure. The music itself was sublime. It filled me like an intoxicating gas, like Esme's blue smoke.

My worries about what was to come began to weaken. By the time the song ended, I felt loose-limbed.

Then he was stood before me, holding out his hand. I took it and he pulled me up. He looked down at me and I looked up at him, the space between us itched. He led me upstairs.

As we climbed, the lulling effects of the music faded, and I could feel the weight of the situation press upon me. I followed his large frame through the darkness; his back barely left room for any light from the candle he held to guide me. I suddenly felt as if I were climbing those steps to the gallows. But my death would be much slower. The walls whispered. Breath on my neck. Something that felt like hair brushed my bare forearm. It made me nauseous. The weeping woman was close. I focused on my feet, counting the steps.

In the bedroom the fire blazed, candles had been lit all around. The thought of Zena preparing the room for this moment left me feeling uncomfortable. Did Isaiah ask her for the extra light? He would want a good look at what he'd bought.

I stood at the end of the bed, my breath shallow. He put the candle down. A shadow flickered at the window. Purdie. I shook my head at her and she flew away. I didn't want her to witness this. Then he was undressing me, examining his purchase. This wasn't like the lustful, shameful encounters I had shared with Charles. This was a transaction.

Isaiah was gentle but still I thought of those dirty hands that had yanked at my laces and torn my clothes. No, I couldn't go there, not now. Instead, I watched the flames in the fireplace, but they only served as a reminder of my devil and the hell that I would be sent to.

Soon enough I was completely exposed like leg of lamb on a butcher's hook. I did not cower. Isaiah held my gaze now, but his expression was difficult to read in the candlelight. Shadows and gold licked his face, distorting his features. The black depths of his eyes held the candle flame like a key to the underworld. Isaiah was the gateway to my doom. And I had chosen this path.

Over Isaiah's shoulder, a shadow shifted in the corner. There was something there. It moved again. A human shape formed. Wild hair, eyes snapped open and looked into mine. I gasped.

Isaiah thought it was for him.

He lay me on the bed, my heart racing.

When I looked to the corner again, there was nothing.

CHAPTER TEN

The next morning, I was instantly aware of the change in circumstance. I lay facing the window, the bed drapes were open, the curtains were open, and the light streamed in. The sky was dotted with wisps of clouds, all in a hurry to get somewhere. Every muscle in my body tensed. If I moved, I would feel Isaiah's body next to mine. I stayed very still and listened.

There was nothing but silence. No rise and fall of someone breathing next to me. The bedsheets offered no resistance. There was no one else in the bed. I turned my head slowly and saw the empty space. Sweet relief. Isaiah had left while I was sleeping. I was impressed he had managed it without me noticing, as I was always woken by the slightest shift in Ma. She couldn't scratch her nose without disturbing me.

It was kind of Isaiah to leave me sleeping. So far, he had shown nothing but gentlemanly kindness, even when making love. I was lucky. But a deep sense of dread weighed heavy on me. It didn't come from Isaiah or the house, or even the eccentric people in it. I had vowed never to let another man touch me; I had vowed never to let my belly grow.

And a power greater than anything earth-born had accepted that vow. I had made a soul pact.

And now I had broken it.

* * *

I saw no one that morning. Isaiah wasn't in the sitting room for breakfast, which was slightly worrying. What if I had done something wrong? I had hardly been the most welcoming bride. It had all felt a little cold.

Breakfast was hard to swallow with the thought of that ritual happening every night. It wasn't Isaiah who repulsed me, it was myself. I had what Ma would call "unrealistic expectations". I had once felt the hands of love upon me, or what I had thought of as love.

The passion, the fire, the wanting of another. I would never have that again. Would I ever feel anything for Isaiah but indifference and gratitude for saving my life? I knew that gratitude towards another never lasted long. It would soften into obligation and eventually harden to a bitter disdain. Especially as allowing him to save my life was brought about by my own cowardice, my fear of death. A sin in itself.

I needed to be outside. The stone walls and dusty carpets were restricting my airflow. The woods called.

It was a crisp, clear day. Perfect for filling my lungs with fresh air and quieting my mind. Purdie joined me as I entered the woods behind the house. She would flit from branches to my shoulder, where she would pull at my hair or nip at my ear. She wanted to play but I was in no mood. Soon enough she tired of me and went in search of berries and bugs.

The woods were different from those at home. My woods were open and clear. The trees stood to attention at regular intervals, giving the squirrels plenty of floor space to run around, and people room to walk without effort. Here the trees grew close, the ground was covered in foliage. The air was warmer and hung heavy in the enclosed space. This wood lived in defiance of the open sea around it. Here was its own world, protected from the sea air with its denseness. The plants were different, too. Their leaves were thick, tropical. The wood was alive; it reminded me that I was alive too.

I found a felled log and sat on it, listening to the sound of the leaves rustling. If I closed my eyes I could see my woods. I could pretend none of this ever happened and I'd be returning to Ma in the cottage soon. I could pretend my lake was just a few steps away. I could see it clearly, I could feel the bank beneath my knees, my fingers cooled as I dipped them in the water. I could see beneath the water, all the way down to the bed, where two small bundles waited for me to join them. But I couldn't escape the sound of the birds. Their voices were foreign and reminded me I was not at home.

A noise, not of the woods, pulled me back to reality. I tensed. Someone else was nearby. I moved to the nearest tree and stood behind it. The noise grew louder. Footsteps. I didn't want to see Isaiah, and he was the only person I could imagine coming out here. I'd yet to see Zena or Esme roaming outside the house. The steps were closer now. I risked a look in the direction of the sound. It was Mathis, carrying his garden basket. He stopped at the foot of a large oak, knelt down, and began carefully digging at the earth with his trowel.

I didn't want to move, but I didn't want to stand there spying on him while he worked either. His face had a determined concentration, his hands worked quickly but gently. His body was relaxed. He was comfortable with the earth.

Purdie suddenly appeared from nowhere, landing right next to me and making a racket of cackling. Mathis looked my way, and I stepped out. His body tensed. He immediately put his trowel back in his basket and stood to leave. Rage swelled in my stomach. I was tired of him ignoring me. I had done nothing to him.

"Is there a reason you avoid me?"

He froze, half turned away from me.

"You can talk to me," I said. My voice dissipated into the trees.

To my astonishment, he didn't look at me and began to walk away. "I'm not good enough for you, is that it?" I called after him, anger getting the better of me.

He stopped and looked at me, interested.

"I'm not avoiding you," he said.

"You abandon whatever you're doing every time I'm near."

"I'm sorry if I've upset you. I hadn't realised."

"It's not important." I waved my hand as if batting this nonsense away, but his indifference hurt. Perhaps I was being unreasonable. This place had put me on edge.

"Can I get you anything, ma'am?"

"Please don't call me that," I sighed.

He nodded.

"I'm not used to being waited on," I said. "A fine mistress I am."

He was going to respond, but decided against it and closed his mouth again, looking at the ground instead.

"I didn't mean to disturb your work," I said. "You can finish."

I walked away. Purdie left the branch she was perched on and followed me. He would see that. I would have to train her.

I emerged from the woods on the north side of the house and stopped dead. Someone was in my bedroom. It could be Zena sorting the fire, or Isaiah. Maybe he was looking for me. But the figure moved in a most unusual way. It glided. There was no rhythm of a gait. Strange how we barely notice the way people walk until a difference so slight as a bob of the head is missing. And it was tall. My windows were high.

I found my feet and rushed to the bedroom. I noticed halfway up the stairs that Purdie was still with me. I shouldn't let her in the main house, but it mattered little now. Without hesitation, I opened my bedroom door and entered with my chin held high, my chest puffed out as if preparing for a fight. But there was nobody in the room. No sign that anyone had been in there. The bedsheets were still a crumpled mess, just as I'd left them in my trepidation of seeing Isaiah at breakfast. The fire hadn't been lit. The air was still, silent, heavy. But a feeling lingered, as if someone had just left through an invisible door. I stood deathly still. Purdie copied me, a taxidermic version of herself perched on the back of the chair.

A soft thud.

It had come from the dressing room. They must be hiding in there. I took a poker from the fireplace, then edged to the dressing room, using the weapon to push the door open.

Purdie flew in before me, screeching as she went. But again, there was nothing.

"Hush, Purdie, we're safe." She perched on the edge of the tub, scanning the room with her beady eyes. She was right to be wary, we had definitely heard something. I looked around the room too. In the far corner, a small bundle was on the floor. I picked it up. A cloth tied with string. I unwrapped it to find a beautiful brooch. It was small but exquisite. Pearls grouped together in circles, surrounding the centre piece, where there sat a miniature portrait of a woman. Brown eyes looked up at me. Her heart-shaped face was framed by golden curls. Her chin lifted in defiance and a cheeky smile curling her lips. A small tiara glittered, and diamonds highlighted her slender neck and smooth shoulders. She looked like a princess.

A rap on the door frightened me and I almost dropped it. I quickly wrapped it up again and hid it at the back of a shelf.

Zena glared at me when I opened the bedroom door. "Mrs Quickly asked for you."

She turned and left. I played my part and followed her, sighing audibly.

CHAPTER ELEVEN

Back down to the womb of the building. Zena had gone back to the kitchen and left me without a light. Tobacco smoke filled the dark narrow corridor leading to Esme's door. The flickering light at its base guided me. It was like walking into a spider's hideout. I wondered if Esme could feel us all moving about the house from here.

As if to confirm my thoughts, Esme called, "Enter" before I knocked on the door.

She was stood behind her chair with an easel. Her back straight, her neck elegant. Her fingers were smeared with paint where she had used them for shading or mixing. The painting was of the house. A perfect replica of my first view of the cove and house from the rowing boat I'd arrived in. It was exquisite. Every detail was captured perfectly. The glinting windows, the birds circling. I could almost hear them screeching.

"Do you like it?"

"It's beautiful, a perfect likeness," I said.

"I'm glad you think so. I painted it for you."

"I… don't know how to thank you. I wish I had something to offer in return."

"You are gift enough, dear."

I moved next to Esme. Here, the smell of her face powder

mingled with the heady smoke. The thick scent settled at the back of my throat. I tried to ignore it.

The more I observed the painting, the more things I noticed: the individual blooms in the garden, the uniqueness of each stone step that climbed the cliff to the castle. She was a true master of her craft.

"Come, sit." Esme settled into her easy chair, picking up her pipe. "Help yourself, child."

The tea and sweetmeats were laid out, tempting me. I chose a marzipan strawberry, relishing the almond sweetness.

"So, my son arrived last night."

"He did. Did you see him? You didn't join us for supper."

"I'm not that kind of mother. I wouldn't want to disturb you on your first married night together." Esme raised her eyebrows. "You found him pleasing, I expect?" She chuckled. "I am just teasing. But we are both women. We know what men want." She puffed on her pipe. "I remember the first night with my husband. I wasn't scared at all. I couldn't wait to get to the bridal bed."

My face burned. There was something disturbing about an old woman talking about the bridal bed.

"I wasn't a whore." Esme laughed. Now I almost choked. "I had known my husband a long time before we were wed."

"How did you meet?"

"We met in Russia about a thousand years ago." Her eyes misted over.

"In Russia?"

"Yes, dear, I am not of English stock." She sucked on the pipe, smoke billowed about her face. "I can see you are surprised. But I arrived here when I was very small, only eight years old, and all my Russian ways are gone.

"It was a harsh winter the year I met my husband. My sister and I had recently been orphaned in some civil brawl and were left on the streets to die. We spent the days begging, the nights huddled in any place that offered some kind of protection from the cold. We would have died, if it hadn't been for my husband.

"I remember his bright red cloak against the drab grey of the streets. I followed him for half a mile offering to work for food, expecting him to swipe at me at any moment. But he didn't. He turned to me and my sister, and looked us deep in the eyes. He tilted our heads and checked our teeth. He said I had a strong determination for one so close to death, and I told him I would never die, not for as long as my sister needed me. He laughed at that. And then, to my surprise, he took us with him. We were on a boat to England, straight to this house.

"Ten years later we were married."

"You were a young bride, then."

"Eighteen. Too old for my liking. I would have married him at fifteen, I was so in love."

"What did his family say?"

"I was lucky. He had no family." Esme cackled. "I didn't have to put up with strange old mothers-in-law," she teased, and I laughed as if she were not strange at all.

"What about your sister?"

"We grew apart." Her tone was clipped, putting an end to that line of conversation.

I sipped her tea, the bitterness not as bad as the last time. I thought of Isaiah. I knew I would never feel love for him like Esme had loved her husband. Ma said the love would come after, but I wasn't convinced it worked like that. Esme had known instantly.

"I'm sorry he's not with you now," I said. "Your husband..."

"He is always with me." Esme smiled. "He defies death."

I thought about the brooch. I wanted to ask. The words were sitting on the tip of my tongue. But the timing felt wrong. I didn't want to throw another dead spouse into the conversation. Maybe I should speak directly to Isaiah about it. Or wait until he wanted to share it with me. Either way, I kept it to myself.

"You'll figure it out," Esme said, as if she knew exactly what I was thinking.

The painting hung on the wall of my bedroom, opposite the windows. It was the perfect place. The midday light exposed the colours in all their glory but didn't hit the painting directly. As I moved about the room, I would catch its shimmer from the corner of my eye. At each moment the painting seemed to offer some new detail. I spotted a mole burrowing at the foot of the trees. Sleek shadows haunted the ocean. A lone bird flew high above the others between the clouds.

There was a gentle tap at the door. Mathis. I felt bad about our conversation earlier.

"I'm to tell you supper is at eight." Mathis looked pale, like he was at the beginning of an illness.

"Are you well, Mathis?"

"I'm fine ma–" He stopped himself from saying *ma'am*. He quickly glanced at the painting.

"Esme painted it for me. It really is beautiful." I stepped back to allow him to see it, and wondered what I was doing. Why did I feel the need to include him? He offered no sense that he wanted to talk to me or even be in the same room as me. He stood before it, examining it carefully, his face revealing nothing as usual.

"She's very talented," I said. Again, feeling the need to talk.

"She is," he said. Though his tone did not suggest praise.

I watched as he examined the painting thoroughly, as if he was searching for something specific. It occurred to me that I knew nothing about him.

"What did you do before you worked here, Mathis?"

He coughed before answering. "I worked at sea."

"Oh, you were a sailor?"

"I was." He offered nothing more.

"Then how did you find yourself here? I thought seamen couldn't bear to be on land for long."

"I found myself on the main island with no work when I heard about this position. I thought it might be good for me to ground myself for a while."

He didn't look at me once while talking, he kept his eyes on the painting. "And I needed work," he muttered. This caveat felt like the truth. Perhaps there was no story to Mathis, just a man wanting to earn a wage. But he had been looking for something, that night in the bedroom. I was sure of it.

When he'd gone, I let Purdie in. I stroked her black-feathered head. Birds are simple. They don't have secrets. They stay out of all things human, and rightly so. "What would I do without you, Purdie?" The bird let out a gentle rapping sound and began pulling loose threads from the tasselled tiebacks.

Supper was at eight. Now Isaiah was here I would have to follow his mealtimes, and I should get ready. Esme and

Mathis had served to distract me for a while from the knot that was tightening in my stomach. I would have to repeat last night with Isaiah, for this night and many nights to come.

I would make myself presentable.

CHAPTER TWELVE

He was playing the piano again. Not soothing like the night before, but fast and rising to a crescendo. The brazen boldness of the music, the reverberating beat of it, shook my insides, causing my heart to beat too fast. I watched his fingers move expertly, furiously across the keys. I was suddenly stripped bare, the memory of standing naked before him the previous night made my entire body blush. But the music swept me up and turned my shame to an unwilling longing. I tingled with the anticipation of being touched again and wrestled with self-disgust.

He made it easy for me, asking me how I'd slept, apologising for having to leave to work so early. I found myself nodding, barely talking. It was a charade, a prelude to the end goal – getting to the bedroom. Not that Isaiah revealed in any way that that was his intention. But it was there, tied like a rope around my neck, loosely for now, with the fibres tickling my throat, but very soon it would be choking me.

As we were about to begin eating, Esme entered the room. She was dressed ready for a ball at the king's court. Huge jewels of every colour dripped from her neck and fingers. A gown of silver with gold lace cuffs and a long red velvet cloak trimmed with black fur trailed behind her.

She sparkled and shimmered in the candlelight. Isaiah and I watched as she shuffled herself into a seat at the table and began filling a plate. I remembered to close my mouth.

"You didn't say you'd be joining us," Isaiah said.

"Do I need an invitation in my own home? A woman must eat, you know. Even an old crone like me." But instead of eating, Esme pulled a familiar box from her skirts, placed it on the table and opened it. Inside was her pipe and tobacco. She set about stuffing the pipe and was soon filling the room with the blue smoke. I looked from Isaiah to Esme. He watched his mother with narrowed eyes. "Or perhaps with your beautiful new bride about the place you'd forgotten I lived here." She winked at me and chuckled, the smoke shooting out in bursts from her nose and mouth. "Have you shown Fortune around the place yet?"

"I've hardly had the time. I only got back yesterday."

"I know. And couldn't spare five minutes to come and say hello to your old mother."

She turned back to me. "I bet he's had time to see your bedroom though, hasn't he?"

My mouth fell open again and I attempted to stutter an answer, "I... well, I..."

"That's not appropriate talk for the dinner table, is it?" Isaiah cut in, keeping his voice low.

They stared at each other for a moment. A battle of wills. The candlelight burned in Isaiah's black eyes and Esme glittered in all her finery. They were family, a whole conversation could occur with a look, and I was an outsider.

"Tomorrow you should take her for a tour, Isaiah. There must be some interesting things to see in this place. I can't remember them myself."

"I'll be working, Mother, you know that." He emphasised

the word "Mother", a warning to back off. Esme was making things awkward. We weren't young lovers courting, we'd been thrown together by circumstance, and Isaiah's good nature. I was surprised by the tension between them. Isaiah was a perfect gentleman, and Esme had been good to me since I arrived, but seeing them together reminded me of how little I knew about them. They had a lifetime of stories and secrets between them, including the one about Isaiah's previous wife. I would stay silent about the brooch.

"I think I've seen everything there is to see already," I added, trying to take the pressure off Isaiah slightly.

Esme sipped her wine and pulled a face. "Why are we drinking this muck?" She pushed the cup away. "Fortune, be a darling and ring for the help, will you?"

Isaiah sighed audibly when Esme said, "the help". I did as I was asked and pulled on the rope. Something I'd never dared do before. I wasn't even sure it would work. Isaiah leaned back in his chair and raised his eyebrows at Esme. She smiled and puffed smoke at his face.

The air solidified as we waited for "the help" to arrive.

"Esme painted a picture of the house for me," I said, trying to offer some relief. "It's very beautiful. Your mother is very talented."

"Did she?" Isaiah asked, not taking his eyes from Esme.

Esme laughed and looked to me. "You flatter me, child. It's just a painting." She puffed on her pipe, looking back at Isaiah defiantly.

I had never before felt relief at the sight of Zena's bony face, but I did when she arrived that moment.

"Oh, finally," Esme declared, rolling her eyes. "Zena, this wine is awful, you must bring a better one." Zena didn't fully acknowledge Esme but came to the table to take the offending jug away. Esme slapped Zena's hand as she reached for it. Isaiah flinched.

"Don't take that one, I'll need to drink something while we wait an age for you to find another bottle," Esme said.

I could feel Zena's fury from the other side of the table.

"And next time, don't boil the carrots so much, they are positively dead." Zena was already walking out of the room. Esme was chuckling to herself as she picked up a strip of floppy purple carrot.

"Leave it," Isaiah said. His voice was firm. Esme was starting to annoy him.

"Ah, we mustn't upset Zena now, must we?" Esme smirked. I looked between them both and sank a little further into my chair. "You know, I think my son loves Zena more than me," Esme said, smiling like the fox who caught the hen. "He would never let her out of his sight in his younger days. It was always Zena this and Zena that." She smirked and puffed on her pipe. The smoke was filling up the room now and pushing its way down my throat. I stifled a cough. Isaiah sighed again, faking boredom. I was intrigued. I couldn't imagine anyone being attached to Zena.

"But these days, of course, he doesn't have much use for either of us. Just two old birds rattling about this tomb, every day one step closer to death."

"That's enough drama for today," Isaiah said. And to my surprise, he stood up and held out his hand to me. "Shall we?" I took his hand and fumbled some comments of goodnight to Esme.

"I'm fine here," Esme called after us. "You two go and do what needs to be done." I could hear her rasping chuckle halfway down the corridor. He led me straight to the bedroom.

CHAPTER THIRTEEN

The sun was rising behind the woods. Its rays reached over the house and across the sea to the horizon, transforming the sky from inky blue to violet to gold. But the sun's embrace didn't warm me. I sat on the chilly beach, night-time still trapped in the shadows between the scar and the sea. The sand was cold. Purdie sat still at my side.

The waves hushed their soporific whispers. Rhythmic, melodic. But nothing could soothe the feelings that had forced me out into the open with the waking of the birds. Every night my husband would take me to bed, and every morning he was gone. I wouldn't see him again until supper. I wondered how long it would take before my belly would begin to grow. The inevitability of it pressed on me like a great weight. Every caress, every thrust, every little death pushed me closer to the end.

Out here was better, in the open air, away from the house. The house itself watched me, judged me. Ghosts lined the walls. I could feel eyes everywhere.

A shadow gliding across the surface of the sea caught my attention. In the sky above, with the morning rays giving it a supernatural glow, was the largest bird I have ever seen. It silently circled. Slowly it descended and came to land on the cold sand a few feet before me.

Purdie hopped back, hiding herself behind me, but didn't fly away.

The eagle was magnificent in size. Her talons, sharp as butcher's knives, were large enough to slice a human throat. Her bright yellow beak curved to a sharp point, powerful enough to tear through flesh The perfect hunting machine.

I rose carefully from my seated position, not wanting to make sudden movements, terrified of scaring the creature away. But I needed to be closer. I had never seen anything so beautiful, so powerful. I had to touch her.

The bird didn't move as I approached. Her left side was facing me, her golden eye fixed on me. I reached out my hand expecting her to take flight, but she didn't move. She would let me touch her.

I ran the tips of my fingers down the bird's back, her large brown feathers as smooth and silky as a well-groomed cat. Feathers splayed from her base as if they had been dipped in cream.

She opened her wings, and I gasped. I heard Purdie let out a squall somewhere behind me, but the sound was muffled. The breeze, the sea, the other birds crying on the cliffs, they all fell away as if I were held in a sacred place. Protected.

Her wings were wide enough to wrap me twice. I let myself fall to my knees as she displayed herself to me, as if I were being blessed by an angel. Then she lifted herself into the air with the grace of a magician flawlessly executing his most dazzling trick, and she was gone.

I sat for a while. Purdie settled on my knee, and I petted her absent-mindedly.

The myriad of beautiful colours in the sky were slowly blocked as a great grey cloud passed over, as if someone were drawing a curtain across the world. It doused the flame that the eagle had lit within me. I was suddenly filled with dread. The bird was an omen, perhaps not a good one.

Breakfast would be laid in the sitting room by now and my need for food brought me back to earth. I couldn't fly away; I would have to face my demons. I had made choices, and choices have consequences. Funny how I had been enticed by the idea of a solitary place. I thought I would be free. I was far from free. I swear Zena could see through walls. Esme and Isaiah had expectations. Mathis was cold. There was nowhere for me to go and nothing for me to do. Every day I stepped a little closer to the inevitable. I would become pregnant, and my devil would be waiting to take the child away. Would the child suffer in the afterlife, or would it simply not exist at all, a soul not given the time to take hold. I hoped for the latter. But why should the child suffer? It wasn't their mistake, and one little one had already atoned for that. Must there be endless suffering and punishment? Ma always said it was those closest to you who paid the price of your ignorance, and I was ignorant. Doubly so for making such a ridiculous vow. There was only myself to blame.

I began to climb the stone steps back up to the house with a heavy heart. Not paying attention to my surroundings, I was caught unawares when my skirt was tugged from behind. Purdie was above me, further up the steps. The sickly smell of sour milk surrounded me. I looked down. A slim hand, muddied flesh and black fingernails had a grip on my skirt. I lost my breath as I followed the arm to its owner. The face was mostly covered with long, curled, matted hair. Only one eye was visible, and it glared at me in fear and anguish, stopping my breath. Her body disappeared into the rock. Impossible. And then I was falling. I was only a few steps up, but the rocks were sharp, and I felt the flesh on the side of my arm being torn by the rough stone as I scrambled for a handle on something. Another pain seared through my ankle as it hit the edge of a step on the way down. I cried out and landed on my back at the foot of the stairs. Purdie flapped about me.

"Hush, Purdie, I'm alright."

I winced at the blood seeping through my torn sleeve. Pain surged up my leg like a hot iron when I tried to lift myself.

Mathis appeared at the top of the steps and deftly ran down them towards me.

"Mrs Quickly, are you hurt?"

"I'm alright," I repeated to him, feeling foolish. I tried to push myself up and let out a whimper as I put weight on my ankle.

"Here, let me help," Mathis said.

He held out his hand and I took it. He put one arm around my waist and placed my good arm over his shoulder. He lifted me with ease, as if I were attached to him.

We made our way up the steps in an awkward dance as I tried not to put any weight on my foot. But I felt that if I'd allowed it, Mathis would have carried me up the steps without losing breath. He smelt of the flower garden, soil was lodged beneath his nails, and his brow had a streak of dirt across it where he must have wiped sweat away while he worked. I glanced back at the rock where the hand had grabbed me. There was only stone. No woman, no way a person could be there at all. But it had been so real. I had felt the tug on my skirt, seen her as clearly as I saw Mathis beside me. She was a phantom, and I had no doubt that this thing wanted to cause me harm.

When we reached the top, I saw Mathis' tools abandoned by the garden. I glanced at his face. From this angle I couldn't see his scars at all. I could see the person he was before the fire had ravaged him. He must have felt the loss deeply as his features were striking. I doubt he would have hidden himself away here if he had not suffered this tragedy. A beautiful face can take you far. It can also bring trouble.

He helped me into a chair in the sitting room and brought a stool, lifting my ankle onto it carefully. When he let me go, I felt a loss. I was alone again. The comfort of his body against mine, the kindness of his coming to my aid, stirred something in me. I missed the touch of another. And not in the way Isaiah touched me. I missed having Ma by my side. I missed her companionship, her generosity, her nagging. I missed the comfort of her warm body next to mine while we slept. I had felt no tenderness since that terrible night I left her, until now.

"Do you mind?" Mathis wanted to take a look at my ankle. I shook my head, no.

With great care he lifted the hem of my dress, so he could see my ankle. He sucked air through his teeth at the sight. It was twice its normal size and quickly changing colour. Very gently, he lifted the offending foot slightly, making me wince. "Sorry," he said, as he slipped off my shoe.

"Can you move your toes?"

I wiggled them.

"I don't think anything is broken."

He still didn't look directly at me when he spoke.

"You know a lot for a gardener," I said. He glanced up at me then. I smiled, and there appeared a hint of a smile in return.

"I'll be back in a minute," he said and left the room.

I looked to the table and there was breakfast laid out, gathering dust, but my appetite had waned.

When Mathis returned, Zena was behind him.

"I need to examine it," she said. My heart sank along with the temperature of the room. I was yet to discover if Zena did in fact chill the air or it was my mind playing tricks on me. Even in the morning light she looked skeletal, no amount of sunshine could raise a colour in her cheeks.

Her bony fingers pressed at the swollen flesh, and I clamped my teeth together in pain.

Black dots gathered at the edge of my vision.

"You'll heal," she said, letting go of my ankle. "It'll take a while. You'll have to stay off your feet. Keep to your room, out of trouble." I was the child chastised.

"Help her upstairs," Zena told Mathis, "and come back for some water to clean her arm."

"Now Zena, there's no need to leave the child like that." Esme's raspy voice proceeded her into the room. How did she even know what was happening? I imagined her watching me struggling to the house with Mathis' arm around me from one of the many windows. She would enjoy making fun of me for that.

"I have something that will help." She practically pushed Zena out of the way and knelt before my swollen foot, which was turning a shade of blue.

Esme pulled a small wooden box from her pocket. She ran her fingers across the embossed lid before opening it. Inside was an ointment. She scooped some onto her finger and began gently rubbing it over the swollen area.

There was a burning sensation which quickly cooled and took a lot of the pain with it.

"How does it do that?"

"It's an old family recipe." Esme smiled. "Better?"

I nodded. My body relaxed; my bones ached with exhaustion. She rubbed some into the cut on my arm, which immediately felt better.

"Don't put all your weight on the ankle just yet," Esme said, rubbing the remnants of ointment into her old hands. "This helps my old aching bones, too."

"Mathis, take Mrs Quickly up to her room, will you? She'll need to rest a while," Esme said.

Mathis didn't answer. His gaze was fixed upon the little box, as if it were sent from the Devil himself.

"Mathis," Esme said more firmly as she put the box back in her pocket.

"Of course," Mathis said, coming back to himself.

Esme rolled her eyes at me as if mourning the idiots about her.

Mathis helped me up. The pain was minimal compared to before. I hobbled out of the sitting room, glad to be away from Zena and Esme. The two of them together made the air crackle with tension.

"I was lucky you were outside," I said once we were out of earshot.

Mathis nodded an acknowledgement.

"I never see Zena or Esme outside." I looked at him, but he didn't look at me, just kept his head strictly forward. The colour in his face had faded somewhat since seeing the ointment, any hint of a smile gone.

"It's a wonder they would want to stay in this gloom when the weather is so fine, and the birds are singing," I said, wondering how I should approach the real topic of conversation.

Why did the ointment jar him?

"Perhaps they like the gloom more," he said absently. I was glad to hear his voice, I didn't think he was going to talk at all. Perhaps the fact that I was clinging to his arm made him more amiable towards me.

"What were you doing, before you came to rescue me?"

"Planting seeds. For rose bushes."

What a strange one Mathis was. Who was he planting rose bushes for in this barren place?

"Did Zena ask you to do that?"

"No. Would you rather I didn't?" he asked, a little abruptly. I had forgotten that I was supposed to be the mistress of this house, and maybe I should be the one saying what flowers are planted where.

"You can plant anything you like. The more the better."

He nodded.

I knew Mathis was hiding something. I just couldn't shake the feeling that he had a reason for being here, and not a good one, after catching him rifling through a random linen closet. But he planted flowers and had come to my rescue on the steps. My husband was nowhere to be seen, and I hadn't even thought to ask where he was.

We reached the bedroom, and I sat by the fire, which Mathis set about lighting. I was glad of the warmth when it began to burn.

"I'll bring your breakfast up," Mathis said as he moved to the door.

I couldn't let him leave without asking.

"Mathis." I stopped him, but he didn't fully turn towards me. "Have you ever seen anything like that ointment before?"

"No," he said, looking to the fire instead of my face. "Never," he added. Then he left, closing the door behind him.

He was not a good liar.

I limped to the window to let Purdie in. She rushed inside, clapping her beak and making short, sharp caws.

"I'm fine, Purdie, hush now."

I stroked the top of her head and tickled her chin as she settled. It didn't last long. She flew across the room to Esme's painting, flapping her wings about it and squawking.

"Purdie, what is wrong with you? Everything is fine."

But Purdie was right, there was something different about the painting. Where the sun had been high in the sky and the cove bathed in light, just as it had looked on my arrival here, now the sky was filled with thick grey cloud, exactly like the cloud that had appeared that morning.

I stepped closer, squinting my eyes at the canvas. How could this be possible? Paintings didn't move. I scoured the painting for any other differences.

There, in the shadows of the cove, was a person. Not just any person: me. Sitting on the cold sand, just as I had done only an hour previous. It was dark and slightly blurred, but unmistakable.

Beside my head, as if emerging from the cliff face behind me, were eyes. Glowing red. Pinpricks of angry light surrounded by long, matted hair. Watching me.

CHAPTER FOURTEEN

Blue tobacco smoke curled from beneath Esme's door. I stood before it, building up the courage to knock. There was also, unusually, the sound of music. It tinkled strange metallic notes.

My ankle had completely healed from the day before. A miracle. Ma had sprained her ankle once and she suffered with a weakness for months after and still gets twinges of pain now. But I was certain my ankle was fully healed, it felt as strong as ever.

If we'd have had ointment like that back home, Ma could have been saved a lot of pain, but I also may have found myself at the gallows like old Rita. Her cures and tinctures didn't work half as well as this ointment, but she had still been targeted. Imagine the fear this ointment would evoke back home. Esme would be hanged in an instant.

Then there was the painting. The moment I had taken my eyes off it, it had returned to its previous state. I was starting to think I'd imagined it, but Purdie had seen it too. Both of us couldn't be wrong. But what would that mean? That Esme was a witch? That she was casting spells, brewing potions, and dancing with the Devil when the moon was full? That was nonsense. Esme was eccentric, but not evil.

I knocked on the door.

"Enter," she said.

The tinkling music was coming from a large contraption in the corner that looked like an overgrown cabinet. It must have been there all the time, but the room was packed with furniture. and I'd paid it little attention, assuming it was a writing bureau. Now, however, I was fascinated.

"It's a music box," Esme said. "Isaiah does love his trinkets, and I must confess I'm quite partial to this one. It's far from an orchestra but still, it's better than the silence sometimes."

"It must get very quiet here," I said. Esme must get lonely with only Zena for company most of the time. Her surly mouth would send anyone retreating into the depths of this house.

"It suits me, for now." Esme started pouring the tea, and I didn't ask her to expand on what she meant by "for now".

"How is your ankle?"

"It's perfect, like I never hurt it at all." I watched her carefully, hoping she would tell me something about the ointment, but she merely smiled and nodded as she focused on the tea. She strained it and scooped plenty of sugar into my cup.

"That ointment really worked a wonder. It looked pretty bad to me," I said, still hoping to entice some kind of explanation from her.

"Looks can be deceiving," Esme said, handing me my cup. "It couldn't have been too badly damaged." She gestured for me to drink. The music box clinked, each note a satisfying metal twang. "I should've joined you for supper last night," she added, "to check how you were feeling."

The conversation about the ointment was over.

"Oh, we didn't have supper. Isaiah sent a message for me to rest for the evening."

"Did he?" Esme's voice raised an octave in surprise. "And is everything well with you and my son?"

"Yes." I felt my cheeks warming and put the cup back on the little table.

"You know, he never has told me why the wedding was so rushed," Esme said, leaning back, her eyes on me, stirring her tea with a tiny silver spoon. She glanced at my stomach.

"He had to leave on business, so we thought it best to marry before he left." The lie made my throat thick.

"I see." The spoon clinked the inside of her mug, adding to the music. "You couldn't have waited until after the business?"

"Well, I..." An ache throbbed in my side as I remembered a fist slamming into it. The angry, beer-filled men surrounding me. Then the crowd parting when Isaiah arrived. I could never tell Esme I was branded a witch. What would she think of me?

"I'm pulling your leg," Esme laughed. "Who am I to question the lust of youth? I suspect Isaiah didn't want to wait another moment to get you into bed."

I laughed along with her, feigning coyness. But Esme's brash comment hid another meaning. There was something *she* couldn't wait for. A child. Marriage was always about children. As much as I enjoyed Esme's company, she was a constant reminder of the thing I wanted the least. The sticks that made up the doll in my pocket pressed against my thigh like thorns. I was an ocean away from my mermaid child, but no distance could remove my heart from the bottom of the lake. The room was hot. I imagined diving into the waters and growing my own mermaid tail, cool and sleek and forever.

"I'm sorry, child, I didn't mean to embarrass you. But we are both women here, and we know what men ultimately want."

No wonder she was desperate for a grandchild in this place. For her it would be a harbinger of joy; for me, one of death. I knew, deep in my heart, that if... when... I lost another child, it would be the end of me too. Even if my devil spared me, I knew I couldn't survive another heartache like that.

"Let's change the subject," Esme said, blunt as ever. "Tell me about your home." She began stuffing her pipe, the music clinked.

"There's not much to tell. It's a regular town, very dull."

"Hmm," Esme said, lighting her pipe and puffing furiously until the smoke enveloped her. "I heard," she said, smoke trickling from her nose and mouth, "that people are hunting witches."

"They are." The memory of Rita's kicking feet returned, the gasps of the crowd.

"You've seen them?" Esme asked, her tone casual.

"I've seen one."

"Hanged or burned?"

"She was hanged."

"A witch?"

"So they say."

"But *you* don't think so?" Esme leaned forward slightly, much more interested in this conversation.

"She was an old woman who blended herbs for ailments."

"So, not a witch then."

"Other people thought so."

"But not you?" She waited for an answer.

I thought for a moment. "No, I don't think so."

Esme leaned back in her chair, a sly smile playing. "You don't believe in the Devil?"

"Yes, I believe in the Devil," I answered, "but I believe that if *I* was the Devil, I'd choose a more able disciple than a decrepit old woman living in a hut with a mangy cat for company."

Esme laughed at that.

"Fortune, child, you are strong-minded. I like it." She puffed on her pipe.

"I saw a burning once," Esme said after a moment. Her voice deepened as she fell into the memory. "A *cleansing* they called it." She leaned back, her laughter gone, blue smoke curled around her powdered face. "Flames melting flesh is something to watch. And the smell. I can still smell it now, like a piece of rotten meat stuck to the back of my throat, and no matter how much I cough or drink or eat to shift it, it never goes away."

I'd experienced something similar when Mr Farley's goats had been cursed with a disease and they all had to be killed and burned. The smell suffocated the town for days, so much so that me and Ma soaked the whole cottage in lavender. But to see a human burn was unimaginable. Hanging was merciful in comparison.

I wondered where Esme had witnessed this, but before I could ask, she spoke again.

"Witches are pesky things. They have to be handled a certain way."

That stopped my mouth.

The music box continued to clink its charming, childlike melody. An absurd backdrop to our dark conversation.

Esme picked up a handful of the sweetmeats that always accompanied the tea and wrapped them in a handkerchief. "Here, take these to your room. I bet Zena never sends you any treats up. And it's good to have some sugar before bed. It brings sweet dreams."

I put them in my pocket.

* * *

"Aren't you hungry?" Isaiah looked at me from the end of the dining table. I hadn't touched my plate. I had been far away, thinking of my previous life, rubbing the little doll in my pocket. My life had been split in two, before and after the death of Amber's child. I hadn't stopped to think about Amber's pain, but as much as I disliked her, she was a mother of a dead child now, just like me. I hadn't wanted that for her. I wouldn't want that for anyone. The past felt like a dream, a world that was slowly disappearing with each new day I spent here. But the doll in my pocket was real and Ma was real, and I had to remember that.

"It's been a long day," I said, picking up my spoon. "Do you know if Zena has sent my letters?" I was feeling lost, and that made me bold.

"Letters?" He had no idea what I meant.

"I've been writing to Ma. I never see any boats, or anybody who could come to collect them. Zena said she would send them. I was just wondering…"

"If Zena said she would send them then she will." I still found his confidence in her completely baffling. "No doubt she already has."

"Hm." I nodded, looked back to my plate.

"I'm sorry I'm not around much." Isaiah put his hand over mine and I stifled my flinch. I hoped he didn't notice.

No matter how many times we were together, I still woke each morning full of dread, hoping that would be the last time. But I knew it wouldn't, not until they had what they needed: an heir for their isolated empire. I didn't dislike Isaiah for that. It was natural for him to desire that. He needed someone to pass his estate to. There was no extended family. He had put his faith in me to satisfy those needs.

He would be very disappointed.

The only blessing was that it would be over soon enough. Isaiah could find a new bride who would provide him with what he wanted.

I hoped they would let the sea take my body and I would find my mermaid child. I imagined that all water was connected in the afterlife. Perhaps I should tell someone my wishes, but I didn't know how to bring it up in conversation.

"Where do you go all day?" I asked. It sounded more accusatory than I intended.

"To my office," he said. "It's just down the hall, past the kitchens."

"I haven't been in that part of the house."

"Don't let Zena scare you, you can go anywhere you like."

"I think Zena could scare the cavalry," I said.

Isaiah laughed. "Shall I play?"

I hesitated, then nodded. I knew by now what this meant. Even though I would wake full of dread, I longed for the piano-playing moments. As soon as his fingers touched the keys, I would forget all about curses and broken vows. The notes would wash over me like too much wine. My skin would tingle, anticipating those fingers turning their attention to me.

Upstairs, with the music faded, my skin would harden again. Isaiah's large body would steal the candlelight, flames would flicker in the blacks of his eyes, like a gateway to the underworld.

The house around us would contract, watching our every move, and I would disconnect from my body. Sometimes, I could hear a woman weeping.

* * *

That night I dreamt of the eagle. She was in my bedroom, her large frame as big as a human sat before the fire. I sat in the chair opposite. Her golden eyes fixed on me.

"What are you trying to tell me?" I asked her.

She opened her huge mouth, revealing her splendid scarlet tongue. From the back of her throat a light glimmered and grew into flame. All at once it burst forth from her throat. I turned my head, and the flames hit the side of my face. I screamed as my flesh melted away.

I woke holding my right cheek.

CHAPTER FIFTEEN

The next day was a perfect spring morning. Blue skies with thin light clouds and a refreshing warm breeze. The kind of day that pushes everything that happens in the dark into the back of your mind. There couldn't possibly be anything bad happening on a day like this.

Instead of going down to the cove as I'd become accustomed to doing in the mornings, I headed into the woods.

I left the screeching clifftop birds, who were busy catching their morning meals for their chicks, behind me. The hush of the woods muffled their sound as I entered, replaced by the chirruping smaller birds who took cover here.

I was hoping to see some young in their nests or being led by their mothers along the forest floor. Instead, I came across a wall.

It was very old, made of grey stone slabs balanced on top of each other, mismatched in size and shape, but solid, chest height. Moss covered the stone, and vines curled through the cracks as the woods tried to conceal this blot on its beauty. Some parts of the wall had crumbled. In time, there would be no sign of it, the woods would slowly and silently reclaim it. But for now, it was holding out. There was a gap where I assumed a gate used to be.

Beyond the wall was a cemetery. A family burial place for the Quicklys. Some stones were elaborate, far too extravagant for the setting. Angels and cherubs stood guard over the lost souls with broken wings and bows, mossy green feet and blank eyes. Saints wept above the dead, their heads in their hands.

I stepped onto the hallowed ground. The air was different this side of the wall, cold and stagnant as if it stopped moving once it entered the space, this holding place for the dead. An angel peeked through her fingers at me as I walked by, her stone eyes following my every move. I shivered, but continued on my path, driven by the need to see the names on the gravestones.

Edward Quickly and his wife Margaret – 1367.
Fredrick Thomas Quickly, aged 7 months – 1345.
Elisabeth Quickly, Mother and Grandmother – 1352.

I looked for Esme's husband, Isaiah's father. He must be buried here somewhere. But there was nothing more recent than two hundred years ago. I presumed they had a new plot elsewhere. I touched each of the headstones as I passed them.

A stone dog caught my eye, his tongue out, mid-pant. His ears were chipped. But he looked peaceful nestled in the grass, lying on his belly. A stone before his front paws read: *Brute – a fierce hunter and honest friend.* It was nice to see the pets were appreciated.

As if I'd summoned her, Purdie appeared and landed on Brute's head. She cawed and shook out her feathers. I was glad of the company, the air in the cemetery was seeping into my bones and filling me with melancholy. These people were forgotten. No one had tended them, cut the grass back or cleared the moss away. Roots pushed up out of the ground from the surrounding trees. I could imagine the skeletons beneath, being rolled and turned in a slow dance as the woods pushed and pulled at them. This could be where I ended up. Sadness came upon me like a great wave.

Another raven arrived and perched on top of the spying angel. I looked up to see more ravens circling above me. One by one they began to land on the stones about me. They were restless, hopping on their feet, giving out short cries. More and more arrived.

"What is wrong with you all? I think your friends have gone mad, Purdie." I stroked Purdie's delicate head, but she didn't respond with her usual nudge against my fingers. She looked past me.

I turned to see Mathis standing at the opening, as still as the headstones, his gaze fixed on the birds that now covered the cemetery.

The birds took flight all at once and rushed towards him. He ducked and covered his head as they flew straight towards him, swerving left and right at the last moment, narrowly avoiding collision.

We stood looking at each other for a moment in shock. Birds always brought me trouble. My *familiar*, that man had called Caesar. It wasn't a crime to like birds. But people thought it odd all the same. Now Mathis looked at me like he had walked in on something he shouldn't, which in turn made me blush with shame that quickly turned to indignation.

"Are you following me?" My words broke the tension. Mathis raised an eyebrow slightly in surprise.

"I saw the birds gathering…" He took a small step back, readying himself to leave.

"And?" I said. "Birds often gather."

"I was worried. I saw you head this way earlier."

"So you *were* following me."

He looked back in the direction of the house, surely wishing he could be there now, away from me.

"I can see you're well, I'll get back."

"Why wouldn't I be well?" I said, my tone abrupt. I didn't like myself; I knew I was making him uncomfortable because I felt uncomfortable, but I couldn't stop. "I can look after myself."

He nodded and tried to leave but I stopped him again.

"I was looking for Esme's husband," I said, changing the subject, "but there are no recent graves here. Is there another cemetery nearby?"

"I'm not sure, it's possible there is another I haven't come across yet."

"You started working here not long before I arrived, didn't you?"

"Not long, three weeks before."

"And you haven't had time to explore the entire wood?"

"Esme kept me busy preparing the house for you."

"For me?"

"Yes, ma'am."

That was impossible. No one knew about our marriage until I arrived with the letter from Isaiah.

"But you said you arrived three weeks before me."

"I did."

I was glaring at him. He shifted his weight uneasily, looking behind him again, desperate to be away.

"That's impossible," I said aloud.

He didn't answer, his brow creased in confusion.

"Tell me what Esme said when she offered you the position."

"Just that Zena needed help now old age was claiming her."

"But me? What did she say about me?"

"She didn't mention you to me. I heard her talking to Zena afterwards. I'm sorry, I shouldn't have mentioned it…"

"No, I'm glad you did. What did they say?"

"Just that things would change when the master's new bride arrived."

It didn't make sense. Why would they be talking about his new bride before Isaiah had even asked for my hand? The air felt thinner, forcing me to take quicker, shorter breaths.

"Here, sit down." I hadn't noticed Mathis coming towards me. He helped me onto a square memorial block. My legs were numb.

"You're pale. I could run back and get you something sweet to drink."

"No, stay." I reached for his arm, surprising myself, suddenly fearful of being alone. The contact steadied me. It didn't make sense. How could they possibly know about me?

Mathis sat down next to me. As he did so, Purdie took the opportunity to investigate Mathis. She pulled at his trouser legs, then hopped up onto his shoulder and rummaged through his hair. Mathis tried to lean away from her but was too scared to push her off.

"She likes you." I smiled. "Come here Purdie, leave him alone." She settled down on my other side, her warm body pressed against my skirts. I stroked the top of her head. The three of us sat in silence. Above us, treetops whispered to each other in the gentle breeze. My mind was scattered, searching for a plausible explanation.

"Did you bring Purdie with you?" Mathis interrupted my thoughts.

"Purdie?" I looked to Purdie and back to him. "No, she lives here," I said, as if that were obvious. "Why would I bring a bird with me?"

"She's very tame," he said, "for a raven."

"She is greedy and silly," I said, but my voice was soft, and I ruffled the feathers on her head. I remembered another silly bird.

"I've never seen that before," Mathis said, and I tensed. "Someone tame a bird so quickly, I mean."

"She's not tame, she's just company."

Mathis nodded. He didn't say anything else, but I could feel unspoken questions hanging between us. I put my hand to my cheek where the eagle had burnt me in my sleep. She had warned me, had she not, to watch out for him? He was not a friend. Why had I asked him to stay?

I stood up and brushed down my skirts, although nothing was wrong with them.

"I'll get back."

"I'll escort you," Mathis said as he stood up, "you might feel unwell agai–"

"No," I cut him off. "I would like to walk alone."

He didn't argue. Unsure if I could trust his account of Zena and Esme preparing for my arrival, there was only one other person I felt I could ask about the misunderstanding.

Esme. I had another question for her, too.

CHAPTER SIXTEEN

I went straight to my room, found the brooch, put it in my pocket, and went to see Esme.

As I reached her door, I realised I had never arrived at her room unannounced before, she had always called me for tea. This was not appropriate. I hovered outside. Golden light slipped through the crack at the bottom of the door. The smell of tobacco lingered. Esme must be inside, but that didn't mean she was ready for guests.

"Enter," Esme called.

My heart skipped a beat. I hesitated before opening the door.

"I could hear you thinking out there." Esme smiled.

I gave a nervous laugh.

She was painting again, but the back of the easel was facing me so I couldn't see what it was.

"I do enjoy my paints," she said. She swept the brush over the canvas in a circular motion before dipping it in a cup of water and leaving it to rest on the palette. She glided over to her chair and sat. Her arms were speckled with paint up to her bony elbows. She was dressed, as always, as if she were about to go dancing at court.

"What is it, child? I wasn't expecting you today."

"I'm sorry to disturb you, I just wanted to see you."

"You're lonely here," she said as she settled herself into her chair and searched for her tobacco box on the table. "It's a harsh place for the young. No markets, no dances." She found the box and started filling her pipe. There was no tea today.

"I'm not lonely," I said. "I've never been a lover of markets or dancing." But I did miss Ma. My heart ached each day for her, like an invisible wound that opened anew every morning.

"And yet, you've come to see me." She held the small flame of a taper into the tobacco and puffed the thing into life. Smoke billowed about her head. "People *think* they want to be alone, but really they always crave company. Eventually. It's in their nature. Humans are drawn to each other, like flies to a carcass."

"It must be a big change for you, having two new people about the place?"

"Two?"

"Mathis and I."

"Ah, Mathis." Esme blew her smoke out slowly. "He is quite the handsome lad, isn't he? Shame about his face. Is he a distraction for you dear?" She cackled.

"No."

Esme laughed at my discomfort, which then morphed into a rasping cough. She couldn't help but tease.

"Zena wanted him about to help out," Esme said. "Said things were too much. She's always complaining."

"Does it bother you, having new people about?"

"Not really, dear. I barely see the boy. And I like having you around. Your perfect face is a much-welcomed sight."

I noticed her gaze move to my brow, then sweep down my cheek to my chin. I squirmed under the inspection.

"What? You do not think your face is perfect? Are your eyes too big? Your nose too long? Your chin too pointy? Not pointy enough?" She barked a laugh. "None of that matters, child."

She leaned towards me, whispering, "Do you know what does matter?" She beckoned me to lean in as if we could be overheard in this dungeon. I leaned towards her. She stroked her bony finger down the side of my cheek and held my chin between finger and thumb, her touch cold and tough.

"Your youth."

Candlelight flickered in the black of Esme's eyes, clear flames in a face blurred with old age. She glanced over my right shoulder at the portrait of her young self before letting go of my chin.

"Youth is fleeting and coveted. Enjoy it while you have it." She stopped a moment before continuing. "You know, when I was young my husband loved nothing more than to show me off to the world. Well, perhaps he enjoyed one thing more." Esme winked, chuckling to herself. "Is my son taking care of you?" She looked me up and down.

"Yes, very good care."

"So he should!" But still she observed me quizzically. "He's so withdrawn these days. I did wonder."

"Is he? I can't imagine him being any different than he is now."

"Oh, he used to be full of life! Parties, dancing, drinking."

I could imagine Isaiah at parties. He would quietly navigate the room, taking in his surroundings, and then he would play. His music would draw the crowds. People would hang on every note.

"What happened?" I asked.

"It's not really for me to say," Esme teased. Her eyes glinted with gossip.

"I wouldn't mention it to him. We don't converse very much," I said.

"I see," said Esme. "Better things to do, I'm sure." She raised one painted eyebrow.

"I didn't mean, I just meant..."

"It's fine, child, I know what you meant. Isaiah is a closed book. He doesn't let anyone in. You can't imagine how pleased I was when he wed you. I never thought he'd do it again."

"Again?" So he had been married before, no doubt to the woman on the brooch.

"Oh dear, I'm afraid I've let the cat out of the bag."

Esme stood and poured two glasses of wine from a side table. "Here," she said, sitting back down with a sigh. "You might need a drink, and I have no tea."

I gulped the wine.

"I'm sorry, I didn't mean to tell you like that. He has been married before, yes. She died. In childbirth." Esme paused before adding, "The child too."

It was a shock. That could explain why Isaiah felt so distant. Maybe he was scared of that happening again and suffering all over again. He knew what it was to lose the person you love and your child. We had more in common than I thought.

A familiar prickle started at the base of my neck, as if fingers had lightly brushed the fine hairs there without touching the skin. It must be her. Isaiah's wife. She was the one tormenting me, the ghost that walked this house.

"That must have been terrible for him, and you. I'm so sorry." I put down my glass, my hand shaking a little. "How long ago was it?"

"Years now. We've moved on, but he loved her deeply. She could do no wrong."

I nodded. If he had married for love and lost everything, it made sense that he would marry for convenience this time. The fact that he saved me in the process showed what a good heart he had. His heart had led him astray, though, as hearts do. I wasn't the person for this job, and his deceased wife knew it. She wanted me to leave, and I would oblige her soon enough.

I knew I would never hold a child in my arms, feed her, watch her grow. I couldn't see it. If I ever allowed myself to imagine it, the images would blur and fade or simply wouldn't come. It would never happen. A pregnancy would be a death sentence for us both.

And Isaiah would have to live through the hell of losing a wife and child again. I was sorry for that.

"She wasn't strong enough," Esme said. "A sickly, insipid little thing she was." She sipped her wine. "I don't know what he saw in her. I told him from the start he should have chosen her sister. It was a terrible business, actually."

I was gobsmacked.

"Terrible business," she said, puffing the pipe back into life with a candle. "That poor girl."

"It is terrible, to die birthing."

"No, child, I was talking about her sister." Not a hint of compassion was left in Esme's voice. "She was a much better fit for my Isaiah. Strong-willed, determined, a mind of her own. She wouldn't have died in childbirth. But she was cast aside. Imagine. Being scorned by the man you love and then lose both him and your sister? She went mad with grief. Flung herself from the cliff top."

I sat wide-eyed.

"You're not like the insipid creature, though. You're healthy and strong with a good mind. I suppose Isaiah learnt from his mistake, which is a good thing if he wants an heir." Esme smiled at me. "Don't worry about all that I just told you. It was a long time ago. Best forgotten. I only thought of it because" – she paused, taking a puff on her pipe – "it happened on this day."

"It's the anniversary of her death?"

"It is. So you must forgive Isaiah if he seems a little distant."

I fumbled in my pocket for the brooch. I unwrapped it. "Is this her?"

Esme looked over her pipe, still puffing. The smoke came out in bursts. "Yes, that's her," she said. I waited to see if she would ask to keep it or ask where I found it, but she said nothing.

"Would you like to keep it? Or should I give it to Isaiah?"

"No." She looked away from it and said no more.

I left Esme to her painting.

CHAPTER SEVENTEEN

Isaiah was waiting at the table at supper, and I wondered if I was late. The door was open. I saw him before he saw me. He sat in the candlelight, his large, elegant frame sitting straight, looking at the table before him. How had I not noticed the deep melancholy that surrounded him? I had assumed he was a rich man who had everything he ever wanted, that things always went his way. But now I could see the cloud of loss pressing upon him. The sitting room was filled with candles and lamps, but the light struggled to brighten the space. Isaiah's presence suffocated the flames.

"I'm sorry if I'm late," I said. Isaiah jumped slightly at the sound of my voice but then turned and smiled.

"You're not late."

I joined him at the table. He dished the food onto our plates as usual.

"There's something on your mind," he said when our plates were full. I was surprised. We didn't have a strong connection as husband and wife, and I thought he barely noticed anything about me. Maybe I had underestimated him.

"It's nothing," I said. I had no idea how to broach the subject or if I even should. *I found out today that your wife and child died. I have a dead child too* – it's hardly a newlywed's topic of conversation.

Perhaps I could mention finding the graveyard and how I couldn't find his father's stone. Again, not the best topic.

"I visited your mother today," I said instead.

"I see." His tone implied that visiting his mother was enough to give anyone worrisome thoughts. He sighed and started eating. I should have stopped there.

"She mentioned your first wife." He stopped chewing the meat that was in his mouth.

The flames on the candelabra at the centre of the table glowed brighter for a moment. I instantly regretted bringing it up.

"I see," he said. He chewed his food slowly before swallowing. "What did she tell you?"

Sometimes my own stupidity astounds me. Had I not said to Esme that I wouldn't mention it? There was no turning back now.

"That she died in childbirth." I cleared my throat before adding, "And then her sister died too."

Isaiah looked down at the food before him without seeing it. He was looking into the past, remembering the tragedy. No doubt reliving that awful day, and it was all my fault. "I'm sorry, I shouldn't have mentioned it. It must have been terrible for you."

"No, I'm sorry," he said, taking a breath. "You shouldn't have found out that way. I should have told you I was married before."

"It was thoughtless of me to bring it up. We all have a past."

"Then shall we forget these sad things and enjoy our evening?"

"I'd like that," I said.

Since Isaiah had returned, these evenings had been the

worst part of my day. I knew with every passing night, every time we made love, that I was closer to the inevitable. And now it was worse. Isaiah had already lost a child and had no idea that I was incapable of providing another. Perhaps I should have let them hang me.

The brooch was still in my pocket, nestled beside my stick doll. I could tell him. I knew his past; it would only be fair to share mine. Maybe he would forgive me for misleading him. But I couldn't do it. Not now. Maybe another day.

I'm at the graveyard. The moon is full and low. It lights up the stones and they shine silver. I know I'm dreaming. The eagle has led me here. She circles above. The scene flickers from bright to dark as her magnificent wings block the light of the moon each time she crosses it. The air is thick and still. Sounds arise as if I'm underwater. A growl reverberates, echoing around me. I focus on the graveyard. Three giant dogs, pelts black as the Devil and eyes red as hellfire, are growling and snapping at something on top of a high tomb. It is Mathis. He is muttering a prayer, eyes closed, head down. His head snaps up. "I've found her," he says. "You need to leave."

"Found who?" But he ignores me. He returns to praying and whimpering.

Another sound arises. A cry. I don't want to look but I have to. In my arms is a baby, swaddled in black lace. Her face crumples, readying to let out a screech, and then it comes.

So loud my ears hurt. The dogs turn, their eyes glowing in the darkness.

I run, but the baby is heavy, and my legs don't move fast enough. The dogs race up to us like thunder rumbling. Their huge paws crash on the ground, barks bellow and echo. There is no escape.

Sharp teeth sink into my ankle. I feel pain, but the fear is worse. I twist as I fall, to protect the child. The dogs circle me. As one jumps for my throat, I wake. The horror of what would happen next was too much to bear.

Outside, the moon was low and full, just like my dream. The room was lit up with the ethereal light. This was the time when dreams and reality mingle. Anything can and does happen beneath the light of a full moon.

Isaiah had left already. I still didn't know where his bedroom was. Would it be wrong of me to ask? I got out of bed, wanting to bathe in the moonlight for a while at the window. The island looked peaceful, magical. Isolated. We could fall off the end of the Earth here and no one would know. Who would find us if we suddenly all died in our sleep? To be so alone is to lose a sense of reality. Everything that had anchored me had gone. Ma, the town I grew up in, my chickens, my work. Before, I had a place in the world, a purpose, however small. Now the people around me had impossible expectations, and I had nothing to do except wait for the inevitable.

Purdie appeared and circled before the window. Her usual purple sheen shone silver. I let her in. She stayed quiet, as if she were attuned to my mood. We sat in silence, gazing at the moon. I found myself asking for protection. The moon had watched me that night by the lake, she had seen what had happened, and here she was now, watching me again. Perhaps she could speak for me in the world beyond this one. She could ask for mercy on my behalf.

A sudden cry from the depths of the house chilled my bones. A newborn babe's cry. I had my answer. I would not be forgiven for what I had done. I knew by now there was no babe hidden in the house, it was the ghost of the weeping woman trying to scare me into leaving. If only she knew I would leave if I could.

I heard movement outside my door. Purdie cawed in protest at the noise, trying to protect me as always. I heard the patter of feet running away and I shivered, as if a cold finger had just traced the length of my spine.

I moved quickly and quietly to the door, opening it carefully to make as little noise as possible. I looked down the corridor. There, at the far end, past the bedrooms, at the corner that led to the top of the stairs, was a woman looking back at me. Matted curls fell to her waist and covered most of her face in shadow. Dark hollowed sockets instead of eyes reflected the fear in my heart. The woman was quietly weeping. She raised her hand towards me, pointing at me, accusing me. The stench of rotten milk filled the space. Then a burst of action as she bolted towards me. I screamed and covered my face, falling to my knees.

Then… nothing. No impact. I opened my eyes to an empty hallway. Footsteps, light and quick, scurried down the stairs. I was compelled to follow. My feet worked independently of my mind, which was screaming to run back to Purdie and hide in the comfort of my bed.

As I reached the top she disappeared to the right, just the tail end of a gown trailed around the corner.

I followed the smell to the sitting room. The door was slightly open. I went inside. The piano and its surrounding furniture by the window were visible but the rest of the room trailed into complete darkness. I stood for a moment, listening.

Nothing.

I went back out into the corridor. A weak light glimmered from the direction of the kitchen. Someone was awake. I remembered the last time I was down here this late, and Esme and Zena had been talking about me. I wondered what I would hear tonight. I crept towards the kitchen, but the light wasn't coming from there. It was from a room further along on the left, one I'd never been in before. Someone was moving about inside.

I held my breath as I reached the door. It was probably Isaiah, I told myself. He'd said his office was at this end of the house. The door was slightly open. I pushed it all the way.

All tension released, my lips parted and then closed again, not sure what to say. It was Mathis, searching again. He was crouching down, searching the underbelly of a huge desk that sat before the window. The room was lined with cabinets full of little drawers. This must be Isaiah's office.

There was no denying it now. Mathis was up to something.

He stopped what he was doing and straightened up, dropping papers back into the drawer he was searching. I felt affronted. Had being with Isaiah finally given me a sense of ownership of this house? Or was it just disappointment that the weeping woman had disappeared into the night? Either way, she had led me here, to Mathis.

"I was just–" Mathis began.

"Don't lie to me," I cut in, my voice harsh and unfamiliar. "What are you looking for?"

He looked down at the desk, searching for an answer, a story.

"I lost something," he muttered.

"And you thought my husband may have found it and stored it in his desk?"

"I just…"

"I'll go and ask him, shall I?" Of course, I couldn't do that as I had no idea where Isaiah was. Mathis didn't panic, but his left fist clenched slightly, and I knew he was concerned.

"Please, don't disturb him. There's a simple explanation."

A simple lie, I thought, but I let him continue.

"I dropped something when I was cleaning earlier and only just noticed it was missing now. I meant no harm." His voice was steady and calm, as if he were telling the truth, but the story was so ridiculous it couldn't be true.

"And do you always clean the inside of your master's desk?"

He didn't respond to that.

I had a choice. I could wake the house and have Mathis removed from service, or I could let it go. For now. There was a reason the waif had led me this way, and there was a reason the eagle had shown me Mathis in my dreams. Logic told me he was hiding something, something he didn't want Isaiah to know. I should have felt scared in his presence, or at least wary, but I couldn't deny that I felt most comfortable when I was with him. I should have been running to inform the others, but my strongest instinct was to stay and help him search. He had helped me when I hurt my ankle, and he was the only other person here who hadn't lived in this house for an eternity. We were both outsiders. I had never been so conflicted about a person in my life.

"I'm going to bed," I said, finally. "I suggest you do the same."

Mathis lowered his shoulders as he released the tension. He had been scared because of me. I didn't like that.

Back in bed, Purdie sat on the pillow beside me while I lay thinking about the weeping woman. I knew this house had secrets. All old places do. Ghosts of people past lingered in the halls, the stone itself reeked with memory. The nights were filled with strange noises. Paintings moved. But this spirit was becoming dangerous. Isaiah's first wife must have really loved him, so incensed was she that he had married again, and now it seemed she wanted Mathis gone too.

I got up again, found the brooch, and took it to the window for the best light. The fair lady in miniature gazed out at me, beautiful and dreamy-eyed. How could this woman be the same spectre that haunted me now? The moonlight dipped as a cloud passed before her and the colours in the picture were muted. Her light blonde hair turned a shade darker, and I realised… it wasn't the same woman. The ghost that visited me had long, thick brown curls. A wider frame. She couldn't be this petite, fair beauty. But then who was the ghost? Esme had told me she had a sister. A strong-willed woman. A will strong enough to cross the boundaries of life and death, perhaps? She had been scorned in life, and it seemed her resentment had continued in the afterlife. She had loved Isaiah deeply, enough to take her own life, and now here I was, a new enemy. Another woman to take Isaiah away from her again. I would have to be careful.

Purdie gurgled at me and tucked her head beneath her wing, ready for sleep. I nestled back beside her but lay wide-eyed, watching the moon move across the sky.

CHAPTER EIGHTEEN

The following day was quiet. Not surprisingly, I didn't see Mathis anywhere, but then I didn't venture far from my room. Too many things were forming to create an uncomfortable picture, and my mind was spinning with theories about Mathis and Isaiah and the ghosts of this place.

I watched from the window as the sun sank towards the horizon.

Purdie tried to brighten my mood by leaping from the sill outside, flying high up in the air and then diving towards the garden below, flipping onto her back and straightening herself again just before she hit the ground. She would change course at the last second, brushing the flowers with the tip of her wing. There was nothing more beautiful in the world than watching Purdie play.

It was almost time for supper. I lit another lamp, as the bedroom was darkening, and I still had to dress.

There was a tap at the door. Not Mathis' gentle knock or Zena's rap. This was new.

"May I come in?"

Isaiah!

He didn't wait for an answer. I felt a rising panic as he stepped inside. He was often in my room, of course, but never before supper. His visits upstairs were kept for the late hours. I looked down at my smock and stockingless feet but there was no time to do anything about them.

"I'm sorry to disturb you," he said on entering the room. The twilight suddenly dimmed a notch. Night was pressing in. Isaiah stood a moment, taking in my appearance. His eyes followed the low neckline of my smock, down to between my breasts. I thought perhaps he wanted to skip supper tonight. But then Zena stepped into the room, stopping at his side.

Her bone-cold stare sucking away any warmth there was between us.

"Zena is going to examine you," Isaiah said. "It will only take a moment." He nodded to Zena, and before I had time to understand what was happening, she was leading me to the bed by the elbow. I looked back at Isaiah, willing him to see my fear and offer some explanation, but he didn't come to my aid. His face was unreadable.

"Lie down," Zena said. I stopped next to the bed.

"Isaiah?" My final attempt to elicit help from him.

"It's fine, do as she says."

I lay down on the bed, my heart thumping, wondering exactly what Zena was going to examine. Outside, Purdie was back on the windowsill, hopping about restlessly. I needed to calm down, Purdie could sense when I was upset.

With one sweeping motion, Zena lifted my smock and put her hand low on my stomach. I flinched at her icy touch. I looked away, out to Purdie. Zena pressed her fingers gently into my stomach, just above my most intimate parts. My face burned with humiliation. Unsure whether to push her away, or shout at her to leave me alone, I was paralysed by confusion. Then she removed her hand, pulled down my smock, and it was all over. I slowly stood up. My dignity lost.

Zena nodded at Isaiah. It was hardly noticeable, just a tilt of the head as she passed him, and whatever that meant he understood. I was still an outsider. They could communicate through a look; I could barely discern if Isaiah was happy or not. We shared a bed, but nothing else.

"Fortune," Isaiah said as he came towards me. It was a struggle not to step away from him after what he had just allowed to happen. "I knew it wouldn't take long." He took my hand in his. "You are with child."

The world fell away, and I was in some kind of bubble. Just as I had been when I touched the eagle. Isaiah's mouth was moving, but the words didn't reach me. Purdie flapped at the window in slow motion, her beak opening and closing, revealing her scarlet tongue.

Purdie is a completely different colour on the inside. Black and red. Red and black.

"With child?" My voice broke the spell. I had cut Isaiah off from whatever he was saying. I looked to Purdie, and she settled. My hands instinctively went to my stomach, and now that he'd said it, couldn't I feel something there? A heaviness.

"I'm afraid this good news is to be tarnished by some bad."

No, there was no good news. A child was not good news for me. He moved me to sit on the edge of the bed. He sat beside me.

"I have to go away on business," Isaiah said. "For a while." His brow furrowed in concern, but it felt fake, like he was pretending to care for a child. "I'll be back before the birth." He stroked my cheek with his thumb, as if he were brushing away tears, but my cheeks were dry.

"Where are you going?" I forced myself to ask, more out

of politeness than curiosity. I didn't care where he went. This whole thing, this game I'd been playing, was over. A deep knowing settled over me and inside me. It numbed my skin, it slowed my heart, it quieted my mind; this child would never be born alive. And I would not survive that again.

"It's a long, boring affair. I have to travel east."

I nodded.

"You are strong, and Zena will look after you."

I found it very hard to believe that she would care a wit about my wellbeing. "Of course she will." I smiled, hoping he would leave soon.

"I'm sorry, it was unexpected."

"Don't be sorry, your business must come first."

He kissed my hand before leaving. I didn't watch him go.

Outside, Purdie sat patiently at the window. I should let her in, but I couldn't move.

Not just yet.

How did Zena know? It must only be days old. A seedling. Less than a seedling. I closed my eyes and sent my mind within, as if I might come across an image or stumble over a foreign object like an unexpected bump in the road. But there was nothing. Zena could be wrong. I wished for something tangible, some sort of proof, something I could hold. I thought of my stick doll, but that didn't feel right. The doll was for my mermaid, not this seedling.

Purdie suddenly lifted off, wings fanned wide. She turned towards the cove and was soon out of sight. I stared at the space where she had been.

Then she was back. There was something in her mouth and she tapped at the window with it. I let her in, and she dropped a smooth, flat pebble into the palm of my hand. It was three fingers wide with a satisfying weight to it, worn to a cool shine by the rough sand and salty water. Its surface glinted in the remnants of the setting sun. The top dented slightly, forming the rough shape of a heart. But the pebble was as black as boot polish, the colour of Purdie's coat. The colour of darkness.

I rubbed it gently between my finger and thumb. I wanted to go to the woods, breathe in the damp, musty air, but tiredness filled my bones, and my mind.

I didn't go down to supper to sit alone at the table. I didn't think I would ever go down again. Perhaps I'd simply curl up in this room forever.

I moved to the chair to sit by the warmth of the fire, but I couldn't feel it. I stared at the flames until I could see nothing else. Demonic shapes formed in the orange and red. Screaming faces jumped out at me, beasts appeared and disappeared. Ma always said that if you stared at a flame too long you glimpsed the depths of hell. I wanted to see where I was going.

The door to my room was opened suddenly, shocking me back to the present. Zena stood there, holding a tray.

"Could you please knock, Zena, you frightened me half to death." I was surprised by my boldness. Zena had always turned me into a fumbling child. The woman's black eyes narrowed, sending a chill straight through my heart. I sank back a little in my chair and looked away, the bold energy expended.

Zena put a bowl and spoon before me, placing it down a little harder than necessary. The contents slopped up the sides. I guessed it was some kind of stew, but it was red as blood. The meat was unrecognisable and appeared almost raw from the colour of it.

"What is it?" I asked, repulsed by the texture and colour of it, but my hand was picking up the spoon.

"It's for the babe. You'll eat it each night."

I barely noticed her leaving, so intrigued was I by the food in front of me. I scooped it up hurriedly and filled my mouth. It was surprisingly delicious. I wondered why Zena had never served this before. Surely Isaiah would have loved it, too. I ate greedily, hardly chewing the fleshy pieces of meat. And when I could no longer fill the spoon, I lifted the bowl and licked it clean. Streaks of crimson ran down my chin. I picked up a cloth and wiped my face. It looked like it had been used to clean an open wound.

The supper gave me a flush of energy. I would leave the bedroom after all.

Twilight cloaked the beach in mystery. The moment before the island slipped into the world of night, the realm of the other. An orange glow cloaked the earth like steady candlelight, streaked with rays of violet and plum, as if God himself were shining his last blessing before handing the reins to the moon goddess. Her silvery light would provide a thin veil between this world and the next. It would let the dead roam, especially here, out on the edge of the world.

Gulls played in the light breeze, calling out to each other, appreciating this moment of magic.

The surface of the sea glittered, but I knew that beneath its sparkle was a vast black hole, promising nothing but death. It would carry you to the underworld in an instant. The breaking waves were small, they lapped onto the sand, tempting those ashore to dip their toes in, but there was always a price to be paid for temptation.

The seals let out their final calls from the rocks just out of sight. The gulls began calling their loved ones home to rest. Purdie hopped from rock to rock. I had removed my shoes, my feet pushed into the wet sand. It squelched between my toes and clung to my skin like syrup. I stayed just out of reach of the water.

Seaweed lay in small lumps, spat from the sea. Out in the water something broke the surface, then disappeared. I thought the twilight was playing tricks on me, but then it happened again. I squinted into the distance. The surface broke again. Dolphins! One jumped high out of the water, turning onto its back so it slammed into the sea, creating an enormous splash. There were smaller ones, too. Babies followed their mothers in the pack. A pain crept into my chest at the sight of them, something deep and inexplicable. They were free.

My own predicament suffocated me in its hopelessness. There was no one here I could rely on. Ma was a world away. Isaiah was gone. By the time he returned I might be gone too, buried in the woods with the ancient headstones.

The seedling was growing inside me and there was no stopping it. Just as the dolphins had no say over the ebb and flow of the tides. They simply had to navigate their way through it as best they could.

Purdie hopped over and dropped something small and white from her beak. "What have you got, Purdie?" As I picked it up it broke in two. I held the pieces together and saw it was a tiny skull. A bird's skull. I placed it gently into a rock pool, hoping the wet sand would provide good burial ground. Nature has a way of taking back bones with little effort.

A creeping sensation filled me. I had an intense feeling I was being watched. I looked back at the steps. At the top,

I saw Esme turning back towards the house, her long silk shawl flowing behind her. Esme never left the house. Had she been looking for me? She may have heard the news and wanted to celebrate. But then why didn't she call out? I worried that she had seen something she didn't like. Mathis had already mentioned Purdie. I looked at Purdie, who was pulling at molluscs in the rock pool. Surely there was nothing unusual in that. I decided to go after her and check everything was alright. As I climbed the steps, the final rays of gold disappeared. Twilight was over. Darkness was falling.

I reached the top and saw Esme inside the house, walking along the right-hand corridor which led to her room, lighting up each window as she passed it with the glow of her candle. She didn't look outside, she didn't know I was watching her. I called out and waved my arms, but she couldn't hear me from this distance, and even if she did look outside all she would see was her own reflection in the glass. The candlelight making the darkness beyond it impenetrable.

By the time I entered the house, she was out of sight. I headed straight for her room. The smell of beeswax and rosemary mixed with tobacco was the only evidence Esme had come this way. Her door was open a crack, but there was no light.

I stepped inside her room.

"Esme?" I whispered, then wondered why I was keeping my voice low. There was something unsettling about this. Esme wasn't there. There was no other exit. It was as if she had performed some cheap vanishing trick. A sense of dread came over me. I had seen her come this way with my own eyes. But my eyes had played many tricks on me of late.

CHAPTER NINETEEN

I was summoned to Esme's room early the next day. Zena would have told her about the seedling, no doubt. I wasn't sure I had the strength to be enthusiastic about this recent revelation just to appease my mother-in-law, but what choice did I have?

Esme sat with a wry smile and an explosion of sweetmeats before her. Excitement crackled in the air.

"Sit, my child, sit!" The room smelled different. There were herbs scattered about in small bowls. Rosemary, lavender and Lady's Bedstraw. Together they made me feel slightly drowsy.

"I must congratulate you, my dear! With child after just a few weeks. I knew it wouldn't be long, I could feel it."

Esme's enthusiasm instantly made me feel guilty. She would be expecting me to gush with happiness, but I could hardly force a smile.

Esme packed her pipe; tea was already in the cups. I took a sip. The bitterness made me grimace and I set the cup down. She chuckled. "Took over your taste buds already, has it? That's the sign of a strong child." She put the flame to the pipe bowl and puffed it into life. Tobacco added to the herb scent and ignited an ache at the base of my skull.

I looked down at my stomach. The same size and shape

that it was yesterday. How ridiculous that everyone was taking it as a certainty that I was carrying a child. How could Zena possibly know?

"How does Zena do it?" I asked. "How could she tell I was with child by touch? It was like a magic trick." Esme's face straightened a little and that made me feel somewhat better. She shouldn't be so happy.

"She's always been able to tell these things," she said, smoke trailing from her nose and mouth as she talked. "There's nothing mystical about it. Something to do with the hardening of your stomach." I'd never heard of any midwife with such a power, even Old Rita wouldn't be capable of that.

"Did she do the same for you?"

"For me?" For a moment Esme looked confused.

"With Isaiah?" Esme stared at me blankly. "When you were with child?"

"She did." Esme took a sip of her tea, her excitement settled into memory. She glanced over my shoulder at her portrait as she often did when the past was mentioned. "Zena has a lot of experience birthing children, you're in safe hands."

"I thought Zena had always worked here?"

"It certainly feels that way," Esme laughed, "but she wasn't born here, she did have a life before." She looked at me quizzically. "You are very quick, my dear. I bet no one could ever keep a secret from you." Esme took a drag on her pipe and exhaled slowly as she spoke. "That's a very good quality to have as a woman. We must be on the lookout for secrets."

My face stayed neutral, but my insides twisted. If only she knew of the secrets I had kept from her. The real reason

Isaiah and I had married so quickly, and my other, much more painful secret that lived at the bottom of the lake back home.

"Zena worked as a midwife in her youth, before she came here."

"Oh, I see." But I didn't see, not really. That still didn't explain her seemingly supernatural gift of checking for pregnancy, or why she would leave her previous life to come and be a housekeeper at the edge of the world. Was she running from something? Was everyone in this house running from something?

"Has she ever been wrong?" I asked, hoping the question sounded flippant, an innocent query, but Esme saw right through me.

"You're scared," she said, leaning back in her chair, a knowing smile playing on her lips. "It's perfectly natural to be scared, child, especially the first time. It's a woman's greatest calling to birth a child, but unfortunately it is also often her greatest sacrifice." She puffed on her pipe.

Esme didn't have to enlighten me about sacrifice. The last ten years of my life had been a sacrifice.

"But don't you worry, dear. Like I said, you're in good hands."

The smoke in the room was starting to choke me.

"You know," Esme continued, oblivious to my discomfort, "Zena has seen some difficult labours, but she has never lost a child or mother. Not once." I found that difficult to believe. "She used to tell me stories of some babies being born arse first. One had only its arm hanging outside the mother for hours. It turned blue and big as a man's. But still she managed to turn him and save them both. She said that arm got sucked back in like a snake retracting its tongue. The slapping sound it made haunts her still." Esme chuckled. I thought I might vomit.

"But what about Isaiah's first wife? Did Zena help with that birth?"

Esme stopped chuckling. "That was different. It wasn't the birthing. The child died hours after. As did the mother."

"Oh, I see, but couldn't Zena–"

"Forgive me." Esme cut me off, forcing a smile now. "This isn't helping, is it?" She picked up a bowl and started filling it with sweetmeats. "Here, take these to your room, you'll need the sugar." She shoved the bowl at me. "All I meant to say was, you're in good hands."

I took the bowl. I was drowning in tobacco and rosemary, even the powder Esme wore was scratching at the back of my throat. How did the old lady cope in here with no fresh air?

"You look after that child now," Esme said. "Don't be exerting yourself."

Zena brought supper that night. The same red stew. My mouth watered at the sight of it.

There was also a cup of tea rather than the usual jug of ale. "It'll help the growth," Zena said. "Make sure to drink it all." The tea was pungent, and some leaves floated on the surface, but I was ravenous and ate the stew and drank the tea in minutes.

Pain suddenly cut through my stomach, rivalling that of childbirth. I ran to retrieve the bedpan from under the bed and began vomiting. The colour! The scarlet stew was regurgitated into the bedpan and splashed the floor around it. Unable to stand from the cramps in my stomach, I dragged the sheets from the bed and crawled closer to the fire. I shivered violently while my skin burned.

It was the tea. Zena had made me ill. She wanted this child about as much as I did. But what could she possibly hope to gain by this? Isaiah would return and I would be with child again. It would only prolong the misery.

The walls began to contract, and my vision blurred. I was vomiting again. The sheets were covered with it, glowing red as if a wild animal had been butchered right there on the rug. The room swayed. The painting came alive. The sea crashed; the birds flew. From the bottom of the cliff in the cove, red eyes glared. A woman began crawling out of the cliff face. A woman with long, thick curls to her waist. She stood up and walked across the sand, then into the ocean. But she didn't disappear. She walked straight towards me, getting closer and closer until her head took up half the painting. She raised her pointed finger to me and pushed through the canvas into the room. Her sour smell hit me as she forced her arms out and grabbed the wall either side of the painting, pulling herself through. Water dripped from her hair and threadbare clothing, pooling on the floor.

I shuffled back, my heart racing, but the floor was rocking beneath me, and I fell with each attempt to move. Purdie was screeching. She was scared. The woman was dragging herself down the wall as if pulling herself from a well. I could hardly breathe and pulled at my dress.

"Mrs Quickly."

The woman tilted her head towards me.

"Fortune."

Hands were upon me. I screamed and thrashed the best I could.

"Fortune!"

I recognised the voice. Mathis. He had a grip of my shoulders. But his face swayed, I couldn't focus.

"The woman…" I tried to explain, to protect him from her. But I threw up instead. A cool cloth wiped my face. Mathis held me half sitting and I sank into his steady embrace to stop the swaying room.

"Be still," Mathis said. I closed my eyes and prayed for sleep.

When I woke, the room was still. The fire had died down, lighting the space with an orange glow. There was a pillow beneath my head and a blanket over me. Mathis sat on the floor beside me, his back leaning against the end of the bed, his head resting on the mattress. He had dozed off. His hands were clasped between his thighs, his legs crossed at the ankles. He looked young, and peaceful, and beautiful. My heart reached out to him, a physical ache. My eyes watered. He had stayed for me.

"Mathis," I whispered.

He stirred. There was a brief moment of innocence as he came to, like he was waking in his own bed, unaware of where he was. It felt almost sinful, too intimate. But he quickly remembered the situation and sat upright.

"I'm sorry, ma'am, I fell asleep. I was worried you would be ill in your sleep."

"Thank you," I said. He rose to his feet and I tried to sit up. Pain swept over me. My limbs were so tired I could barely lift myself.

"Here, let me help." Mathis lifted me to my feet but I was unsteady. He helped me to the chair. He placed the pillow behind me and the blanket over my knees. There was water to drink, too. The soiled sheets had been cleared away.

"You were very kind to stay, Mathis."

"I didn't want you to come to any harm," he said.

"How did you know I was sick?"

"I heard you screaming."

"I'm sorry."

We sat in silence for a few moments before he said, "What woman were you talking about?"

"A woman?"

"When I came in you said there was a woman."

"I must have been seeing things. Everything was blurry. I didn't even see you come in. I'm sorry, I must have frightened you." But was I seeing things? She had seemed so solid, her smell so vivid, and that sound. That dripping. I could hear it again now. She was real. I knew it. Mathis would think me mad if I told him that.

"I'm just glad you're alive."

"Hmm." I looked into the fire. "Would you stay a while longer?"

"Of course, ma'am."

"Please don't call me ma'am," I sighed. "I preferred it when you called me Fortune."

"I was trying to get your attention. I don't think Zena would like me calling you that."

"Maybe just when Zena isn't around, then?" I smiled. He nodded. "Did you tell Zena I was unwell?"

"I couldn't find her. She disappears sometimes."

She didn't want to help me; she needed the poison to do its work. It was so strong I feared she wanted to kill me too. She could try it again. I had thought Zena unpleasant and rude, but not a murderer. Whatever her reasons, it was very clear she did not want me to stay here and become part of her family. If only she knew I didn't want that either. This night may have given me more time to think. I was certain the pregnancy couldn't withstand this. I had felt like I was dying, as if all my insides had been turned out. Isaiah was going to be away for months, so Zena may have given me another year or so before I had to confront this problem again. She had unwittingly helped me.

I looked to Mathis, his profile glowing in the embers. He had come to my aid twice now. A guardian angel, protecting me from doom. If only he could protect me from the past. How different things might have been if I had met him earlier, back home. I fought the urge to move closer to him, to curl up in his arms. Even the house settled when he was there. The night-time was usually filled with shadows and the scratchings of ghosts and vermin, but now it was still, peaceful even.

There was still the question of what Mathis was hiding. My mind questioned his purpose here, whereas my heart felt nothing but honesty from his. But he *was* looking for something and the eagle had come to me in my dreams to warn me about him. Hadn't she? The idea of Mathis as a thief or a rogue didn't fit with the man who sat before me now, concerned for my well-being.

"What did you lose?" I asked.

"Lose?"

"You said you were looking for something, in the study?"

"Oh." His eyes widened, surprised by the question. "A necklace." He looked down as he said it.

"Was it valuable?"

"Not to anyone else. My sister gave it to me."

A sister. I'd not thought about Mathis having a family, or a life, or anything outside of this place. This island made you forget the rest of the world existed.

"Oh," I said. "Will she be disappointed you lost it?"

"I doubt it. I haven't seen her for a long time."

This was the first bit of real information I had had from him. "I'm sorry," I said. My body was still weak. I rested my head against the pillow.

"Are you feeling any better?" He looked at me like Ma used to when I had a fever. "You look pale," he added. "Maybe I could warm you some milk, or bring some tea."

"No. No tea." Another pause. The fire crackled.

"I'll leave you to rest," Mathis said and headed to the door.

I didn't want him to go, and I didn't want to sit in this room alone for months on end either. Purdie was fine company but not much of a conversationalist. I craved human compassion.

"Mathis," I blurted.

He turned back to me.

"Do you play cards?"

"I do."

"Would you like a game? Tomorrow after supper."

"I'll look forward to it," he said, and managed a smile before closing the door behind him.

CHAPTER TWENTY

A flurry of snow had been falling for the past hour. It coated the island like a dusting of sugar on one of Esme's sweetmeats. Spring had blossomed into summer. The heat down here on the edge of the world was thicker and stuffier than back home. Summer had melted into autumn, a final burst of colour before the island accepted its fate of bare branches and grey skies. Some green clung on, but now it was hidden beneath white.

The cold crept into the bedroom like dead fingers searching for the living, but they pulled back from the heat of the fire that enveloped myself and Mathis.

"What do I win this time?" I said, laying my cards on the table.

"My respect, of course." Mathis smiled. "And I'll steal some more sugared plums from the kitchen for you."

"For someone who claims to have made money from these games in the past, you're very bad at it."

"I swear I did," he laughed.

"Then you're letting me win! I don't need your pity."

"And you will never have it."

I smiled and rummaged through my pocket for some breadcrumbs, scattering them on the table. Purdie hopped on and pecked happily, ignoring the two of us.

"Purdie is always the real winner," I said. I pulled myself from the chair to stand but it was difficult with my extended, perfectly rounded stomach. The seedling had stuck.

My body was alien now, an entity with its own laws that I didn't fully understand. Eight full moons had passed since Isaiah left. My hair had grown, and I could manage a small plait or some pin curls when I had the energy to do it, which mostly I did not.

As my stomach grew, my frame weakened. My soft curves were replaced by angles, my face drawn and hollow like a wet rag. Sometimes my teeth hurt. The child sucked me dry, bringing us closer to our end every day.

Mathis rose from his seat to help me. His skin had filtered to a creamy white now we were in the depths of winter. I took his hand, solid and strong, and he pulled me up with no strain at all. *I am featherweight*, I thought. *I am disappearing.*

Each night Mathis brought the tray up and sat with me while I ate the unidentifiable bowl of scarlet stew. Then we played cards or talked into the night. Our warm pocket surrounding the fire glowed orange and red and pink. This space had become our sanctuary, a lifeboat in the expanse of a black, midnight sea. No one came near. Each day I longed for the moment of his arrival. Just like Esme and Zena, our boundaries had blurred. We were no longer gardener and lady of the house, we were friends. I denied the other feelings; the tingling of skin when his hand brushed mine, a look held a moment too long. I pushed those thoughts away. It would do nobody any good.

I had stood to do something. The window. I opened it. The ice-cold air caught in my throat. I was still here, still living. The outside world still existed, whether I wanted it to or not.

"You'll catch your death," Mathis said.

"The snow is beautiful."

Mathis stood next to me. The snow had put everything to sleep. Only the crackling fire and our breath could be heard. I slowed my own to match Mathis' steady flow.

"I'm sure Mr Quickly will be back soon." Mathis broke the spell.

"Do you think that's what I'm looking for?" The darkness outside was impenetrable. Why did he have to remind me that things were going to change?

"Why are you still here?" I asked, turning to him. His eyes widened in surprise.

"I…"

"You said you loved to travel," I said, my tone hardening, "so why are you still here, in this damned place? There's nothing keeping you here."

He didn't answer, he didn't need to. He was there for me. I broke eye contact first, looking back to the silent snow. He couldn't protect me from the child that would soon rip me open, and the fate that awaited us. The thought of Isaiah returning filled me with dread.

The baby kicked. A foot in my side. I winced; my hand instinctively pressed down on the area.

"Are you well?"

"I'm fine," I snapped. The baby would arrive soon. Isaiah said he'd be back in time for the birth. "You should go."

Mathis nodded and began clearing away, placing the bowls and cups on a tray.

"No, I mean, leave this place." I slammed the window closed. "This house, I mean. Leave this house. Find work somewhere else."

"You don't mean that," Mathis said, standing straight.

"What do you think will happen when my husband returns? Do you think we'll continue to play cards every night?" The blood rushed to my head, my heart beat faster, panic rising at the thought of our nights together coming to an end.

"Zena will tell Isaiah as soon as he returns that you've been here every night. Do you think he'll let you stay? You should leave now, before he returns."

Mathis stood still for a moment. "No," he said simply, with an air of finality, and continued to clear the plates and cards from the table.

The windows were mirrors. There was no world outside, just the inside looking back at me. The sea in Esme's painting rippled in its counterpart. I ignored it. I had taken to ignoring a lot of things in this house.

The child pressed a hand against my stomach; a wave of nausea followed. I might not live for much longer, and I didn't have the strength or the righteousness to force Mathis to leave when I needed him more than ever.

He abandoned the dishes and came to stand beside me again. We looked like a family in the glass. A couple waiting for the birth of their child, with a blazing fire and each other to keep them warm while the world turned to white, their whole lives ahead of them. My devil was taunting me, showing me all I could not have. The image twisted my heart, wringing it out like a wet rag. I wanted to cry. I wanted to hold him. I wanted and wanted.

"Leave with me." He said the words quietly. They floated on the air like sea foam rising. If I pretended I hadn't heard, would they sink back into the water again, forever forgotten?

"Don't," I said.

"Why not?" His voice was still low, as though someone might overhear us. "I fear for you. Something bad is happening here."

"What, are you a gypsy now?" He was right, of course, but running away wouldn't stop it. I couldn't run from my fate.

"There's something wrong here. A doctor should have been called. You're fading away."

"I'm well enough."

"You're not well," Mathis hissed, anger boiled beneath his words. "This…" he grabbed my hand and held it aloft, "is *not* acceptable." Slim bones protruded from beneath a waxen layer of skin, my veins throbbed violet rivers. I pulled my hand away.

"It'll be over soon, when the child is born."

"And what if it's too late by then? What if…"

I died? Those were the words he couldn't say.

"Why do you care?" I said. He looked at me. Beaten, crushed, broken. I knew why he cared.

"It doesn't matter now," I said. "The baby will arrive soon. I can feel it." I swallowed a growing lump in my throat. "Just go, Mathis, there is nothing to be done. There is nothing here for you."

I saw the anger and frustration behind his eyes. I thought he might shout, or hit something, or set the fire between us alight with a kiss. Instead, he turned and went back to collect the tray.

"You have barely eaten," he said. "Do you even want to live?" He waited for an answer, but finding me mute stormed from the room, slamming the door behind him, making me flinch. It was a very good question. Did I want to live?

I thought I did. But since the seedling made its presence

known, I had been sliding into acceptance. I took the stick doll from my pocket, pulled a strand of hair from my head and began wrapping it.

I'd had no letters from Ma.

I was afraid for her. What if they hadn't let it go? What if they had taken her to the gallows when they found me gone? I would drive myself mad thinking of it. There must be another reason she hadn't replied. A simple reason. Perhaps Ma had decided to go somewhere else, and I was sending the letters to the wrong address this whole time. Confusion made my head ache.

How I would love to go back to the lake. For my belly to be flat and to sit with Ma by the fire in the evening. Caesar would rest on my lap as we sewed. But that life was long gone, it felt like a dream now. How quickly memories fade and distort. I strained to picture Ma's face. Slowly it came back to me: the soft curve of her jaw, her worn rough hands, the smell of lavender she would soak her clothes in.

Do you even want to live? I stared at my reflection. It showed a haggard woman, alone, tired and used. No hint of Ma's playfulness. There was nothing to be playful about. If I was lucky, I might simply fade away in my sleep without the messy drama of childbirth. All that pain and blood. It was unnecessary.

Purdie suddenly squalled in alarm and her fear surged through me. In a moment she was on my shoulder facing into the room, her tail beat against my breast in time with the knocking sounds coming from deep in her throat. A shadow moved in the glass, and I froze.

The room grew colder. My heart raced.

In the reflection, I watched as a form took shape by Esme's painting. Long dishevelled hair, hands covering the face. The smell of sour milk and the sound of quiet weeping filled the room. I had almost forgotten the weeping woman, convinced myself she was a dream. I willed myself to turn and face her, but my body was paralysed, every muscle locked in fear. Her hands moved slowly down her face, revealing deep gaping holes where eyes should have been. A red spot bloomed at the centre of her chest, like a rose spreading its petals wide, straight from her heart. The centre of it blackened and streaks of red ran down her ragged smock. Misery overcame me. A sorrow so strong I struggled to breathe, the weight of it crushed my chest. I blinked tears away, not wanting to lose sight of her, afraid she would reach out, touch my aching back, and lock me in this hell forever.

The door opened with Mathis saying "Fortune, there's something I have to..." before he realised something was very wrong. But he broke the spell. The gripping pain in my chest released like a hand letting go, and I gasped and gulped at the warm clean air, one hand clutching my chest, the other clinging to the sill to steady myself. My whole body shook. Purdie began flapping about the place where the weeping woman had been, barking into the empty space as if telling her not to return.

"What happened?"

Mathis held me up, guided me to my chair.

"It's nothing," I said, still shaking, but glad to be back beside the fire. Mathis covered me in a blanket, and as he went to move back to his chair, I took one of his hands in both of mine and held on tight. I needed his solidness. I was losing myself in this place, in this pregnancy, in this fear. Mathis was my anchor. He pulled his chair next to me and sat down, placing his other hand over mine. I leaned my head on his shoulder and wept. I cried for a long time.

She was not a figment of my imagination; she had been there. Why return now? It had been months since she had emerged from the painting on that terrible night. I placed a hand on my stomach. It was my devil reminding me that time was creeping on. The day was near, and this illusion of happiness I had created with Mathis was at an end. It was a cruel trick, to allow Mathis into my life only to take him away. The fear of the weeping woman receded quickly with Mathis there, but my sobs continued, accompanied now by the previous image of this false family in the glass. Mathis didn't stop me, just rubbed his thumb over the back of my hands until I settled.

Eventually he asked, "Do you want to tell me what happened?"

I shook my head, no. "Will you stay here tonight? At least until I fall asleep?"

"Of course." He wiped the tears from my face, pushed sticky strands of hair from my forehead. If we were lovers this is when he would kiss me, take me to bed and hold me in his arms until I slept. But we were not lovers.

Purdie had settled by my feet, and she ruffled her feathers now, ridding herself of any remnants of what had just happened to us.

"What were you going to say?" I said, trying to smile a little.

"What?"

"When you came in, you said there was something you had to… do? Tell me?"

"Now isn't the right time."

"I think it's the perfect time. I'm far from sleep, and who knows what tomorrow has in store." I looked to my stomach.

He sat back in the chair, his hands before his mouth, fingertips tapping. Whatever it was, it was important. I sat up a little straighter, intrigued.

Purdie, who had been steadily cleaning her feathers for the past few minutes, stopped and sat still, her beady eyes trained on Mathis. He let out a long breath of air, closing his eyes as he did so. Mathis' silhouette flickered unsteadily in the firelight. The snow continued to fall outside, silent and secure, and for a moment the world was still. "When you first came here you thought I was a thief."

I was stunned. Why was he bringing that up?

"I think it's obvious to you now that I'm not." The fire crackled loudly; Mathis' voice was low. "But I *was* looking for something." He hesitated, glanced at me, a moment of doubt.

"I know, you told me, a necklace," I said, but he was shaking his head.

"No, I lied. I was looking for evidence of my sister, Anna. Not her necklace."

"I don't understand."

"My sister was married over fifteen years ago, and I haven't seen her since."

"I'm sorry," I said, thinking how marriage had taken me from Ma, "but I still don't understand. Why were you looking for her here?"

Mathis paused again. He looked into the fire, contemplating, before deciding to continue. He rubbed his palms along the length of his thighs. "Anna would never have left me." This didn't answer my question. He saw the concern on my face. "Just, please, bear with me." I nodded, and he took a deep breath. "My mother died in childbirth, with me. My father never forgave me. He was a cruel man. It was Anna who raised me.

"But one night a man came to our home. Father was doing his best to make a good impression, and even at my young age I knew it could mean nothing good for me or Anna.

"She came to our room that night and told me she was to be married, but she said her husband seemed kind and she would speak to him about coming back for me. But she never did, and I've been searching for her since."

"I'm sorry, Mathis."

"There's more," he said, looking at me now, regret in his eyes. "The night the man came to the house, I watched him and father talk." He paused a moment, as if the words were stuck in his throat. "It was *him*, Fortune." A knot exploded in the fire, making us all jump. Purdie hopped onto my knee, and I pulled her close. "It was Isaiah." He paused a moment. "I'm almost certain it was."

"Your sister was married to Isaiah?" I could hardly believe it. Anna was Isaiah's first wife who had died in childbirth? If that was the case, then Mathis had no idea she was gone. "Why are you only telling me this now?"

"I'm sorry. But I wanted to be sure before I mentioned it to you."

"Sure of what? Why didn't you just ask Isaiah about her?"

"I planned to. I meant to." He was getting flustered. "But then you were here, and I wanted to stay."

"But if he was married to your sister, he would let you stay anyway. And not as house staff."

"I don't know." He ran his hands through his hair. "It's complicated. Please don't mention it to anyone. There are some things I need clear in my head first."

"Of course, if that's what you want." I thought back to Esme's story. "Do you have another sister?"

"No, just me and Anna."

That couldn't be. Esme had said Isaiah's sister-in-law had been in love with him.

"Esme told me Isaiah had been married before." I hated to tell him. "I'm so sorry to tell you. But she said she died, in childbirth." His face didn't change, no shocked reaction. "The child too."

He nodded, looked at the floor. "I thought as much."

"Wait." I could do something for him at least. "I have all the evidence you need." I left the safety of my chair to find the brooch, which was exactly where I left it, wrapped in cloth in the washroom. I hoped this small token might ease his suffering.

"I found this. You should have it."

He unwrapped the parcel, revealing the miniature portrait.

"What is this?" His brow furrowed in confusion.

"Your sister," I said, surprised. "Isaiah's first wife."

"That's not my sister."

CHAPTER TWENTY-ONE

The eagle was in my dream again, carrying a mother and child on its back. It skimmed the waves that glimmered silver in the light of a plump full moon on the horizon. The mother was dressed in flowing white, the baby swaddled in gold-trimmed lace. A picture of beauty; gliding, diving, cutting through the sea wind. But as they flew closer to the house, I saw how the mother gripped the bird's feathers so tight her knuckles were white. Tears streamed her face. A sad wailing came from the swaddled bundle. The mother shouted something to me as she passed by my window, but I couldn't hear her. The giant eagle, twice the size of its burden, circled far out and then returned for another pass. The mother shouted again, her mouth moving rapidly, her face anguished. "I can't hear you," I cried and banged on the glass, watching helplessly as she flew out of sight. Then, out of the darkness, her face appeared close to the glass. "Move," she said. The windows exploded inwards. I raised my arms to protect myself, but shards sliced into my arms and face, waking me with a start.

I felt I had barely slept an hour, but there was the grey dawn. I pushed the sheets back and went to the window. The snow was still thick, shrouding the island. With each passing day we seemed to move further and further away from the real world. My life before was a distant memory. I struggled to remember Ma, our cottage, Caesar, my chickens. They floated in the back of my mind, out of focus and so very far away.

I was beginning to think Isaiah would never return, and if it were not for the size of my stomach, I might have believed he'd never been here at all.

The brooch was still on the table. I hadn't the energy to touch it again last night. I told Mathis it was my mistake, that I'd found it and jumped to conclusions. Esme had told me that woman had been Isaiah's wife. It was possible he had more than one previous wife, he was old enough. Esme may have thought it wise to keep that to herself, or let Isaiah tell me. But Isaiah told me nothing.

Mathis said it had been fifteen years before. He was a child then; a child's memory was not a reliable source. I didn't know what to say to him. I didn't have the heart, or the courage, to tell him he could be wrong.

I wrapped the brooch, put it away in the washroom and began to dress. I would go outside today. The snow had tempted me.

Zena arrived with a breakfast tray. These months had not been kind to her. Her bone-white skin did not sag in the manner of old ladies, instead it became thinner and brittle, stretched so tight I feared it would split and reveal a skeleton that would immediately turn to dust. Her limbs had stiffened, as if she were turning to stone before my eyes. She scanned my outfit, taking in my boots and jacket.

"It's not a good idea to go outside. You'll catch a chill."

I laughed silently to myself. A chill was the least of my worries. I grabbed an extra shawl in answer.

"Your master will be home soon. It's almost time."

I flinched.

"He's my husband, not my master," I said.

"He is your master."

I bristled at the word. Zena added to my fury by being so constantly loyal to Isaiah. Even when we hadn't seen him for months. Even though he had abandoned us. With breakfast untouched, I left the room. Zena didn't follow or try to stop me.

Outside, the clouds were beginning to break, sending rays of violet and orange across the snow. It crunched beneath my feet. Purdie flapped her wings in a small drift against the house, playfully flinging the snow about her. She would join me when she was ready. With hardly any breeze, the sea was quiet. A great beast slumbering.

On the woodland floor, the snow was an uneven blanket. Branches sagged. I ran my gloved hand along one, pushing all the snow onto the ground, then I felt bad, as if I'd stripped it of its magic. Purdie arrived and landed on a snowy branch. She lifted off again, leaving the imprints of her talons behind her. She was enjoying herself, but I was already becoming tired. My weak body frustrated me, and no matter how tightly I bound my stomach, the weight of it dragged on me. Despite that, I was feeling more alive than I had in long time. The air was so crisp and fresh, like drinking from a stream recently thawed.

Footsteps approached. I knew by the gait it was Mathis.

"It's good to see you out," he said.

"I'm afraid I've exhausted myself already. Did you want to walk?" We occasionally walked in the woods, but it had been a couple of months since our last one.

"No, I was hoping I could show you something back at the house. Unless you need to rest first."

"Lead the way," I said.

Inside, I expected Mathis to stop at the sitting room, but he continued on, past the kitchen, stopping at Isaiah's office. The house was cold and dark in winter; most of it was uninhabitable. I stayed close to the fire in my room. Down here the shadows had taken hold, anything could be hiding in the darkness. My skin tingled. I was afraid. Of the weeping woman? Of Zena finding us? I had become weak-willed, a hollow casing of my former self.

"Where's Zena?" I asked, looking back at the kitchen, expecting the old crone to appear like a spectre behind me, then chided myself for caring.

"She's not here. She always disappears for a few hours a day."

"Where does she go?"

"I don't know. I've never had the courage to ask."

"Don't you ever follow her?"

"No."

Zena's whereabouts each day was surely more interesting than anything Mathis had to show me.

"Ready?" he asked, his hand on the office doorknob. He was nervous too, or excited.

Either way it made him agitated. Dancing on pins, as Ma would say.

I nodded, and he opened the door.

The room looked the same. Mathis went to the right-hand corner and moved one of the casings that was filled with little drawers. It moved much easier than I expected.

"There's a door here." He was right. It was covered in the same wainscoting as the walls and blended in almost perfectly. He pushed the secret door open. I didn't move. This was Isaiah's private space. My husband. But my curiosity was too strong, and I had a right to know if he was hiding something.

I stepped into the secret room and was met with disappointment. No scandalous leaflets, no dead bodies. Only portraits. Lots of them. They lined the four walls of the room, stacked up against each other. None of them were hung. My spine tingled. So many eyes watching me. Old men in all their finery, beautiful young women, children sitting in a circle, women dressed in black. Faces everywhere.

A family faced me: a father, mother and three children. All fair. The smallest child's hair so light it was almost silver in colour. They were blurred beneath a layer of dust. The room was full of it. Cobwebs gathered in the corners, thick and grey. Balls of dust had scattered across the floor with the opening of the door, blown out of place by the breath of foreign air. No light came from a small window high up that was smeared with some kind of black tar.

"Who are these people?"

"The Quicklys," Mathis said. He lit a candle, instantly adding colour to the faces surrounding us, animating them in the inconsistent light. Heads seemed to twist towards me, eyes rolled in their sockets. Mathis was stood before a round table at the centre of the room.

Upon it was a large open book.

"This is their family tree." He lightly traced his fingers over the page.

I moved close to him, our arms touching as I took in the lines and names on the old pages. "Edward and Margaret," I read, "married 1325. They were who we saw in the graveyard."

Mathis nodded.

"I don't see Esme or Isaiah. Wouldn't they be at the bottom of the tree?"

"They're not there," Mathis said, "and this family tree stops two hundred years ago." He sounded excited, like he had just solved a mystery or proved a point, but I didn't know what the point was.

"I can see that."

"Don't you think it's strange?" He looked at me as if any moment now I would come to the same conclusion as him without further explanation.

"Why do you think they gathered all the family portraits here?" I asked, looking around at the unsmiling faces. If I could get any closer to Mathis, I would. The place was chilling me to the bone.

"I don't know," he said. "Unusual, isn't it? It's like they gathered every portrait from the entire house and hid them in here a long time ago. Perhaps... two hundred years ago?"

"They could have started a fresh family tree elsewhere," I suggested. "Families are strange. They hold grudges, they might have secrets in their past they want to forget."

"I think you're right about that part." Mathis walked over to the family portrait with the silver-haired child and held the candle close. "Do these look like the ancestors of your husband? Green eyes, white hair, oval faces?"

"What are you suggesting?" I was getting frustrated with him now. *Just spit it out.*

"I'm suggesting that *they*," he pointed at the picture, "might not be related to the people who live here now."

"But they are the Quicklys. Family characteristics change with every marriage. It means nothing."

"Then where are their names in the book? Where is the record of deaths? Where is Isaiah's father buried?"

"I'll speak to Esme about it if it's really bothering you," I said. He shook his head.

I walked over to him and placed my hand on his arm. He was trembling beneath his shirt.

"You're not listening," he said. "They're not who they say they are."

"Please, tell me what this is all about."

"This is a clue. Don't you see? It leads one step closer to finding Anna."

I pulled back, releasing his arm. "Anna? But Mathis, Anna is dead." As soon as I said the words, I regretted them. Was Anna dead? Had she been married to Isaiah at all? The stories from Mathis and Esme didn't make sense in my mind. But still, Anna was long gone. That much was clear. I understood the pain of losing someone, but I was surprised to find he was still looking for evidence of Anna.

"I need more than their word for that. I need evidence."

"Why don't you speak to Isaiah? He could tell you exactly what happened to her."

"I can't do that. There are things, other things. I need to know for sure first." He was becoming erratic, pacing and wringing his hands.

"You're worrying me. It's becoming an obsession, a fixation. You were a child when your sister wed. It's not a certainty she was married to Isaiah at all."

"I am sure," he said, his voice firm. "And there's something not right here. I know you feel it too."

I couldn't deny that.

"It is strange," I agreed, "but it's the isolation. It distorts everything. It makes people question their senses." I thought of my devil waiting, and the weeping woman, and wondered if Mathis was experiencing something similar.

My curse had spilled over onto him. I had gotten too close to him, and he was paying for it.

"I'm not mad," he said. "They're not who they say they are."

"Then who are they?"

"That I don't know." He went back to the book and flicked through the pages as though this time it would reveal some secret. "Why are these portraits hidden? Where is Esme's husband buried? And where is your husband, for that matter?" He turned back to me, accusation in his tone.

"Away on business, as you know." My cheeks flushed. Should I know more than that? I felt like a fool.

"What kind of man leaves his new wife to suffer bearing a child alone?"

"One with an insignificant wife, I suppose." I gritted my teeth.

"I'm sorry, I didn't mean that. You're not insignificant."

"We both know that I am."

"You're not." He mumbled this more to himself than to me, then flicked through more pages. He slammed it shut, making me jump, and started rifling through the portraits.

I watched him, confused and grasping, moving portraits around with no obvious purpose. I was unsure what to do. Dust motes flew as he shifted the paintings. I coughed.

"You should go back upstairs. The dust will do you no good." He didn't look at me, still intent on unfolding the mystery in his head.

"Mathis," I tried, but he barely noticed. This place was getting to him. It wasn't right for him to be here. His jawline was severe, his breeches sagged a little. I wasn't the only person wasting away.

"Mathis, please stop." I moved towards him and grabbed

his hands away from the paintings, turning him so he would have to look at me.

"I'm worried about you," I said. He was full of defeat.

"You think I've gone mad. You think this place has addled my brain."

"I don't think you're mad."

"Then you believe me?"

"About what? I don't know what you're saying."

"That they're not who they say they are. They're not the Quicklys."

"Who are they then?"

Mathis hesitated before answering. "I don't know yet. But I'll find out." He pulled his hands from mine and turned back to the paintings.

"Please, just leave me here. I don't want you to become ill."

I watched him a moment longer, hoping he would stop and speak to me, or walk me to my room. Or shout at me. Anything to distract him from this troublesome mission. But he didn't. So I left him to it.

CHAPTER TWENTY-TWO

It was time to visit Esme. We had fallen into a regular pattern of tea every other day. I barely saw her otherwise.

Tea and sweetmeats were laid out before her as usual. She reclined in her chair, smoking a particularly pungent tobacco. While I had expanded at the waist and withered everywhere else, Esme had simply withered. Her fine clothes hung on old bones. Her skin wrinkled and sagged. Her movements had slowed somewhat. However, the larger my belly grew, the wider her smile became. Nothing could suppress her joyful anticipation of the arrival of her grandchild. I thought of Ma and fear crept over me. I remembered her last embrace, the fear in her eyes. I'd never see Ma again.

I sat down with a groan.

"You look pale, child. What's on your mind?" She puffed her pipe into life. The smoke had an orange hue to it. I breathed in deeply, filling my lungs with it, relaxing.

"Oh, I'm fine. I've been out in the snow, that's all. It tired me out." I imagined Mathis still frantically searching through the portraits. I hoped he'd given it up.

"It's snowing?" Esme's thin, painted eyebrows lifted in glee. "I should take a walk myself."

"You should, it's beautiful outside."

"Hmm," Esme said, noncommittal.

Playing cards were laid out on the table before her, but it was a game I didn't recognise.

"Sorry, I've disturbed your game."

Esme scooped up the cards with a practised hand and shuffled and stacked them effortlessly. "Nonsense, I don't care about cards when you come to see me. Here." She poured the tea. "Drink." She puffed on her pipe. "I wish you would smoke; it does wonders for the constitution."

"I'm useless at it." I had tried puffing on Esme's pipe in the past. It only brought on a hacking cough. "I'm breathing it in anyway."

I picked up a marzipan. The sweet burst of sugar set off a sharp pain in my head. I pressed my hand to it, waiting for it to pass.

"I know your secret," Esme said, and I tried not to panic. She couldn't know about me and Mathis in the secret room, could she? "You are scared," she added. My chest relaxed and then tightened again. "It's getting close."

Esme took a long drag of her pipe. She pointed to my stomach. The seedling. Esme wouldn't notice anything beyond that. "I'm not going to sugar-coat it. Childbirth is no easy task. But your body will tell you what to do, you just have to listen." *I've done it before*, I thought, *I know what to expect*. "And Zena and I will be there to assist."

"You'll be there?"

"Of course! I wouldn't leave you alone with only Zena for company at such a moment."

The thought relieved me a little. Esme wasn't Ma, but she was a world better than Zena. Better than being alone. My hand slipped into my pocket, my fingers found the little doll and I rubbed it.

"Isaiah said he would be home by now," I said.

"No, he said he would be home for the birth, and he will."

"How can you be so sure? What if something has happened?" It was wishful thinking on my part. I had grown used to him not being here. I enjoyed my solitude, sharing my bed with only Purdie and sharing my evenings with Mathis. Isaiah's return would change all that. But what did it matter anyway? Everything would be over soon. This seedling would wither and die, and me with it.

"Nothing has happened. He will be back." She gave me a sidelong glance. I flushed. Sometimes I thought Esme could see straight into my heart. "Maybe you don't want him to come back."

"Of course I do." Did I hesitate?

"I'm not judging you, child. Isaiah is older and practically a stranger to you. I see the boy, Mathis." Esme chuckled. "You like having him around."

I was dumbstruck.

"The two of you make quite a pair. I wouldn't blame you."

"I haven't, we aren't…" My face burned.

She was cackling now. "Calm down, child, I am teasing." She rested the pipe on her lips, still smiling.

"I wouldn't blame you," she teased again, and laughed to herself some more. I searched for something else to talk about.

"What if Isaiah doesn't want to be here for the birth? What if there are too many bad memories for him? From the first time?"

"Ridiculous. Of course he'll be here, you can count on it."

"But he must have been affected by his first wife's death," I ventured. "She died in childbirth, didn't she? What did you say her name was?" I hoped I sounded casual. If I knew her name, I could confirm to Mathis that Isaiah was never married to a girl called Anna.

"Don't you worry, I won't let anything of the sort happen to you." Esme wasn't forthcoming. She blew smoke rings into the room, her jaw clicked as she pushed the little circles from her wide, rouged mouth. She wasn't in the mood for storytelling today.

I was glad to climb the familiar steps up to my room. I let Purdie in and lay on the bed. She settled on the pillow next to me. "What's it like to fly, Purdie?" I whispered. "I think I'll find out soon." Purdie looked at me as she always did when I spoke my secrets to her – with determined indifference. I had always imagined death as flight. I would leave this body, grow wings and take to the air. I would see as far as the ravens, as high as the eagles. I'd be free.

The room was warm, and I dozed. The seedling kicked. I pushed my stomach into the mattress. I didn't want to feel it. I didn't want to love it. It would be easier if I pretended it had never been alive in there. My eyes closed.

The lady who rode the eagle is here. She's in the bedroom, watching me sleep. The bundle in her arms writhes. Her hair is matted, dried tear tracks streak through the dirt on her cheeks beneath the blackened holes for eyes. She reaches out her hand to touch me. As the tips of her fingers touch my shoulder, she is yanked away. A rope around her neck lifts her from the floor. Invisible executioners hold it steady. Her feet kick, her arms reach to her neck and the bundle falls. I watch with a bird's eye as the babe falls in slow motion. The swaddle loosens, an arm is freed, pink and plump. I see the crease at the wrist, the dimple for an elbow.

"Wake up," I'm shouting, or thinking, I can't tell. I can't do anything. I only observe. Time speeds up again. The bundle hits the floor with a thud.

I woke gasping and quickly froze.

Someone was in the room. My muscles tensed as I listened. Nothing. I pulled myself up into a sitting position.

"You're awake," a voice said.

"Christ! Are you trying to kill me?" Mathis was sitting by the fire. The day was dark, or was it night already? It was hard to tell.

"I'm sorry," Mathis said and left the warmth of the fire to come to my bedside. "I brought your supper but didn't want to wake you. You've had a difficult day."

I raised my eyebrows at him.

"I made your morning difficult," he corrected. Purdie left her preening and hopped onto Mathis' shoulder, nipping at his ear. "Stop it," he said, trying to brush her away, but she was persistent. I couldn't help but laugh. Mathis smiled, too.

"I'm sorry about this morning," he said, serious again.

"You've nothing to apologise for. I know what it's like, to lose someone." It could send a person mad if they weren't careful.

"She was a good person," he said, looking towards the window as if he would see her there, flying by on the back of a giant eagle. But it was dark, and we could no longer see outside. Only our own reflections. "My father disappeared when she left. Anna's husband had compensated him for her loss, and he took it and ran. As if money could ever compensate for her absence."

"You loved her very much," I said. "I'm sure she held onto that, too."

Mathis turned to me. "I hope he died in a ditch. Father.

I hope that's why he never came back. I imagine him spending all that money on so much ale that he choked on it." His voice was low. "I've tried to forgive, but I can't."

I didn't know what to say so I stayed silent. I knew the rage of wanting someone to choke. Many times I'd dreamed that Charles would fall beneath his horse or be accidentally shot while hunting. But Mathis didn't need to hear that right now. I squeezed his hand instead.

"I think that's why I can't let it go. I've searched for her ever since. This was the most promising lead, but it's time for me to admit that maybe I was wrong. It feels like I'm giving up on her."

"I don't think any sister could have a more loyal brother than you. You'll see her again."

He nodded. "You remind me of her," he said, brightening a little.

"Me?" I laughed a little.

"You're strong, just like her."

"I feel far from strong."

"But you are. You're a survivor."

"I can barely shift my backside right now."

"Here," he said, pulling a vial from his pocket. "I made this tincture for you. It should help you gain some strength. It's strong, though. Just a couple of drops in your jug before bed."

I was surprised that in the midst of Mathis' pain, he still stopped to consider me.

"Thank you."

"I'll leave you to rest," he said.

"I've already rested." I didn't want him to leave. Our nights were numbered. My chest tightened a little at the thought. "Do you not want to stay for a while?"

"I thought maybe you'd seen enough of me for today."

"Don't be foolish. Who else am I going to beat at cards? Purdie is useless." Purdie cackled at the insult from the crossbeams above.

"Cards it is," Mathis said.

"But do you mind if we play here? I don't think my bloated body can cope on the hard chairs right now."

"Why do you always do that?"

"Do what?"

"You talk about yourself as if you're not beautiful."

"Tsk." I swiped his words away with my hand.

"I'm serious, it's like you hate yourself. Or you hate…"

"What?"

We both knew what he was going to say. I hated what was growing inside me. I hated the thought of what was to come. *Don't say it.*

"Nothing," Mathis said. "Just… drink your tincture."

He gathered up my supper and the cards while I fixed my pillows into a comfortable position. Best to eat, enjoy Mathis' company, and pretend that this was my life for a little while longer.

CHAPTER
TWENTY-THREE

In the woods the snow melted away. Mathis and I were silent as we walked. My steps had slowed, my strength had faded. The air about me hung heavy with sadness. I could see it weighing Mathis down, too.

Even Purdie was subdued. She played half-heartedly in the last drifts of snow. I was wrapped up well, but the cold still seeped through to my skin. I shivered.

"We'll head back," Mathis said, "you're cold."

"In a minute." The thought of going back inside made me nauseous. I'd spent months in that room not wanting to go anywhere, and now that I could barely move, I needed the fresh air and the trees and the birds. Typical.

My stomach made it difficult to see the forest floor, and on my next step the ground disappeared beneath me. A small ditch, most likely a rabbit hole, brought me down. My hand hit a sharp rock as I reached out to protect my stomach. I heard a crunch before I felt the pain shoot through my hand, up my arm and down my side. Blood dripped from an open wound in my palm. A flash of white bone. I cradled my wounded hand at my chest, turning flat onto my back. The clear white sky was visible between bare branches, which interlocked like a giant bird's nest. The pain surged. I tried not to whimper.

Mathis helped haul me into a sitting position. He looked at the blood dripping from my palm and winced.

"I think it is most certainly time to go back to the house. What do you think?"

I raised my eyebrows at his cheekiness, but I soon stopped smiling when I tried to stand. Shooting pains crippled me as Mathis pulled me up. I focused on his arm around my waist, the soothing strength of his body. Purdie flapped about my head.

"I'm fine, Purdie," I heard myself say, and then vomited into a shrub. Mathis wiped my mouth with the cuff of his shirt.

My feet were moving but the world was getting darker with every drip of blood. My dress would be ruined. There would be a trail of scarlet behind us. Mathis half carried me up the stairs.

Then Esme was there. I must have fallen asleep or passed out, because I hadn't seen her arrive.

"Are you trying to kill yourself, child? You shouldn't be out at all, especially not in this weather."

I wondered where Mathis was. Esme's powder and tobacco made me feel nauseous.

I tried to sit up to look for him. "Oh no you don't," Esme said, and pressed on my hand. Pain shot through my body. I screamed. It soon subsided, and I could feel Esme's fingers gently rubbing the palm of my hand. She turned it over and rubbed the back. The pain was disappearing, melting like the snow. My heart slowed to its regular beat and things began to focus.

"Better?"

I nodded. "Thank you."

"No more going outside, do you hear?" She continued to gently stroke the palm of my hand until I slept again.

When I woke up, Mathis was sitting where Esme had been. The room was dark, only the fire and a candle beside the bed bathed the room in an orange glow. The shadows crawled. My hand was wrapped in cloth but there was no pain.

"How are you feeling?" Mathis asked. "I was worried."

"I feel... good." I made a fist, then spread my fingers and twirled my hand about easily. "How silly to react so badly to a little cut."

"It wasn't a little cut," Mathis said, and I noticed that he didn't appear to be happy at all that I was well. His face was stern, determined. "You broke bones in your hand, Fortune. Your body is too weak, and the fall broke your hand."

I felt chastised. It was somehow my fault that my body was failing.

"They should have taken better care of you," he added. It wasn't me he was angry with.

"It couldn't be broken, look," I said, holding up my hand and clenching and unclenching my fist again. "It doesn't hurt."

"Earlier you were vomiting and fainting from the pain, and now there is none. Doesn't that strike you as odd?"

"You must have been mistaken. And I overreacted."

"No," Mathis said. He shook his head. The candlelight flickered on his burns, making them dance, as if his skin were on fire right now. I waited for him to speak.

"Remember when you hurt your ankle?"

"I can hardly forget."

"Remember the ointment that Esme healed you with?"

I nodded, confused.

"She used the same ointment today, but a more potent concoction." He paused. "It fixed the breaks."

"That's impossible, there's no such thing. It would be a miracle."

Mathis let out a long sigh, looked to the floor. "There was only one person who could make such a thing." He paused again, looking back at me.

"Who?" I asked.

"My sister. Anna."

"I don't understand. You're saying Anna had the ability to make this potion too?"

"I'm saying there is no other person in the world who could have made it. It's impossible. Only Anna had this gift."

"But you don't know for certain if Anna was ever here."

"I was beginning to doubt that she was. I'd almost convinced myself that the day I saw the wooden box with the ointment I was imagining things, or it was just a coincidence. But that box *did* belong to my sister.

"You know, my father couldn't believe his luck when Anna was taken off his hands. Witches were already being targeted in our town, and I was afraid Anna's gift would be discovered. In the past he had charged people for her ointment. But then no one would come near us. It was only a matter of time before she was hanged. That ointment *is* Anna's. She was here, I'm sure of it. Or perhaps…" He stopped.

"What?"

"She is still here," he said quietly.

"How could that be?"

"I don't know." Mathis stood up and paced, then stopped,

looking at me. "But what other explanation is there? Anna is the only one who can make the ointment. I often asked how she did it, but she always said there was a secret ingredient that came straight from her heart, that she couldn't explain, she could only feel. I thought she meant love at first, but as I grew older, I realised that the ointment was a wonder, like nothing else on earth. Magic, even. It was her gift, and hers alone. Esme has used two different strengths, which means there is someone still making it."

"But Mathis, listen to yourself. Where could she be?"

"I don't know." He sat down again, defeated. His eyes were pleading. "But there's another reason I think Anna was definitely here."

"What's that?" I asked, intrigued. The solid, real world around us had slipped away. We were in the realm of secrets and dreams now, just the two of us floating in the orange glow, the shadows twisting and contorting. Anything was possible. It was a dangerous place to be.

"You."

I was brought back to myself. "Me? Why?"

"Because you are like her."

"I don't know what you mean. I can't make powerful potions." Except I knew he meant something else. I willed him with every muscle in my body not to say what he was about to say.

"The birds."

Purdie ruffled her feathers above us, as if aware we were talking about her and she didn't like it.

"You control the birds," he said.

I went inside myself. I didn't want to hear it. The birds just liked me. I fed them.

That's all it was, all it ever was.

"No, Mathis," I said, as if he was a small child I could manipulate to believe my lie, "the birds just like me. I feed them." I had heard myself say those words many times. But this time was different. Mathis didn't smile and brush it off. He held my gaze, waiting. My attempt to defuse the conversation had failed. He wouldn't let it go.

The truth that had nestled hidden inside me was cracking open, a chick hatching into a hostile world. If I said it, if I allowed the words to leave my lips, they could never be put back. And what would happen to me then? I thought of Old Rita, her feet slowing to a stop. Her fate wasn't so bad, at least it was over fast. I should have put an end to everything months ago. I should have accepted my fate instead of the hand of marriage. I had only delayed death, and this time round he would be even more cunning and cruel.

But there was no one there to hang me now, and Mathis had just admitted his own sister had a gift. Esme painted pictures that moved and possessed an ointment that healed broken bones. We would all be hanged together.

"It's alright," Mathis said, "you're safe with me."

"I know," I said, "but I can't control birds."

"Yes, you can," he insisted.

"Sometimes they appear when I'm lonely or sad or angry, like they can feel my emotions. But that's all." It was terrifying admitting out loud what I had only ever held in my heart. But Mathis wasn't satisfied.

"Ask Purdie to do something," Mathis said, as if I hadn't just told my deepest, darkest secret. I stared at him. I knew I had a connection, but I couldn't tell birds what to do.

"Fine," I sighed. "Purdie, go to my chair."

Purdie flew from the crossbeam to my chair before the fire, perching on its back.

Mathis looked at me, slightly triumphant.

"It's a coincidence," I said, "she likes to sit there." But the secret inside my heart was breaking out. I pressed my hand to my chest as if I could push it back in.

Mathis nodded. He went to the window and opened it.

"Ask Purdie to go and get you something," he said, "but only in your head. Don't say the words out loud."

I thought of something, and Purdie flew out the window.

"What did you ask her to bring? And we'll see if she does it."

"Some holly from the woods," I said. My voice shook slightly.

We waited in silence. I could barely breathe. But I already knew.

Purdie returned quickly, bringing a brisk breeze with her, a flash of colour shining at her beak.

She dropped the bright red berry onto the bedclothes before us.

"It doesn't mean anything," I said, still clinging to the old truth.

"Fortune." Mathis' voice was soft, pleading.

"What do you want from me? To say it out loud? That I'm marked by the Devil?" I glared at him. "Because I already know that. Nothing good will come from speaking of it."

"But don't you see? This connects you to Anna–"

"No," I cut him off. "Nothing connects me to Anna except you. She's not here."

I almost shouted the last part, and although Mathis stayed firm, I could see the words hitting him like shards.

"Isaiah connects you. He knew."

"He didn't know anything. Isaiah saved me from witch hunters. And he'd proposed to me before anyone had

even considered me a witch. But they were right. This" – I
pointed at the berry – "is witchcraft. I should have let them
hang me there and then."

"You're not a witch. Neither was Anna." He paused. "You
don't cast spells or curse people or dance with the Devil."

"I need to get out of this godforsaken bed." I threw back
the bedsheets to stand, but as I pulled my legs over the edge
a sharp pain hit the side of my stomach and I let out a cry,
my hand instinctively pressed against it.

"Fortune!" Mathis reached out to me and almost placed
his hand on my stomach.

"Don't touch it," I snapped. I was burning. Anger flamed
through me, hot as the fires of hell. My breath came in rags.

Mathis let his hands drop and waited for the moment to
pass. He was so steadfast I wanted to hit him, I wanted him
to feel what I was feeling. I gripped the sides of the mattress.

My knees almost touched his, his chair was so close to
the bed.

My breath slowed down. The fire receded.

"You called the babe 'it'," Mathis said. I winced at the
word "babe".

"It's not a babe yet," I said unkindly.

"All this time I've never seen you touch your stomach, or
refer to the babe, or talk about when it arrives."

"Please, don't," I said, but Mathis continued.

"All you ever say is that it's a burden. Your body is wasting
away, and you've done nothing to stop it."

He wasn't accusatory, his tone was kind, inquisitive. He
was putting all the pieces together. "Did you even drink the
tincture?"

I looked away.

"I see," he said. "Are you afraid?"

"I'm afraid of nothing." Of course, that was a lie. I'm afraid of everything. I reached for my stick doll, but my pocket wasn't there. I was wearing only my smock.

"What do you keep in your pocket?" Mathis missed nothing.

"I don't want to talk about this. I'm tired, and you're talking nonsense."

"Which is it, then? You don't want to talk, or you're tired, or I'm talking nonsense?"

I huffed and tried to move away from him, but he took one of my hands in both of his and rooted me to the spot.

"There will never be a babe," I said. "I'm cursed and there's nothing that can be done about it."

"What do you mean?"

I couldn't look at him. The berry had stopped short of falling off the edge of the bed in my rush to get up. It looked like a perfect drop of blood. I remembered Ma pricking her finger, and the blood that ran down my legs at the lake, and I sickened at the thought of all the blood to come.

"This isn't my first pregnancy." I watched Mathis closely as I said it. I needed to see the disgust in his eyes, watch as he ran from me. But he did none of those things. He was listening intently, without judgement. He stroked his thumb over the back of my hand, and I couldn't bear it. I pulled my hand away.

"Maybe we should–"

"I'm not going anywhere," Mathis interrupted.

He had stuck with me these past months. He deserved to know what was going to happen.

"There was a boy in my town. I was young. Fifteen. I thought he loved me."

I glanced at Mathis, but still there is no judgement, just a slight nod of the head. The bedside candle burned a little brighter for a moment, a sign for me to continue. Whoever the ghosts were that walked these halls, they were telling me it was alright to talk, and I felt it too.

"Of course, he didn't." I half-smiled at my naivety. "I bore the child alone in the woods by my home. But she didn't survive. Her cry never came. She was just a shell. It was for the best, really." I paused. Mathis waited.

"I wrapped her up and left her in the lake. She rests at the bottom with the other shells."

"I'm so sorry," Mathis said. "But that doesn't mean that this babe will…"

I glared at him.

"There's more," I said, and he was silenced. "I thought the birds were the only witnesses, but I was wrong. Something else watched my pain from the trees. And while it looked on, I stood before the lake, in the light of the moon, and I made a vow." I stopped a moment. The shadows crept further into the room, their talons reaching. "That I would never let another man touch me, and I would never allow my belly to grow.

"You said that witches dance with the Devil, that they cast spells. I think that's what I did. I didn't intend to. I was so angry, so afraid. I didn't think." I swiped at tears, cleared my throat. "I called something in, something evil. It followed me home. I was tired and wet and bleeding. Then it appeared before me. A man's body with an eagle's head. Ram's horns jutted from its crown. It was a demon, a devil. He touched my forehead. I knew he would be watching and waiting always, and the moment I broke those vows, he would take me down to the depths of hell where I belong.

"Now do you see? I broke those vows. I put my life before anything else. I was a coward. And I couldn't let Ma watch me die. Isaiah saved me from the noose, and Ma from seeing that. But I have to pay for my sin. The Devil is waiting for me. This babe will not survive, and neither will I." I looked down at my stomach. "I wouldn't want to."

Mathis held my hand again and squeezed it gently. A gesture of acceptance. He could see it now. There was no future for me or the seedling.

"Fortune, I..."

The bedroom door opened without warning, and there in the shimmering light, radiating darkness, was Isaiah.

CHAPTER TWENTY-FOUR

Time stopped while Isaiah took in the scene before him. My smock: Mathis and I huddled like conspirators. The conclusion of what these things meant.

Mathis stood up, pushing the chair back. It screeched against the floorboards, and time sped up again.

"Isaiah," I said, trying to sound happy, but instead sounding guilty.

He didn't look at me.

"Thank you for bringing my wife's supper up," he said to Mathis, "that's all she'll need for tonight."

"Yes sir," Mathis said. His voice was low, but he held Isaiah's gaze. Brave or stupid, I wasn't sure.

Mathis didn't move for a second or two, and the tension rose. The room was too hot, the air stuck in my throat. I willed Mathis to go. He suddenly walked quickly towards the door, where Isaiah blocked him. I held my breath. But then Isaiah stepped to the side and let Mathis pass.

"You're home," I said. I sounded pathetic. My heart was hammering so hard, I worried he could hear it. I had expected some kind of announcement when Isaiah returned. I had gotten so used to spending my nights with Mathis, sharing everything with Mathis, that I had become complacent. In a moment I had lost them both.

Mathis now knew the truth of who I was, and would surely leave.

I could only imagine what Isaiah thought of me right now. Whatever terrible things he thought, he was right. It was shameful of me to sit in my smock with a man who wasn't my husband. I could see it clearly now. But this place, the loneliness. It skewered expectations, the rules of the outside world didn't apply. But Isaiah was the world returning. Judgement day was here, and the outlook was grim in this world and the next.

"You should get some rest," Isaiah said. "It is late." He didn't come any closer. "I'll see you tomorrow." He left me alone to my suffering.

I wrote to Ma again, in desperation this time, telling her that I wanted to leave, and she should come here if she could. I didn't hide my fear and begged her to respond. Then I sat very still for a long time, before crawling back to bed to hide beneath the covers and wish I could close my eyes and never open them again.

When I woke, I was alone. Completely alone. Purdie was not on the pillow next to me. The letter was gone.

I heaved myself over to the window and opened it. I called her name. Nothing. Panic fluttered in the pit of my stomach. I couldn't *feel* her. I pushed the panic down with excuses. She was just out playing in the breeze, she didn't hear me when I called, she was spending time with her own kind. All nonsense.

She would be back. I could wait.

The winter air was biting so I closed the window. As I did, I heard a breath behind me. A soft sigh. I turned but there was nothing there. Esme's painting shimmered. It wanted me to see something, but I wouldn't look. I couldn't bear any more bad news. Instead, I dressed and sat by the fire. Zena had been in while I was sleeping, I could tell by the layout of the logs. Mathis piled them differently. His were chaotic in comparison. Zena's fire burned more efficiently; it warmed my feet and chilled my heart. It had been a while since Zena had done it. I tried not to think about what that could mean.

Hours passed in bleak anticipation. Zena came and went with meals, but I daren't ask her anything and she didn't offer any information. Purdie did not appear at the window. Mathis did not knock at the door. This was the beginning. It was time to pay my debt.

I couldn't take it any longer. I went looking for them instead.

In the kitchen I heard chopping. Zena was preparing supper. The door was open, and I risked a quick look to check if Mathis was there. He was not. I walked the garden and the herb garden. He was nowhere to be seen. No Purdie either. I walked to the top of the steps to the cove. Mathis wasn't on the beach.

The sea roared instead of soothed. *It's alright*, I told myself, *it's nothing. I've gone a whole day without seeing Mathis before.* But this day was different. And never had I gone this long without seeing Purdie.

I felt the birds before I heard the beating of wings. Within moments they appeared from either side of the cliff face and filled the cove. An unkindness of ravens. But no Purdie. They called and shrieked. I wanted to shriek with them, but if I did it would be an admission that Purdie was lost to me, and I wasn't willing to believe that yet.

The birds swooped and dived, perfectly navigating the frenzy.

Night-time was creeping in. With the weight of loneliness bearing down on me, I headed back to the house.

There was a light on in the sitting room. I didn't want to enter, but I must. I had to face him. Isaiah was sat at the table with a large, covered silver dish before him. I could hardly look at him after last night.

"I've been waiting for you," he said.

Not all the candles were lit. The wall behind him disappeared into the darkness. His face distorted in the candlelight.

"Sorry, I didn't realise." I sat opposite him. He was angry, of course he would be.

"It wasn't what you think. I know that situation wasn't exactly appropriate, but it has been so quiet here, and nothing has ever happened between us..."

I stopped rambling when I finally looked to him and saw that he offered no response. His face was unreadable. The candles flickered. I knew so little about the man before me. I braced myself for a reaction. My muscles tensed, readying my body against an onslaught.

Words or fists; I had no idea what Isaiah was capable of.

He held my gaze until I shifted in my seat. Awkwardness forced me to look away.

Then he removed the lid of the silver dish.

It was a bird.

Golden brown and stuffed with herbs and spices where a neck and head should be. It was the perfect size. The light contracted, dimming and brightening.

He picked up the carving knife and gently cut through the tender breast. I watched in horror. The knife edge glinted gold. He placed the meat on my plate, then his.

"Eat," he said.

I stared glassy-eyed at my plate. It couldn't be. He wouldn't.

He watched me intently. His hands rested either side of his supper. He had no intention of starting before me. He wanted to witness my pain.

"Eat," he said again.

I couldn't do it. I would vomit if I tried.

"She should be in bed." Esme's voice came from the doorway behind me, and I felt a rush of relief.

"Oh, I don't know," Isaiah said, "she seems very capable of doing all kinds of things."

He smirked at me.

I was stunned into silence. I would rather have taken a beating; it would have hurt less than the pain in my heart right now. Could he really be this cruel? Purdie was innocent.

"The child," Esme hissed at him, and Isaiah relaxed back into his chair. Esme took this as a sign to take over, and her papery hand took mine. "Come, child."

Out in the darkened corridor Zena's white face appeared to float in the shadows. I wondered if she was really there or just a vision. But Esme spoke to her. "Tell Mathis to bring her supper," she said.

Mathis. He was still here. A seed of hope sprouted in my barren heart.

"But Isaiah," I said. "He won't like it."

"You leave him to me," Esme said.

In my room she helped me into my chair by the fire and

covered me with blankets and shawls. "You're freezing. You need to take care of yourself." She sat in the chair opposite. "I must insist you stay inside now, dear, you're very close."

"I know," I said. I was heavy with the exhaustion of it all.

There was a knock at the door. Mathis. Esme called him in. I tried not to react in any way. Mathis laid my supper on the table. It was the usual stew. He didn't glance at me once.

"I'll leave you to eat," Esme said. "Isaiah won't disturb you." She stood up. "You leave him to me," she said again. She gave a warm smile and left us alone.

"I shouldn't stay long," Mathis said, but he sat down.

"I was worried, I thought…"

"That they'd kicked me out?" Mathis sighed. "I thought they might, too. I've stayed out of the way. Been waiting all day for something to happen. But nothing has." He paused. "It doesn't mean it won't, though."

"Mathis." The words were building up inside me, bile rising. "I think he killed her."

"Who?"

"Purdie. She's not here, I can't feel her. There was a bird on the platter. I… she's not here…" The golden glint of the knife haunted me.

"Fortune, there is something very wrong here. With him." Mathis knelt next to my chair. He brushed a tear from my cheek and the touch of his hand comforted me. "We should leave. You've seen it now. You know he's not the gentleman he said he was. There's a boat on the other side of the island. I know how to hide; I could protect you and the baby. There's still time."

I shook my head. "There is no time. I thought you understood. There's no way out of this for me. Wherever I am, it is the end for me. It goes beyond Isaiah, and you."

This could be the last time I ever saw him. I touched his cheek, the first time I had ever done so. He closed his eyes, placed his own hand over mine and sighed gently. I longed to kiss him.

"Listen to me," he said, now taking my hand in both of his and resting them on my lap. "I know that you think what you saw and heard was true, but Fortune, you were a child! A child who had just given birth and was mad with exhaustion and pain. Can you really trust what you saw that night?"

I pulled my hand away from him. "I thought you understood."

A bang against the window startled us. A loud incessant cawing, wings beating against glass. I threw off the shawls and blankets and rushed to open the window. Purdie came flying in, shouting and flapping her wings, until settling on my arm that I held out for her.

"Purdie, you stupid bird," I croaked. My throat was choked with tears and laughter. "Where have you been? Where have you been hiding, eh?" I rubbed my nose into the side of her neck and she pulled at my hair. "Silly bird," I said, laughing still. "Silly, silly bird. You frightened me."

"I'm glad she's back," Mathis said. He wasn't laughing. "But this doesn't change anything. We should leave."

I sighed. I didn't want to hurt him. "I'd rather die here in this bed than in the hold of some ship or hiding in a cave somewhere." Purdie made a gurgling sound that she does when she's happy. I tickled beneath her chin. "This is as good a place as any," I said to her.

Mathis didn't argue. I didn't look at him. I only heard the door close behind him.

"But I do wish you could be with me," I said.

CHAPTER TWENTY-FIVE

Something woke me in the night. The moon was bulging, lighting up the room. I stared at Esme's painting. Something had changed. The house and sky all appeared the same, the cliffs muted to a dark grey. But there, in the cliff face, was something new. A light orange smudge. I got up, unable to ignore it, and stood before the painting. It was a lamp. A window had appeared, as if rooms were built inside. I lightly ran the tip of my finger over it. It felt just the same as the rest of the painting. But it hadn't been there yesterday, and no doubt it would be gone by morning. I was numb. The events of the day had wrung me out. A shadow passed across the room. A bird outside flying through the moonlight. Purdie slept on my pillow, her head tucked beneath her wing, breathing softy. I listened to the house. If I stilled myself long enough, I could almost hear it breathing. But then, another sound.

Music drifted into my room, creeping through the cracks of my bedroom door, barely audible. My heartbeat was louder. Esme's music box? No, the sound could never carry this far. I closed my eyes. It was the piano. Isaiah. I didn't want to hear him, didn't want to ever see him again. I climbed back into bed. But the music became louder. The longer I listened, the calmer I felt. The hairs on my arms lifted in awe of the music and a great sadness washed over me. It was calling me. It was only right that Isaiah had been angry with me, and he hadn't cooked Purdie after all. I should go to him. That's exactly what I should do. The music was telling me so.

I put on slippers, grabbed a shawl, lit a candle. Its glow drowned out the moonlight, but the hallways were dark. I would need it.

A melancholy march led me to the sitting room. My bones ached. The music filled the house with sorrow. The sound of a woman weeping somewhere just out of sight called to me, vying for my attention, but I ignored it and pushed on. By the time I reached the sitting room I was ready to run to Isaiah, tell him how sorry I was and comfort him. But the instant my fingertips touched the doorknob, the music stopped.

"Isaiah?" I pushed the door open and went inside. The sitting room was empty. Black and cold. Whatever spell was upon me lifted and I shuddered at the thought of running to Isaiah. How could music force me to abandon my better judgement? I shivered and pulled the shawl tighter around me.

A rustle behind me. The hem of a dress on the stone floor. I turned quickly, almost extinguishing my single candle. Nothing.

The rustle came again.

I crept back into the hallway and caught the edge of a white lace gown disappearing around the corner, towards the entrance hall. For a moment I was frozen in place, my heart beating a chaotic rhythm. I had heard weeping. Could it be the woman that haunted me? Or had Esme passed by without seeing me? I followed.

The full moon plays tricks, causes havoc with the senses. I knew I shouldn't trust anything on a night like this. Perfect conditions to thin the veil between this world and the next, and my devil was already closing in. I was asking for trouble.

I reached the entrance hall. No sign of a woman. But then came a child's cry. Soft, but distinct. I should turn around, go back to bed and wait for the sun to clear all this up. But the cry was coming from the direction of Esme's room, and I couldn't help myself. I pushed on.

At Esme's corridor, the cry faded to nothing. Her door was slightly open. Legions of candles were lit as usual. It was very late for Esme to be up. I crept towards the door. Voices.

Esme's voice was clear and sharp. A deep, rumbling tone answered. Isaiah.

I blew out my candle, needing to get close enough to decipher words.

"It will be done very soon. You can make sure of it, can't you," Esme said. Isaiah's response was indiscernible.

I barely breathed as I approached the door. I could see Esme now, dressed elaborately in green-and-gold brocade. Another step and Isaiah came into view. Something about this meeting felt wrong. They were stood very close to each other towards the back of the room, where Esme would often set up her easel.

"Now, dear, don't be disheartened, it'll work. I know it will," Esme said. She took Isaiah's hand in her two. For a moment they stood, Esme looking up at him, him looking down at her. Esme then lifted his hand to her cheek, pressed his palm against her powered skin and closed her eyes, breathing in the scent of him. My heart skipped. I thought of Mathis and the intimacy of a similar moment we had shared.

I felt like a thief in the night. I shouldn't be spying on this tender moment between mother and son. I should leave but my curiosity, and the fear of being heard, held me fast.

Esme then put a hand to his cheek, and he turned his face towards her palm. She ran her hand over his slicked-back hair and all the way down his back, resting at the base of his spine. She pulled his body close to hers. I could feel bile rising. This was wrong. Something was very wrong.

My darkest thoughts were confirmed as Esme gripped Isaiah's lapels and pulled his face to hers. They kissed. Not the chaste kiss of a family bond. An open-mouthed, lovers' kiss.

I stifled a sob with my hand over my mouth.

Isaiah pulled away. "Not now, *mother*."

"I know I disgust you right now. But soon you'll be calling to me again. Soon." She traced a finger along his jaw. Isaiah didn't look angry or disgusted.

"Soon," he said. "I'll leave you now." He stepped back from Esme. This was it, the moment I would be discovered. I should have left earlier. There was only one way in and out of this room. Isaiah would walk right into me.

"You would leave me for her?" Esme asked.

Isaiah sighed. "It will never change with you, will it?"

He didn't wait for an answer. I looked about me in panic, ready to flee. Isaiah would find me. I would lie, say I'd just arrived. Saw nothing. But instead of moving towards the door, Isaiah lifted a large tapestry on the back wall and stepped through. A hidden door. The tapestry fell back into place behind him. Esme turned, huffed out some air and rapped her nails on the top of her chair as though thinking about what to do. I pressed myself into the wall behind me, wishing it would swallow me whole. I was cloaked in shadow, but with Esme facing my direction I felt utterly exposed.

With a sudden decision made, Esme followed Isaiah through the hidden exit.

I didn't run, or cry or scream. I was paralysed with fear.

Slowly my senses came back to me. The wall was cold against my back. The smell of rosemary and herbal tobacco was strong. Overwhelming. My fingers loosened their grip on the candleholder. My nails made sucking sounds as they pulled from the skin of my palm, leaving little half-moon indents.

Esme's room was eerie. The candles had been left burning for no one. I could go and find Mathis and tell him he was right. Instead, I stared at the tapestry. Fear that they would return set my nerves on edge. I should leave and pretend this never happened. But I had to know more.

Time passed. I don't know how long. When I was certain they wouldn't return, I stepped into Esme's room. The comforting familiarity of it made me baulk. Everything was the same as it always was. Her tobacco box at the side of her chair. A pack of cards and an empty teacup on the table. The easel was folded and pushed to the far-right corner of the room, the paints and brushes neatly stacked beside it. Then there was the tapestry.

I stood before it. It reached from ceiling to floor. The image was a bird's-eye view of a tree stump, the rings of the tree exposed. The stump was surrounded by wings, a pair at the top, a pair at the bottom, as if protecting it from further harm. They could be angel wings, or those of a large bird. But they were disembodied. I had never paid it any attention. The room was full of large hanging tapestries, and this one wasn't in my line of sight when I sat with Esme for tea.

I lifted it. The weight was surprising. Esme had pulled it back so easily. The door behind was like any other in the house. Oak wood and black iron hinges set into the wall. I pushed at it tentatively. Any resistance and I would turn back. But it did not resist.

The air behind was much colder than Esme's suffocating room, but not fresh. It was stagnant, like old pond water filling my lungs. Stairs descended into darkness. The point of no return. It wasn't too late for me to turn back. And hadn't Esme said Isaiah was leaving her for me? Was this simply another route back to the main house? The chill rising from the darkness told me that wasn't the case. Something awful was down there. A terrible, dreadful secret. The truth isn't always the best option, ignorance can be kinder. But I had been ignorant long enough.

I relit my candle and descended the stone stairs.

At the bottom, tunnels stretched left, right and straight ahead. I went straight ahead.

This labyrinth was cut directly into the rock that the house resided on.

Damp, mouldy air clung to my skin like cobwebs. Isaiah and Esme were down here somewhere in this dreadful place. I watched where I placed my feet, terrified I would kick a stone or trip on the uneven floor and they would find me.

Water dripped somewhere in the gloomy distance, creating a disembodied echo. My back ached from supporting the weight of my stomach. The tunnel narrowed, the air became ever colder, thinner. *I will suffocate down here*, I thought. A dull pain started in my chest, as if the damp had seeped inside me and things were growing there, like mushrooms in mould. I put my hand to my chest. I should turn back. I couldn't see when this tunnel would end and I was tired, so tired. The place filled me with worry and grief and unease and fear. So much fear. My candle lit only a few feet ahead. I stopped. I would go back.

A scratching froze me to the spot. And then *she* was there, a breath away from my face. Her eyes blacked out, her hair dishevelled, covering her face in matted strips. Her mouth opened wide, her lips black, her teeth broken and yellow. She screamed. The stench of rotting milk and flesh on her breath hit me. I stumbled back. And then she was gone. I was left alone in my circle of light, my heart hammering. The water dripped in the distance. My chest ached, but not with fear. With grief. With a loss that I had felt long ago in the woods, walking into the lake with a bundle. I knew now that this weeping woman was not my devil taunting me. She was something else, something connected to this place. I kept going.

A door appeared from the murk facing me. The passageway split to the left and right. The door was thick iron with wide, elaborate black hinges. They were oiled and shining, often used. The dripping had stopped. Only the sound of my own ragged breath was audible now. The seedling squirmed, sensing the oppressive fear. A tiny hand pressed against me from the inside. The seedling and I did have a connection; we would die together. I should have been kinder, offered her love while she was here, even if she would never see the world. I had been selfish yet again, thinking only of how to protect my heart. I pressed back, but gently this time. *I am here.*

I pushed the door open. Inside, the air was musky and warmer than the tunnels. A rectangular stone altar sat in the centre of the room. Scenes were carved into the sides. Facing me, a woman held up a sword in one hand

and a man's head in the other, his body lying at her feet. A battle raged behind her. I circled the altar. A pack of wolves devoured a large animal. A bull, perhaps? The back showed men rising from their graves, an angel above them trumpeted their awakening. The final side depicted Death, his sabre held high, his cloak flowing. Children lay at his feet. Horror and death. There was nothing on top of the altar, just a smooth surface.

The walls of the chamber were hidden in shadow, but I held out my candle and saw more stone structures. Smaller than the altar, and square. I stepped towards them. I could now see three within my circle of light. Sarcophagi. Each had the same scene depicted on its lid: a pregnant, naked woman being dragged and scratched by many demonic hands into the fires of hell. Their chests gaped open where their hearts should be.

On the wall behind each coffin was a portrait. In the one before me, a young woman cradled a newborn babe in her arms. The sitting-room piano was behind her. In the corner it was labelled *The Musical Bride*.

The next painting was almost a replica of the first. This woman was blonde. Her skin ashen and drained. She too held a babe. Behind her was an easel bearing a blank canvas. She was *The Artist Bride*.

I didn't want to look any further but couldn't help myself. The next painting was worse. I gasped as I recognised the waist-length curly hair. Her eyes were no longer black holes. They stared out at me, pleading, longing, dying. The colour of a ripe chestnut. She held her babe, exactly like the others. In her free hand was the little wooden box that Esme kept her ointment in. *The Healing Bride*. Anna.

The square stone beneath was no more than three

feet wide or deep. I knelt before it. Every movement was involuntary, as if I were watching myself from the rafters like Purdie would. I put my candle down, slipped my fingers beneath the lip of the lid, and lifted.

Off-white bones lay at the base, gathered in a pile. Two skulls, one much smaller than the other. My tears dripped on them. I cried for their loss, and Mathis, and myself. I pulled the lid back into place.

There were many portraits. *The Herbal Bride*, *The Trickster Bride*, *The Empath Bride*, *The Necromancer Bride*! It went on and on. A gallery of brides. Of women, just like me, whose lives had been cut short.

I had to get out.

Back in the passageway, I heard voices. Esme and Isaiah were close. Their voices seemed to come from the way I came. I turned right. I couldn't think or breathe or even understand what was happening. All I knew was I could not see them down here, or it would be the end for me. And this was not how I was planning to go. Not like this. Not crammed into a tiny secret tomb with my child.

I moved forward, hoping for a miracle. Hoping I was far enough away from them that they didn't see my light. My prayers were answered with a set of ascending stairs. A strip of dim light signalled a way out. The door at the top was thin and short but certainly a door. I had no idea where it led. I blew out my candle.

I held my breath and listened. I cursed my heart for beating so loud. I couldn't be sure what was on the other side. I couldn't hear anything. I pushed it open a crack and was relieved to see a small room lined with shelves full of boxes and crates, bags of grain leaned against them. I was in the kitchen, in the larder. The door to the kitchen was closed and I waited for a long time, listening. I heard nothing, and eventually garnered enough courage to open it. The kitchen was flooded with moonlight. Mercifully empty. I stood, unable to move. The horror of what lay beneath the house screamed inside my head as if the weeping woman was there right now, screaming and crying in my face. Not a nameless, faceless woman anymore. Anna. But what could I do? What could I do?

I crept swiftly through the kitchen and into the house.

CHAPTER TWENTY-SIX

I couldn't stay in the house. I went straight out the front door and down to the cove. The icy sea breeze swept away the damp that clung to me, but the taste of sour milk on my tongue lingered. Purdie arrived as I descended the stone steps. She hopped on the rocks and barked at me, occasionally nipping at my dress or hair. I ignored her.

Then I was at the water's edge. The waves lapped my feet. The wind whipped my hair and slapped my nightgown against my legs. The cold had teeth, but I couldn't feel it bite, my body was numb. I needed my mind to be numb, too. Isaiah and Esme. It wasn't natural. All this time I had been waiting for my punishment, to be killed and flung into the depths of hell. But I was already in hell. I had been so focused on an elusive afterlife that I'd missed the true evil circling me daily. Devils that had served me food and tea and tended to my needs, wed me and bedded me. I had allowed it all.

The brides. All those brides. They had killed them all and stolen their gifts somehow. It all fit. The power of Isaiah's music, the painting, the ointment. They were using those women's gifts. But why the children? If the seedling did survive, what then? Buried in a cold, dark crypt, forever trapped with the other babes. My fate to evermore walk the halls, weeping with the other brides. Powerless.

I couldn't let that happen. I would choose our death.

Mathis. He should know that Anna was here. Is here. That her bones and those of her child were resting beneath his feet the entire time. It would break his heart. Better for him never to find out.

I walked into the ocean.

The water resisted me, pushing me back. I pushed forward, harder. Purdie was fretting now, flapping about my head, tugging on my nightgown. I barely noticed. All I could see was the black ocean, the gateway to the next world. My mermaid would be waiting, somewhere in the water. I would find her.

My stomach submerged. The seedling squirmed. Then the sea threw out a large wave that knocked me back. Beneath the waves I was cut off. It was pitch dark, but not quiet. The water roared. I tumbled in the current until it slowed and I could stand again. I coughed and spluttered, but kept walking. It wouldn't be long now, the sea would soon cover my nose and mouth, and that would be the end of it.

Purdie had gone. I was glad, she shouldn't see this. I pushed on, walking deeper and deeper into the ocean. The seabed was rough and uneven. The water was at my neck. I took another step and was sucked beneath a wave, the sea finally embracing me. I let myself fall into the darkness where the water pushed and pulled me, a child playing with her doll. My chest screamed in pain, desperate for air.

A hand gripped my arm and pulled me up and out. I gasped. A voice echoed through the water in my ears. Mathis was there, pulling me back towards the beach. I tried to fight him off, but I was no match for him. I didn't have the strength to fight him and the sea. I let him guide me.

We fell onto the sand. Mathis pulled me into a sitting

position between his legs, my back against his chest. Maybe this was a final mercy, and I would die there in his arms instead of alone in the vast ocean.

But I didn't die. We sat until my breath regained some kind of rhythm and I started shivering. My senses were returning. A thousand needles pricked my skin all at once. My chest hurt with every breath. I was cold, so cold. I thought I would never feel warmth again. I didn't want to. I didn't deserve to.

"What were you thinking?" Mathis' voice was clear despite the ringing in my ears.

Things were becoming sharp again.

"I won't let them take us," I said. My words barely made it out as my jaw shook violently. Did Mathis even hear me?

"We need to get you upstairs. Now," Mathis said. He lifted me from the sand. We stumbled up the steps, dripping and shivering. "You should leave me," I said, over and over, but Mathis didn't pay me any mind.

We were back in our lifeboat. The fire blazed. I sat wrapped in blankets before it. The needles were slowly dispersing. Mathis had been staring into the flames for the last few minutes. I had been watching him. My mind raced.

"Why?" he asked.

"How did you know?"

"What?" He looked at me, confused, then sighed. "Purdie." Purdie clicked her beak from the back of my chair. "She came flapping at my window. I knew something was wrong."

"Yes, something is wrong. Something is very wrong." I stared at the fire. The portraits appeared one after the other in my mind. "You should have left me."

"So that's it, is it? You think that you and the baby will die, so you thought you'd offer yourself up without a fight? All because of something you think you saw when you were fifteen?"

Rather that than a secret sarcophagus. "No, it's not that," I said.

"Then what?" Mathis raised his voice. "I'm sorry," he said, calming himself.

I hated what I was doing to him, but it would be worse if he knew the truth.

"I'm sorry too," I said. "But you must prepare yourself. This seedling will never sprout, and I'll go with it, one way or the other."

"It's already sprouted, Fortune," he said. "That is a fully formed babe in there. She moves. You can feel her, can't you? Soon she'll come out and meet you. And what then? Have you even considered that? What if she lives? What if you live?"

I couldn't speak. *She*. He'd called it *she*.

Mathis waited for a response, shook his head, and looked back at the flames.

I looked down at my protruding stomach. The weight I had hefted and complained about. The thing inside that I tried not to think about. I remembered my beautiful shell at the side of the lake. Her eyelashes, her perfectly formed lips. Now I could see those eyes opening, her mouth suckling. Pink instead of blue. Grey skin suddenly flushed with colour.

I thought about the other brides. I had accepted that I would die in childbirth. I had envisioned my second shell being born and my soul going with hers. We were supposed to die in bed. Not spend eternity in a dungeon.

Perhaps there was still time. Mathis and I could leave,

and I'd have the babe somewhere else. I would be with him and my child, and death would be better greeted then. I couldn't stay trapped here, my afterlife spent walking the halls and weeping over my dead child.

The brides were here in spirit. I could feel them watching from the shadows. They had tried to warn me. Anna had tried. But I hadn't listened.

"Do you still want to leave?" I said.

Mathis lifted his head from his hands and looked at me, surprised.

"Do you mean it?"

"Yes."

"Why? What's changed?"

"Don't ask me that. Can we do it? Can we leave?"

Mathis looked at me, no doubt considering the terrible state I was in. "It would be risky..." He shook his head.

"Yes, but is it possible?"

"There's a boat on the other side of the island."

"Good, let's go." I began removing the blankets.

"We can't leave with you like that." He stopped me pushing the blanket off and picked one up from the floor that had fallen, placing it over my knees again. "You need rest. It'll be a walk to the boat, and I need to gather supplies. I can't carry you as well as all that we need."

I knew he was right, but fear stirred within me. If we didn't leave right now, then something would prevent us. We would never get off this island.

"You must sleep. We'll leave tomorrow. Once Zena has made sure you've had breakfast, she'll not disturb you again for a while. That will give us some time. She normally disappears for a while after that. Isaiah's office faces the cove and Esme's room has no windows, so we should be able to leave unnoticed. It'll be much easier to navigate the woods in daylight."

Zena would be beneath the house, in the catacombs. They were in it together, a team.

A coven?

"You must sleep. I'll arrange everything," Mathis said. "Please, drink the tincture. You need rest if you want to have any strength for the journey tomorrow." I nodded and drank it to appease him. I had worried him enough.

I tossed and turned in the bed. Worried that Isaiah would appear at any moment and drag me down to the crypt from which I would never return. I had felt fear before, many times. But not like this. Fearing for your soul wasn't the same as a living, breathing threat. I couldn't fight off a man the size and strength of Isaiah. Mathis couldn't either. Every creak, groan or whisper the house made set me on edge. I wouldn't be able to sleep until I was far away from this house and the people in it. The tincture had only succeeded in making my head ache.

Behind the anger and disgust there was another, deeper hurt. I had thought Esme was a friend. She had stood up for me when Zena was happy to leave me in pain. She had joked with me about Isaiah. We had spent hours drinking tea and eating sweets and playing cards.

She had sucked me in, an experienced spider catching an ignorant fly. I had trusted her.

How had I let my guard down so willingly since I came here? The brides and their gifts were a part of it. I thought of Isaiah's precision commanding the keys, and my longing when I heard him play. How relaxed I became as the music swallowed me whole. Esme's painting. Every time it had shimmered or changed, I brushed it off. I accepted it as a trick of the light or my imagination. Anna's ointment had healed me more than once. They had barely hidden anything from me. But I was completely blind to it. They had stolen these gifts. What else had I been subjected to? The companionship I felt with Esme, was that real? What about the food I ate? Did that have power over me, too? I could trust nothing in this place.

All this time I had been guarding against the wrong thing. I looked to my stomach. I had cut myself off from my own heart to save me some pain. But I realised then it was my job to bring this seedling into the world and fight for her at all costs.

I stroked my stomach.

"I'm sorry," I said.

CHAPTER
TWENTY-SEVEN

I must have dozed off in the end, because I woke to Purdie nuzzling into my messy hair, looking for bugs, tugging at strands. I let her continue; the gentle pulling comforted me.

"You saved me, Purdie," I said. She didn't respond, too focused on her task. I enjoyed this peaceful, soothing moment, cocooned in the soft warmth of the bed, a world away from the previous evening, an ocean away. Then it all came flooding back in a wave of nausea. A fleeting moment of contentedness replaced by images of incest and tiny white bones.

The seedling pressed against my stomach. Her movements were fewer now. She was too big to move around much in there. It wouldn't be long.

We would leave today. It terrified and excited me. I feared what would happen if they caught us, but a glimmer of hope shone in my heart at the thought of having my child away from this place. If we stayed, she would be murdered alongside me down in the catacombs, spending eternity folded in a small tomb alongside the other brides. The certainty of this death forced me to question the certainty I had had in my devil. Beneath this house was proof that both our lives would end. I had no such proof of my devil. What if Mathis was right, and all this time I had believed a falsity? A fiction of my own making. *What if my child lived?*

I dressed, stoked the fire, and waited.

Mathis arrived with breakfast. As he entered the room, I opened my mouth to speak, but he stopped me with a slight shake of his head. He quietly began to lay the table before me. Zena appeared just behind him. She carried linen to the dressing room, and we listened to her shuffling about, tidying up. Mathis laid out the breakfast as slowly as possible, but now it was done, and Zena still hadn't left.

"Could you get more logs for the fire and build it up? I'm feeling the cold today." I said it loud enough that Zena would hear.

"Yes ma'am," Mathis said. We looked at each other. Everything we needed to say was conveyed in a glance. He felt the same as me. Nervous, excited, terrified. He left the room.

Zena appeared from the dressing room. She had been waiting for Mathis to leave. She stood before me. Her bone-white face chilled me. My heart hammered. This woman could see into my soul, I was sure of it. And what if there had been a bride who could read minds? No, they would have known I'd discovered their secret. She could most definitely sense my terror. *The Sentient Wife*. But Zena was just the housekeeper. Even if Isaiah and Esme had been stealing the brides' gifts somehow, Zena only served them. I sure they wouldn't share with her, no matter how blurred the boundaries.

"It won't be long now," she said.

"No," I said.

The fire crackled. Purdie shifted on her perch in the rafters. Zena stared.

"It won't be easy," she said.

"I know."

She waited another moment before adding, "You'll do well."
Then she left.

It was the kindest thing she'd ever said to me. That's if
she meant I'd do well giving birth. She could be referring to
what they had planned for me after. I shuddered.

I tapped the arm of my chair and Purdie joined me. I
broke some bread for her. She took it to the floor, where she
liked to play about with it before eating. My heart swelled
with gratitude for Purdie. Her love and loyalty had helped
me through many lonely nights. I wished my gift extended
to growing wings and flying away.

Mathis returned with the logs and closed the door behind
him.

"Meet me at the cemetery in an hour. It'll look suspicious
if we're seen heading to the woods together. Make sure
you are wrapped up warm. Extra layers. Two of everything.
And as many shawls as you can carry on your shoulders."
He walked to the window, assessing the weather. "It's calm
today. We should have good sailing."

"Mathis," I said. "I'm sorry I didn't go when you asked. I
should have trusted you."

He opened his mouth to say something but then changed
his mind. Instead, he came and crouched beside my chair.
"How are you feeling?" He put his hand on my forehead.

"I'm well."

"Are you strong enough to go today? You had an ordeal
last night."

"No, we go today."

He nodded. "You don't have a temperature at least," he said,
removing his hand. My forehead was left cold without him.

"The cemetery. One hour."

"I'll be there."

He took my hand and squeezed it, hesitating before releasing me. I didn't want him to let go but there was no choice. He left me to my meal.

After breakfast, I put on extra stockings and a second underskirt. I filled my pockets with leftover bread and sweetmeats I kept wrapped in napkins in a drawer.

"We'll be fine," I said to Purdie, offering her some crumbs which she gobbled up. "We'll make it." But my confident tone did not reach my heart. I had no idea who my husband and mother-in-law were. *What* they were. Or what they were capable of.

And what of Mathis? He deserved an explanation. He was the one who had known there was something very wrong with this place. With Isaiah. His sister was here, for heaven's sake. But if I told him about the catacombs he would want to go down there, and I couldn't risk him being hurt. I would tell him after, when we were long gone. Selfish, but necessary.

At the cemetery I sat on one of the low tombs. Decidedly disrespectful, but the occupant was a woman and her daughter. They would surely forgive this pregnant woman for taking a much-needed rest. The cold bled through my skirts. Even with the extra layers, I could feel it. Purdie circled overhead, the chill breeze useless against her impenetrable coat. The graveyard was shielded by its wall and the woods, and although the trees were mostly bare, they offered some protection. I looked at the stones about me. The Quickly name haunted me, whispering at me accusingly from the headstones. "Who are you?" I asked them. The angels hid their faces behind praying hands, and the cupid looked straight down his arrow. Brute's tongue lolled, as always. They knew things, these tombs. The memories of the people beneath them had filtered through the soil and grew into the grass and weeds and were held in the stones that crowned them. I could feel it. They were watching and waiting. Judging. I thought again of the women in their dark tombs, forever deformed, never allowed to stretch out their bones, crying with their babes into the void. There was nothing I could do to help them. There was only hope for the seedling and me, and Mathis. I would get Mathis away from these demons. It was the least I could do.

Purdie cried out from above – Mathis was coming.

He arrived carrying his herb basket as though he were just foraging in the woods. I felt my heart sigh in relief for him.

"Are you well? Have you waited long?" he asked. He opened a bundle at his side and produced a flask of wine. "Here, drink some of this." I took a drink to appease him, but it burned my throat. I held it down. "I've brought food and some extra clothes, but it doesn't take too long to reach the main island. I know someone who will help hide us there until we can sail." He tucked the flask of wine away.

"Will Purdie warn us if anyone is following?"

His faith in my connection with Purdie gave me confidence.

"Yes," I said, glancing up at Purdie, who was still at her post as lookout above.

"This way," he said.

I followed him through the woods. Each step was too loud, each scenario that ran through my head was more terrifying than the last. I kept checking the skies for Purdie, afraid she might disappear suddenly. But she was there, gliding across the treetops, back and forth like a soldier on guard. My feet hurt and my back ached. I felt like a traitor. Mathis had a right to know, but he would want to go back, and I couldn't go back there.

The woods ended abruptly. This side of the island was much lower than where the house stood. We skirted along the rock until they formed into a small natural harbour.

Mathis stopped abruptly. Half a boat was tied to the rock. The other half had been smashed to pieces. Planks of wood drifted on the surface of the water, like shattered dreams.

Mathis stared. Then he ran and knelt at the water's edge, pulling the solid half closer to him, as if that would fix it. "No, no, no," he muttered as he looked it over.

My heart pounded. I had known, had I not, that it wouldn't be this easy. The whole escapade felt like child's play. A silly dream. Now it was over. There was no escape from this dreadful place.

"He did this," I said. Purdie came and landed on the bank beside me. The horizon began to sway. "He must know, then, what I saw."

"What did you see?"

"I'm sorry, Mathis. I've trapped you here with me and I don't know what will happen."

"Fortune, please, tell me what you saw. I can't do anything to help if–"

"I'll tell you," I said, but I turned pale at the memory. Mathis helped me onto one of the larger rocks at the bank and sat beside me. To sit was a blessed relief.

"I saw Isaiah and Esme… together," I said. Mathis looked confused. "Kissing," I added. I fought back the bile.

Mathis' brow crinkled in confusion. "Do you mean they were greeting each other, or–"

"No," I stopped him, "they were kissing like man and wife."

The sea lapped gently against the rocks; birds called to each other in the woods. Purdie had settled on a high branch above us. The natural world continued, oblivious to my torture.

I could see Mathis willing his brain to accept this information. I knew that in this moment a million things were rushing through his head, searching for another explanation. He wasn't ready to believe it. It is difficult to believe something you haven't seen with your own eyes.

"There's more." I stopped his ticking brain. I took a deep breath. "They left Esme's room through a secret door. And I followed them."

"A door? Where?"

"Behind one of the tapestries at the back of her room. There were stairs. I followed them," I said again. I couldn't say it. I couldn't tell Mathis that his sister was dead.

"What did you see?"

"Mathis, I..."

"What did you see?" He was growing afraid, and I wasn't being fair.

"There's a dungeon beneath the house. In the cellar. It hides a chamber filled with portraits. And... tombs."

"Portraits of who?"

"Of women, of new mothers, just like I will be soon."

"And the tombs?"

"They were small, the lids lifted easily." I could see it again. Taste the stale air in my mouth, feel the sadness emanating from the fragile bones. "There were the skeletons of mothers and their children."

"Are you certain?"

"As certain as I can be."

"What else? What did the women look like? Were any of them Anna?"

The desperation in his eyes was a knife in my heart. "Yes."

Mathis hung his head and stared at the ground for a long while.

"Are you sure? It could have been someone else. The ointment was new, stronger…"

"It was her," I said more firmly. "She was holding the box in her portrait. And bones lay in the tomb beneath it, just like all the others." Every word hit him like a blow to the chest. It was destroying him. "They all had gifts, too, just like Anna. You were right. That's why I'm here."

"And you didn't tell me? You were going to let me leave without seeing this for myself or giving my sister some justice? Or a proper burial?"

"I'm sorry," I said, hardly able to look at him. "I thought it would be better if…"

"You thought it would be better?"

I flinched at his anger. "I knew how much it would hurt you. And I knew you'd want to investigate, and I didn't want you to get hurt."

"You mean you needed me to run away." The words stung. He turned away from me slightly, looking out to the open ocean.

"I didn't want to lose you too." I choked back a sob and placed my hand on his arm.

"I'm sorry," he said, turning back to me. "That was unfair. Forgive me. I knew in my heart that she was gone." He put his hand over mine, our fingers linked. I was tired. So tired. Tired of everything.

"I'm so sorry, Mathis."

"I know. So am I."

We sat for a time. Mathis gazed out to sea, and I listened to the natural murmurings of the woods.

"What are you thinking?" I asked.

"I'm thinking about what they do to these women. They are taking their gifts, but how?"

"I don't know, but it has something to do with the children." I stroked my bump.

"I have to see them," Mathis said.

CHAPTER TWENTY-EIGHT

We were going back in. I tried to remember as many details as I could on the walk back. The one Mathis was very curious about was that I had returned to the house through the kitchen. He decided that was the best way in.

"You're not coming with me," Mathis said as I removed the extra layer of clothing.

We were back in my room.

"Of course I am. Do you think I could sit here and worry myself mad? I'm coming. If you find anything else, I think I ought to know." My hand instinctively cradled my stomach.

"I'd say that's a reason to stay here," Mathis said, glancing at my stomach. "I don't want you in any danger."

"It's far too late for that. It's best if we stick together." Mathis was uncomfortable with this, but he nodded in agreement.

"We need to know where they are first," I said. "I'll check if Esme is in her room, you check on Zena and we'll meet in the sitting room."

"What about Isaiah?"

"He'll be in his office, like he is every day."

"Are you sure? Have you ever seen him in his office?"

"No, but I..." I thought about this. I had never visited Isaiah in his office. It occurred to me now that he may not spend his days there at all. His whole life was a lie. I still didn't know where he slept. But then I didn't know where any of them slept. *That's because they sleep beneath the house.* A chill ran down my spine, as if someone had walked over my grave, Ma would say. I shrugged the chill and the voice in my head away. I couldn't lose my nerve now.

"No, I've never seen him there."

"I'll check," Mathis said.

He left first. I counted to thirty before making my way to Esme's room.

Approaching her room with the confidence of a rabbit leaving the burrow for the first time, I sniffed the air. The familiar scent of tobacco mixed with rosemary greeted me. Esme was there. No need to go inside. I turned to leave.

"Fortune, dear, is that you?" came her croaky voice. *Damn.*

"Yes, just me," I called back. I sucked in hard, filling my chest with the smoke, lifted my chin and entered her room. Esme had her easel out with the base of an image started.

Swirls of red and orange filled the canvas. This was good, she wouldn't move for hours.

"Sit down, child, rest your back. You shouldn't even be out of bed." She studied her painting, swapped a brush for her pipe and took a drag. "You know, I'm not even sure what this would be. What do you think?"

The painting screamed blood and fire, bodies burning forever in an endless hell. "A sunset, perhaps?"

"A sunset." Esme nodded. "How beautiful. It's perfect." She swapped the pipe back to a brush. "You do see the beauty in things, innocent as you are."

"I'm not so sure about that." I smiled. I thought of how I had once seen the beauty in Esme. The kind way in which she had taken me under her wing, made jokes about Zena to put me at ease. Made me feel worthy of being here, of being part of this strange and wealthy family. I realised now that I had been desperate to feel some of the comfort I missed in Ma.

But now I saw Esme as she truly was. The mask of friendship concealed a spider, casting her web to catch the flies, each strand a temptation. She hunkered down here in the centre of her web and waited with the kind of patience only a stealthy hunter has. Waited for what, though? I knew the answer. The delicate curve of the child's skull in the small tomb pushed its way to the forefront of my mind. Esme and Isaiah kissing. I had to shut it out or I would flounder. I worried she could hear the blood pounding in my head, or would notice the sweat forming on my brow.

"Have some tea," Esme suggested.

"I'll not keep you from your craft. And I could use a walk." I stood up.

"Do you need company?" Esme said, putting her brush down. This was different, Esme never offered to walk with me. I had to stay calm.

"No," I said lightly. "I'll only make it to the garden before needing a lie down. It wouldn't be worth your while."

Esme picked up her pipe and sucked on it, observing me as I made my way to the door.

Every movement felt exaggerated, every step a giveaway.

"Fortune, dear." I turned to her from the doorway, a smile stuck to my face. "Do be careful."

Was it my imagination, or did her tone differ with those final words? I felt naked beneath Esme's gaze. But Esme didn't falter or fluster. She watched and waited, like spiders do, until the flies trapped themselves.

The sitting room was freezing. The fire was dying. I could hardly believe it was only a few hours since I'd eaten breakfast. My stomach rumbled. I took a piece of marzipan from my pocket and sucked on it. I needed energy. Nothing good would come from what we were about to do. What would happen if they caught us? And Mathis. Seeing his sister in one of those tombs would bring him only more pain. I despaired.

Mathis slipped through the door, closing it quietly behind him. "Zena's gone. She's usually gone for a few hours. I think she goes for an afternoon nap. What about Esme?"

"She's painting."

"Good."

"And Isaiah?"

"He wasn't there."

"We should wait, then, until we know where he is."

Mathis took a deep breath. "I can't, I'm sorry. You stay here, though, or go and warm yourself in your room." He was desperate for me not to go, and I didn't want to go, but the thought of him facing that alone was intolerable, and the fear of him being caught by Isaiah filled me with dread.

"I'm coming with you. I'm not an invalid." I pushed myself up from the chair, feeling exactly like an invalid.

"No, but it would be better if…"

"I'm coming."

We crept to the kitchen. With every step I expected Isaiah

to appear behind us, or Zena's spectral face to appear from the shadows.

"It's in the larder?" Mathis asked, even though he knew the answer. He wanted to break this oppressive silence, and I was grateful. It was like a rope tightening around my neck.

"Have you never noticed another door in there?" I asked.

"Zena goes in there. She gets out everything that is needed for the day. The garden is my domain."

Mathis opened the larder door. I felt a breath on the back of my neck. A shot of panic ran through me. I turned, but of course, there was no one there. But someone was watching, or some*thing*. The ghosts of the house were gathering, closing in on us in anticipation.

Mathis stepped into the larder.

"I see it," said Mathis. "I can see why I never noticed it from the kitchen." The door was textured and coloured to blend in with the cold stone walls. It was unlike any door I had ever seen. I hadn't looked back at it on the way out.

Now I was there, facing that dungeon again, fear crept back in. Not only could I feel the breath of ghosts upon my neck, but my bones were stiffening in memory of the dead cold down there in the darkness. Maybe hell wasn't filled with fires after all, but a lake of ice where people were locked in a state of fear and anguish for all eternity, with only their worst thoughts and feelings to accompany them.

Mathis pulled the door open. Cold air rushed at us, carrying the whispers of the dead upon it. He descended the stairs slowly, his lantern surrounding him in a golden glow, a man on an expedition into the unknown. He held my hand as he led the way.

It was different with Mathis there. More real. Solid. I wondered if we would get down there and find nothing.

As if another pair of eyes would reveal that I had suffered a terrible nightmare, a truly awful nightmare, but that was all it was: a figment, an illusion. I wished it would be so.

We reached a crossing of passageways. "Which way?" Mathis asked. The tunnels were identical. I thought hard, trying to remember my earlier steps and put them in reverse.

"Right," I said.

"Are you sure?"

"No, I'm not sure," I hissed. How could I be sure of my steps when I was in a state of pure terror? But he hadn't seen, he didn't understand – yet.

"There are marks on the wall," he said.

"There are?" I hadn't noticed these earlier, unsurprisingly. They were small, square glyphs of some kind. "What do they mean?"

"I don't know," Mathis said, continuing on.

We turned down another tunnel, slightly wider than the previous one. The scent of must and oil was perceptible. "We're close," I said. These were the smells of human habitation. Oil lamps and wood, powder and rosemary. Esme had been somewhere nearby. The darkness before us was suffocating. All manner of things could be lurking. The lantern held it a few feet at bay, but the darkness pushed back as if it would extinguish the light and smother us at any moment. I forced a slow intake of air to calm my racing heart.

Mathis stopped. He had found the iron door. He stood in complete silence. I watched his chest rise and fall rapidly in the dim light. Then, with a flurry of movement, he lurched forwards, opened the door and disappeared inside. I stood for a moment before following him into this chamber of death.

Inside, Mathis stood before Anna's portrait. His face had turned grey, his knuckles holding the lantern were white.

Their brown eyes and square chin were the same. Brother and sister. She held her newborn child on her lap, just like the other women, and in her other hand was the wooden box that held the healing balm. She wasn't smiling. None of them were. How much had they known about their fate?

Mathis knelt before the small tomb at his feet, placed his lantern to the side and lifted the lid.

He held his lantern aloft and studied the bones inside. Two skeletons. An adult and a tiny child. He stayed there for a long time without moving.

"Mathis, we should…" I touched his shoulder, and he jumped violently.

"Where did you say you heard them?" he asked.

"What?"

"You said a light appeared and you heard them. Where?"

"Further along the tunnel, around the corner."

Mathis was away, moving out of the room and turning left. I followed. The seedling kicked, and I winced. I saw the tail of Mathis' light disappear around the corner.

"Mathis," I whispered.

I had no choice but to catch up. He waited for me before another iron door and held a finger to his lips as I approached. We listened. The hairs on my neck raised. Nothing. No sound.

Mathis opened this door as slowly and as quietly as he could. It offered no resistance. It was a sitting room. Carpet covered most of the stone floor. A large table with three chairs about it was placed in the centre. Tapestries and gossamer curtains covered the walls. You would hardly know you were beneath the ground. There was a door on the left wall, and one on the right. Directly in front of us, where you'd expect to find a fireplace, hung a huge portrait surrounded by heavy velvet curtains, black as a new moon.

Three people were captured. At the centre was Isaiah. He was as he is today. Perfectly cut features, every hair in place. Only his clothes were different. An older style. He was wearing a long royal-blue cloak and a red tunic adorned with laurels. A black hat flopped over each side of his head like a feather cushion, as if he were dressed for a costumed ball at court.

Either side of Isaiah was a young woman, younger than I was now. To his left, the lady was tall and slender with dark plaited hair and sharp features. She wore a gold band across her smooth forehead. To his right was a shorter, pretty blonde woman. The dark woman exuded grace and elegance; the blonde woman encapsulated innocent beauty, with her petite rose-coloured lips, large blue eyes and fresh pink cheeks.

Two women. One the essence of courtly grandeur, the other the essence of mother nature. Indoors and outdoors. Upstairs and downstairs.

"It's them," I said, my voice shaking.

"Who?"

"Zena and Esme."

Mathis held his lantern higher. "Impossible," he said. "Isaiah is the same age."

I turned to him. "You said when he came and took Anna, you saw him, and he looked exactly the same."

"He did, but fifteen years can pass unnoticed in some men's lives if they have a good bearing." Mathis did not look convinced.

"I saw them, Mathis. Isaiah and Esme. Kissing. They are not mother and son."

"But how can this be? How could they be younger than Isaiah?"

"You're the one who has been suspicious all this time. What have you learned about them?"

"Only that there's no family tree or any other evidence of people living or dying here in the last two hundred years. Until now."

"Anna. The other women."

"What's the connection?"

A theory was forming in my mind, but surely it was impossible.

"We need to leave before they find us."

"Wait," Mathis said. "Check the rooms first."

I picked up a candle and lit it with the lantern. Mathis took the door to the left and I the one to the right. My hand hovered at the handle. I heard Mathis open his door and walk inside. I wasn't sure I wanted to see what was behind mine. But there was no going back now. I took a deep breath and pushed the door open.

Inside was a bedroom. A large oak bed with blood-red velvet curtains and blankets to match. I scanned the room and recoiled at the sight of a face. But it was my own drawn features, eyes wide and full of fear, that looked back at me. A looking glass. The room was full of beautiful furniture, every inch was cluttered with ornate candelabras and trinkets, hairbrushes and perfume. It reeked of rosemary.

"It's a bedroom."

My heart skipped a beat at Mathis' voice behind me.

"What's in the other room?" I asked, already knowing the answer.

"Another bedroom," he said, "but not like this. The other is much plainer."

"It would be. Zena doesn't like the clutter."

"Zena?"

"These are their bedrooms. This belongs to Esme."

"I don't understand. A lady and her housekeeper?"

"They're not master and servant. They never have been."

I had to see Zena's room. I scanned the bare space from the doorway and noticed a box beneath the bedside table. The kind you might keep writing paraphernalia in, or even a diary. "She might have something important in there." I stepped into the room, as cold and stony as Zena's face. I knelt before the box and lifted the lid. Inside were letters, bound together by thin blue ribbon.

Unopened.

My letters. To Ma.

"No," I muttered, riffling through them. They were all there. Not one had been sent.

"No, no."

"What is it?" Mathis was beside me instantly, with a comforting hand on my back.

"My letters. To Ma. Zena didn't send them." Dread settled in my stomach. "She doesn't know where I am." My heart fluttered in panic. "She doesn't know if I'm alive or dead."

Mathis gripped my shoulders. "Hey, hey, it's alright. We'll fix this."

"How can we fix this? I'm so stupid. I'm such a fool. I knew in my heart something was wrong, but still I hoped." I clutched the letters to my chest. "I was hoping that..."

"What?"

"...that Ma might save me."

CHAPTER TWENTY-NINE

"What are they?" Mathis asked, more to himself than me. We had made it safely back to my room.

I was exhausted. Fear and a nervous excitement had kept me on my feet but now I was done. Everything ached. I was glad to sit down, but I could barely feel the warmth of the fire. Hope had left me.

"They follow the Devil. They are the real witches," I said. I couldn't even cry. My panic had subsided into an empty void.

"Worse than witches. And much more powerful. Do we agree on what we've just seen? That Isaiah doesn't age. He defies death? Is that really what we're saying?"

"I think we are. It couldn't be an ancestor. How could Zena and Esme be in a portrait with Isaiah's ancestor?"

"But Zena and Esme are old now and Isaiah isn't. They are different from him somehow." Mathis ran his hands through his hair and down his face. "It doesn't make any sense."

It didn't make any sense. What we were surmising was impossible. But it was there, before our very eyes.

Out of the void, at the back of my mind, a question niggled at me. "I don't understand how he knew," I said. I thought back to the events before arriving here. "He asked for my hand before anyone had accused me of witchcraft. And then he saved me."

"Anna hadn't been accused either, although she would have been eventually."

"He knew before?"

"He can sense it somehow." Mathis was right.

"He is stealing our gifts. God knows what he is capable of. Or how powerful he is." I thought about Old Rita and the hanging, the way Isaiah had helped me get away when Charles singled me out. "But Amber's child died, that is what set the horrible events in motion back home. It had nothing to do with me. Charles said the eggs were bad, that they had poisoned her. But they were perfectly good." And there it was, a moment of clarity. I was back in the market selling my eggs and Isaiah... "Oh god," I gasped, my hands instinctively covering my mouth.

"What is it?" Mathis said. "Fortune, what is it?"

"*He* did it. He'd been at my stall that morning. Then I gave the last batch of eggs to Amber. He made it happen. So it *was* my fault. If not for me, Amber's child would have lived." I choked on the last words, my throat swelling. Fear and sorrow rushed back in, filling the void. I feared my body would simply give up. I wasn't strong enough for shock after shock.

"No, you're not responsible," Mathis said, taking my hands. "It's not your fault you have this gift. Isaiah is responsible, and him alone. If he hadn't turned up, you would still be with your Ma, and Amber's child would be alive. It's not your fault."

"They're not gifts. They're a curse. Look at all the death they have caused."

"No." Mathis shook his head. "Anna would never hurt anyone. She was a healer. And you? Did you use your gift to torment and kill people? No. It is all him. Them. Don't forget who the enemy is. You've spent so long blaming yourself for things that aren't your fault, it's become your nature. It's time for that to end. Put the blame where it really lies. On the people who've harmed you." Mathis' voice softened at the end. He was gathering himself, becoming focused.

"I'm so sorry, Mathis. About Anna."

"I think I'd been preparing myself for it. It breaks my heart, but I always somehow knew that I'd never see her again." He sat in the opposite chair and looked into the fire. "I'm angry," he said quietly.

There was a tapping at the window. Mathis let Purdie inside and she brought a flurry of snow with her. It was coming down again. Heavier this time. Even nature was against us. Or against me. Hadn't Mathis suggested leaving before Isaiah had even returned? If I'd listened, we would be gone now. I had missed that small window of opportunity.

"We have to leave," he said.

"Is there another way? Maybe Zena has someone who brings supplies? She must get her meat from somewhere."

Mathis shook his head. "I've never seen anyone arrive. When I arrived, the icehouse and the larder were full. I grow most of the herbs and vegetables. If there is a supplier, they won't be returning anytime soon. They have everything they need."

He stared at the flames, thinking. I knew he would be running over every possible avenue of escape. But hope was waning, the wolves were circling. The noose tightened around my neck.

Mathis rubbed the length of his face with his palms.

"I'll fix it. I'll build a boat, or a raft at least," he said.

"How?"

"There's plenty of wood in this house. It won't be very sophisticated, but it will be good enough to carry us to the main island."

"But the snow," I said. "And how will you hide what you're doing?"

"I'll find a way." He looked at my stomach. "I just need a few days. Do we have it?"

I ran my hand over my bump. "Maybe. I can't be sure."

Mathis nodded. "If I fail, we will have to fight."

"Fight?"

"They are just two old women and one man."

"But they're not. We shouldn't underestimate them."

"We know they need something from you, and we know they're lying about what they are and what they want. That gives us an advantage."

"Yes, but…" I gestured at my stomach.

"You have another advantage," Mathis said.

"What?"

"We know the brides were kept alive until after their babes were born, so we have time. And you still have your gift." He looked to Purdie, who was busy trying to uncork a flask of wine on the table. She knocked the bottle over with a clatter and grumbled her frustration. Hardly a warrior.

"I need some rest," I said, not wanting a conversation about the birds. What use were birds in this situation? "I'll go down for supper tonight, act as if everything is normal." The thought filled me with dread.

"I'll get started on the raft."

Mathis left, and I crawled onto the bed. I pushed a pillow beneath my bump to support it while I lay on my side and watched the snow fall. It was thinning out, the end of the flurry punctuated by some lonely flakes. The seedling shifted, and I placed my hand on my stomach, suddenly very aware of the thinness of the skin that separated us. "Just a few more days," I whispered. I imagined those tiny eyes opening as she greeted the world, the delicate chest rising as it filled with air for her first breath.

Purdie was still clanking about, playing with the bottle. I wished she would settle. The clanking stopped, and she landed on my pillow just above my head. Her preferred place for sleeping. I looked out the window again and held my gaze. What use were birds? They couldn't fly us out of here. They couldn't pick up arms and fight.

A host of sparrows came into view outside. A huge flock that must have been passing through. I hadn't seen them before. Their formation appeared chaotic, but then they moulded into a soft circle that stretched and bent and changed into a V. They circled the air as if putting on a show just for me.

Then another shadow in the distance, separate from the sparrows, barely noticeable in the snow. But I knew it was my glorious eagle on the hunt. The sparrows were too compact.

It would be hard for the eagle to find a straggler.

I focused on the sparrows. One fell behind the group. It started heading straight towards my window. The eagle took its chance. It flew at the sparrow at such speed I held my breath, frightened they would come crashing through the glass. The sparrow was almost at my window when the eagle caught it in her talons, pulling back with her magnificent wings before hitting the window. Her wings were so large, like a blessing from an angel. And then she was gone, her game secure.

The sparrows were gone, too. Frightened off by the predator.

* * *

In the darkness of sleep comes an image. Hazy at first but clearing quickly. It is a ballroom laid out for dinner. Empty tables fill the room. They are circular, covered in silk cloth and laid with gold plates and chalices. All empty. I'm sitting at one. Opposite me sits the giant eagle. It is silent. We stare at each other, knowing there is danger. It is right here with us.

She shifts her regal head to the left. I follow her gaze. On another table, not so far away, sits Isaiah. He is holding a large butcher's knife. It gleams. At his side stands Zena. She is handing him cuts of raw meat. Isaiah slaps them onto the table, blood splatters, soaking the white cloth. He brings the blade down, cutting the meat in two. More blood. He swipes the meat from the table with his knife, into a bucket at his side.

Zena lifts another cut of meat. But this one is different. It wriggles. It is a baby, born before its time. The length of one hand and thin as a reed, but it is alive. Isaiah takes it by the feet. Slaps it on the board and pushes his blade through its neck. He scrapes the knife along the board, plunging the head into the bucket beside him. He looks straight at me and smiles. His teeth are covered in blood. His face and hands are soaked in it, his hair drips with it. He laughs.

I woke in a panic and sighed with relief at the sight of my bump. The evening had arrived, the darkness surrounded me, held back partly by the dying fire. The windows reflected the room back to me. Esme's painting was clear in the glass. Instead of the blue sky of midday there was a blazing sunrise, all orange and red. What could that mean?

A new day is dawning? I turned to look at the painting itself, but in the moment between window and wall the painting had returned to normal. Now that I knew Esme had stolen this magical gift, I wondered if it was her or the ghost of the artist bride speaking to me through the painting.

I would go down for supper. I wanted Isaiah to know that I wasn't afraid. He had frightened me half to death with the bird, it was true. But I had to let him know that I wouldn't be that easy to tame. Everything hurt as I pulled myself awkwardly from the bed. Purdie shifted but didn't wake. I left her to sleep. Isaiah wouldn't be coming back upstairs with me. Unwanted images of our first night as man and wife ran through my mind, followed immediately by Isaiah and Esme locked together. I had to hold on. I had to put on a show so Mathis could make our boat undetected. I daren't think about the consequences if they realised I knew about the dungeon. About them.

I struggled down the stairs silently, fearing that any disturbance would draw attention to my weakness. I wanted to surprise Isaiah. At least for him to see me as strong, even if I didn't feel it.

There was light in the sitting room. He was in there. And he wasn't alone.

I pushed the door open to Isaiah and Esme. Not kissing, thank goodness, but talking intently. Isaiah sat in his chair at the head of the table. I couldn't see him fully as Esme stood, leaning over him. She turned at the sound of the door, her eyes widened in surprise. Now I could see Isaiah's face. He looked at me without expression. No surprise or wonder at how strong I was. Nothing. His hands rested on the arms of his chair, his body relaxed, content, the master of his strange, isolated universe.

"Fortune, child, what are you doing up?" Esme walked towards me, arms outstretched.

It took everything I had not to recoil. She linked her arm through mine, patting my shoulder.

"We've already eaten supper, and you should not be out of your room at this late stage."

"I thought my husband may want me to join him," I said, looking to Isaiah.

Esme looked to Isaiah and back to me. There were far too many candles lit in the room, but Isaiah seemed surrounded in shadow. Did he emanate darkness or did the light fear him? "I'm sure he wants what's best for you, which is your bed." Esme glared at Isaiah.

"My mother is right," he finally agreed. The word "mother" turned my stomach. "Go to bed."

"Come, child," Esme said, and tugged at my arm. I went with her, all the way back upstairs. I was far too tired for this. What had I been thinking?

Esme walked me to my bed. "Fortune, dear, what is that on your pillow?"

"It's just Purdie," I said. There was no point hiding Purdie or making excuses for her. "She's my pet."

I let Esme help me strip down to my smock. "You've never mentioned a bird before. How unusual you are, child. Always surprising me."

I gritted my teeth at the lie. "Oh, she's nothing special. Just a silly bird who I feed and now she won't leave me alone."

"Perhaps *I* should get a pet bird, that would be something new."

I suddenly saw Esme in the future with Purdie at her side while my bones rotted in a tomb beneath the house. Would Purdie stay with Esme? Could Esme force Purdie to do something she didn't want to do? I thought of the little sparrow separated from its flock. I had done that.

Esme tucked the blankets about me and pulled a chair to the bedside. I wished it were Mathis sat there.

"You know, I swear sometimes that painting you gave me changes." What was I doing? I shouldn't be making waves. But I couldn't help it.

She let out a bark of a laugh. "Changes? Whatever do you mean?"

"Sometimes things appear or the sky changes colour." I watched her face intently, but she appeared surprised by what I was saying, as if she had no idea such things could happen.

"Are you well, dear? Confinement can addle your brain, especially in such an isolated place such as this."

She put her papery palm to my forehead and applied a little pressure to force my head back onto the pillow.

"You know, it could be Zena. I wouldn't put it past her to take up the dark arts. She's always had the temperament of a witch." Esme chuckled to herself. She was enjoying this. It was all a game to her. "Rest now. Zena will bring you supper, you'll feel better in the morning."

She left me seething with all the things I wanted to say to her.

Purdie nuzzled my hair, looking for bugs. If I died and Purdie was left here with Esme, she would be trapped with her. I had no idea the extent of my power over the birds.

What would Esme be able to do once I was gone?

I heaved myself from the bed and went into the washroom. The wash bowl was full of water, as I expected. I called Purdie in. I needed to know the extent of the danger, for Purdie and all the birds.

I thought about what I wanted Purdie to do. She cried out, the fear in it was a dagger in my heart, and then she plunged her beautiful head into the bowl. She stayed under the water until her wings flapped wildly, her legs kicked out. She would drown. And then I released her. She emerged from the water crying and squawking and flew away from me to the rafters. She shook the water from her feathers and began preening.

"I'm so sorry, Purdie," I said. She ignored me.

So far, I had only thought about mine and the seedling's life. But it was much bigger than that. Much, much bigger.

CHAPTER THIRTY

The sunrise blazed red and orange across the sky, blackening the figure of someone stood before my window.

"Mathis?"

He stepped towards me. Too large for Mathis.

"Isaiah?"

He did not speak. My heart beat hard, my skin prickled.

He knelt next to me, his face becoming visible as he blocked the light of the sunrise behind him.

"I think it's time we moved things along," he said. He pressed his large hand against my stomach, and it cramped so hard I cried out.

I tried to push his hand away, but my feeble efforts were powerless against his strength, like a wisp of a breeze attempting to uproot an oak. Another stabbing pain, this one lasting longer, going deeper, a knife twisting in my gut. My cry turned into a long moan.

He released me but the pain didn't stop.

He will get someone, I thought. *Zena will be here any moment.*

An hour or longer must have passed with the pain ebbing and flowing and only my dreadful thoughts to keep me company. When I closed my eyes through the cramps, all I could see was the woods back home. A full moon, and something swimming just below the surface of the silvery lake.

Mathis eventually arrived with my breakfast. Isaiah had told no one.

"We're out of time," I said. He rushed to the bedside and took my hand.

"What should I do?"

"Keep building the boat. We're leaving, I swear it."

"I will. But what can I get you right now?"

The pain gripped me again. I gritted my teeth and squeezed Mathis' hand.

"You'll have to tell Zena," I said when it subsided. "Be careful. They know something is wrong."

"What happened?"

"Isaiah started the birth." I was sweating, breathing hard. "How?"

"He placed his hands on me. He said it was time. We have to stick to the plan, though. We have to leave. They won't be expecting us to try. Not after destroying the sailing boat and now the birth. They'll think we've given up. It's our best chance."

"We will," Mathis reassured me. "But right now you need to focus on getting through this safely. I'll get Zena."

I nodded.

"They won't let me back up here once I go." Mathis pushed strands of my hair back from my forehead that had become stuck.

"I know," I said. "I'm scared."

He kissed my forehead. "She'll live, Fortune. She's strong, like her ma. The only devils are the ones here, living and breathing in this house. And we will escape them, and you will grow old with your daughter at your side. I know it."

HIs face was so close to mine. That beautiful, scarred face that I had grown accustomed to, had come to rely on.

I pulled him close and kissed him softly on the lips. He held me until I cramped again and cried out in pain.

"I'll get Zena," he said. "I'll see you after." I nodded, hardly able to talk but not wanting to take my eyes off him. If this was the last time I saw him, I wanted to remember him as he stood there now, worry in his eyes, the taste of his lips on mine.

Zena arrived shortly after. Bowl in hand, towels over her arms.

"How long have you had the pain? Be truthful."

"An hour, maybe longer," I said, hating that I had to share this moment with her. But if I truly wanted to survive, I needed her help.

Zena pulled back the covers and lifted my nightgown. I looked away. I could sense the chill of her hands before she even touched me. I gritted my teeth as she pushed her fingers inside me, the pain worse than the cramps.

Purdie, who had retreated to the rafters at Zena's arrival, now lunged towards her, flapping about her head in protest.

"Purdie!"

"Get that bird out of here," Zena said. I glared at Purdie, annoyed that she too would now have to leave the room. Purdie puffed her chin feathers out and flew out of the window. Zena narrowed her eyes at me. Pain rushed me again and I curled onto my side, pulling my knees up.

"It won't be long now."

I shifted onto my hands and knees, the weight of my stomach pulled downwards. This was better.

The door opened, and Esme's raspy voice followed. "Well done, child, that's it." I didn't answer, all my energy focused on staying in this position, which was more comfortable for my lower regions but putting a lot of strain on my arms.

Esme rubbed something onto my lower back. I was sick at the thought of Esme touching me, talking to me like I was her daughter.

I wanted to hit her, scream at her, but I couldn't do any of that, all my strength was used managing the pain. My back began to cool. I had hardly noticed it was burning. The pain was ebbing. Esme was using Anna's ointment.

I thanked Anna silently for the welcome relief. A whispering surrounded me, seeping through the walls and into my thoughts, a wave of love and affection. Of course, Anna was a good person. She knew the pain of childbirth. She would be happy to help. This gave me strength. I rested on my elbows, my rear in the air like a wild animal. I didn't care.

Esme and Zena were talking, maybe arguing, but I couldn't hear them properly. I knew I should try harder to listen to what they were saying but I was exhausted. Instead, I breathed in the sweet smoke of one of Esme's medicinal concoctions.

I lay on my side again. A moment of respite. The room was flickering light and dark, but it couldn't be, it was daytime. I rubbed at my eyes. The weeping woman was there. Everything else faded to black. But she didn't smell of sour milk and there was no gaping hole in her chest. Her waist-length curls were clean, so was her nightgown. I could see her clearly now, as Anna. She held a finger to her lips – *ssshhhh*. She smiled. I smiled back. I reached out my hand and she took it, her hand solid and warm. Another woman appeared behind her with straight white hair, holding a baby. Another woman beside her, then another, and another, more than I could count. They watched me. They smiled.

This was death, then. I would join my fellow brides, and they would welcome me with open arms. It wouldn't be so bad spending eternity with them. They were just like me. I should tell Anna her brother is close. "Mathis," I started, but Anna held her finger to her lips again – *ssshhhh*.

The pain came again. I closed my eyes as all my muscles contracted. When I opened them again the scene had changed. Nightgowns were now shredded and covered in blood. Their chests gaped open at their hearts. Their eyes were no longer kind but filled with rage for those who had stolen their lives. And they were looking to me, urging me to survive.

Another wave of pain swept through me. I curled in on myself, gripping the bedsheets. When I looked up again, the women were gone. A strength rose in me that I didn't know I had. I let out a guttural roar as the pain swept me again. Those wives could no longer fight, but I could.

My body was being torn in two, but I refused to give up, I wouldn't die. Too many people needed me to live.

Esme shrieked with excitement. A child began to cry.

CHAPTER THIRTY-ONE

Her eyebrows amazed me. Perfectly fine tiny hairs barely perceptible, but I was mesmerised by them. I traced them gently with my fingertip, then followed the line of thick black hair that tufted out in various directions. I brushed the curve of her tiny ear and swept along her jaw to a chin the size of a nail. Her mouth was divine. Perfectly heart-shaped pink lips. It was hard to remember how this serene, beautiful face had looked, flushed pink and screaming only a few minutes earlier.

Zena had shown me how to help her attach and allow my milk to flow freely. It had stung that first time. I hadn't expected it. I hadn't expected anything. I had spent such a long time trying not to think about this moment, fearing a very different outcome. But my child had life in her. I was dazed by it. Exhilarated and terrified at the same time.

This unyielding sense of happiness and terror lodged deep in my heart and settled there, beneath the world, hidden from Isaiah and Esme and Zena, and even Mathis. But directly connected to the little girl in my arms.

Now she lay content, belly full and sleeping. We were alone, and I wished we could stay in this moment forever.

But I knew it would be fleeting. I knew how Zena had developed her knowledge of midwifery. The brides had been here all along, watching and waiting. In the music Isaiah played at the supper, in the paintings Esme produced, in the ointment she rubbed on my skin. They were in the corridors, and the garden, and sitting in the cove waiting for their ships to come in. They walked the woods and settled in walls and slept in the catacombs. They were everywhere and they were desperate to be heard.

Would I be joining them? Would I watch and wait with them when another innocent woman was brought to these shores? Would I scream into the void as Isaiah took a new unfortunate bride to bed, and then cry the months long as she grew fat like a turkey being plumped for Christmas?

A snuffling noise drew me back to the present. My child was suckling in her dreams. Her chin bobbed up and down as her plump lips dipped in and out. It was the smallest movement and the most miraculous thing I had ever witnessed. My heart ached. I pressed my lips gently to her head and breathed in her newborn smell. Purdie was sleeping at the end of the bed, head tucked beneath her wing. The only sound was the soothing crackle of the fire. The world slept, and my eyes grew heavy.

"Fortune." A whisper close to my ear woke me. I dragged myself from the depths of sleep, where I could have stayed for many hours more, but I wasn't angry because it was Mathis at my side.

He sat on the edge of the bed, his body turned towards me.

"Mathis." My voice was groggy, my body ached, my groin throbbed. "You shouldn't be here."

"Nobody is around, I made sure." He paused. "I'm sorry to wake you."

"No, I'm glad you did." My daughter squirmed in my arms where she still slept.

"She's beautiful," Mathis said. "She has a strong look about her, just like her mother."

"Her ma," I corrected, and couldn't help but smile a little, even though the word made my heart break. Ma didn't even know she was a grandmother, and probably never would. I noticed a pot of yellow narcissi from the garden on the bedside table.

"I thought you might like some flowers. I wasn't sure what to bring you."

"They're beautiful." It amazed me how thoughtful Mathis was even at a time like this.

"What's her name?"

"Well, she has hair the colour of Purdie's feathers," I said. "I thought I'd call her Raven. Is that silly?"

Mathis smiled. "It's the perfect name." But his smile faded quickly. "This changes things," he said, looking at Raven.

"No, it doesn't."

"You can't travel in a couple of days' time. You need rest, and we must think of the baby."

"I am thinking of her." My voice was firm. "What is the alternative? Stay here and die?"

"Maybe it won't happen. Maybe the others died naturally or in childbirth. Maybe it's not as sinister as we think?"

"Come on, Mathis. You saw the tombs. You saw the paintings!" Raven squirmed as my voice raised, and I quietened it back to a whisper. "Those babies and their mothers were alive and well and they killed them." I paused, running all the horrible images of white bones and babies' skulls through my mind. "They will not show us any mercy."

"I know you're right," he sighed. "It's just…"

"You're afraid," I finished for him. He nodded. "So am I, but I'm more afraid of losing her. All this time I thought it was impossible. But she is alive, and I intend to keep it that way. When will the raft be ready?"

"Three days. Maybe two."

"Then we only need survive that long. And they won't kill us yet, not without their trophy."

"Trophy?"

"My portrait. I haven't had my likeness captured yet."

His face paled at the thought. He was bereft. His hair was dishevelled, dark rings created hollows beneath eyes that had lost their spark. We were both beaten, but not dead.

"Would you like to hold her?"

His face brightened at that, and he held out his arms. He took her awkwardly at first but soon settled into a comfortable position. He gazed at her little face and some of his worry lines smoothed away. She was a tonic. He stroked her cheek.

Birds circled outside. In the distance a larger shape came into view. "Do you see her?"

"Who?"

"The eagle."

Mathis looked out, squinting into the twilight. "I see something."

The eagle flew closer, her size becoming apparent the nearer she got to the house.

His eyes widened. "She's magnificent," he said, "and terrifying."

"She's been coming to me in my dreams," I admitted.

"What does she want with you there?"

"Nothing. She shows me things. Mostly death and destruction."

"Ah, nothing to worry about then."

I laughed. "It's been a while since you teased me."

The eagle glided past the window two times, three times, and off back to the cliff.

"Once we leave this place, I will be able to tease you all the time." Mathis smiled as he said it, but I wasn't sure he truly believed our escape was possible. "I have to go, it's almost supper." He handed Raven back. "I'll be back as soon as I can."

He opened the door of the bedroom and was met with the cold, hard stare of Zena. I wondered how we hadn't felt her intense hatred penetrate the door. Everyone was struck mute for a moment. Zena's black eyes immediately spotted the flowers at the bedside. I shifted uncomfortably. Zena looked back at Mathis, who suddenly seemed to remember his position and moved to the side to allow her past with the supper tray.

"Bring in the linen before you retire," she said eventually.

"Yes, ma'am."

She enjoyed watching us squirm and stood longer than was comfortable in the doorway. Eventually she brought the tray to my bed. Mathis gave me a final look from behind her, a half-smile playing on his lips, but he couldn't hide the fear in his eyes.

CHAPTER THIRTY-TWO

For the next two days I barely saw Mathis. And if I did, there was always someone else there, either Zena or Esme. Even Isaiah had visited the night before. They were gathering. Hovering around me like vultures, waiting for their moment to strike.

By the third day, I was more than ready to leave. Despite heavy bleeding and an aching body, I couldn't bear to be around those people any longer. My fear was growing and time was against us. Raven, however, was growing stronger by the minute. I was desperate to see Mathis alone so we could make arrangements. He had said two or three days to build the raft, so we could leave by tonight. I just had to make it through one more day.

I held Raven close. "We'll be fine, we'll be fine," I repeated over and over as I washed and dressed us. But I could sense that we were cutting things close. At least, if we died, Raven and I would be together. The thought of being separated was too much to bear. I understood now how Ma felt about me. How difficult it must have been for her to watch me leave, and how serious she was when she threatened to die if I did. How worried Ma must be now, hearing nothing from her only daughter all these months.

Purdie, who was pecking at crumbs on the table,

squawked and flew to the window to be let out. Esme must be coming. Purdie couldn't bear to be in the same room as her. I knew how she felt. I let Purdie out and sat by the fire, preparing myself to act happy to see Esme.

There was the sound of clattering as she approached the door and then her loud rap.

"Come in."

Esme opened the door, and I saw what the noise was about. She was carrying her paints. Behind her, Mathis carried the easel. It was large and cumbersome, and I couldn't see his face. My heart pounded. I could almost hear the death knell. My throat tightened.

"What's all this?" I forced myself to say, laughing slightly with nerves. The brides and their babes were closer than ever. I felt their eyes upon me, watching the final hour, knowing what was coming next.

"I thought this would be a good opportunity for a portrait. Seeing as you're sitting all day anyway, you might as well sit for me." Esme moved one of the chairs to the end of the bed and motioned for Mathis to place her easel where the chair had been. He glanced at me. A moment of connection while Esme's back was turned, and I saw the terror in his eyes. I knew he would come for me tonight. He sensed the urgency just as I did. Esme waved him off and he left.

"I don't think I could sit for a portrait. Not today. I'm still tender. Maybe in a few days?"

"Nonsense, you are fighting fit, and I promise I won't torture you for long."

"But I'm a sorry sight. You wouldn't want to look forever on me like this."

"There is something special about a new mother," Esme

said. "So raw, so vulnerable. You look perfect. I'll get you a cushion."

It was worth a try. Esme always got what she wanted. She placed a cushion on the chair and organised her palette and paints on the table.

Mathis reappeared at the door holding a blank canvas.

"Thank you, my boy. Just place it on the easel," Esme said.

Mathis did as he was bid, only I could feel the weight of his heavy heart. "And bring us some tea and sweets, will you? Make sure there is marzipan." Esme winked at me as if she knew me so well and my soul could be sold for so little. "We're going to need plenty of sugar."

I sat down. Pain shot through my groin.

"That's perfect, child. And how thoughtful of the babe to be sleeping so peacefully. She is a treasure. Just try not to move." She hummed a tune as she began a couple of strokes. "Oh, I know what would really make this portrait sing!" Esme declared as though she had only just that moment had a wonderful idea. "Where is that pet bird of yours? Call him in."

"Purdie's a girl."

Esme gave a chuckle. "Call *her* in."

I made no move at first. Could I allow this to happen? This portrait was destined for the dank wall of that chamber, with myself and Raven entombed beneath it for all eternity. I was knowingly partaking in my own memorial. Esme wouldn't want the painting without Purdie, it would be incomplete without her. "She may not come when I call. She's not a pet dog. She has a mind of her own."

Esme looked around the side of the canvas, her eyes no longer playful. "I'm sure you can convince her."

There would be trouble if I didn't comply, and I needed to keep up the pretence. Just one more day.

"Could you open the window? Purdie is outside."

Esme opened the window, and the moment it was wide enough Purdie flew straight in, almost hitting her in the face. Esme jumped back with a little yelp, and then laughed it off. I smiled to myself. Purdie landed on the back of my chair and stretched her neck out proudly. I envisioned the title that would adorn the bottom corner of my painting: *The Raven Bride*.

"Wonderful! Now we can start."

The weak sun moved slowly across the sky. I fidgeted. Raven grew heavy in my arms. She had woken, cried, fed, and slept again. I had bled through multiple cloths, disturbing Esme with my need to change. Every part of my body hurt, and I willed this to be over. Purdie perched still as stone, as if moving would be some kind of defeat.

"Could I put the babe down for a while?" I didn't use Raven's name. None of them had mentioned names, a small detail of this charade that they forgot, perhaps. I would keep it for myself.

"Just a few more minutes and I'll have her features."

I grunted my assent and focused on the small movements of the hem of Esme's dress as she made her strokes to distract from my pain. Her withered hand appeared from behind the easel occasionally to dip her brushes or change them. The flesh of her hand was marked with old age, dark brown spots and deep wrinkles. The marks much more prominent now than when I'd arrived.

"You can put her down now," Esme said. My movements were stiff as I carefully made Raven comfortable on the bed.

Purdie followed every move, landing on the pillow while I settled Raven and then following me back to the chair.

I found myself staring at the painting of the house. The longer I looked, the more the lines softened, and the waves began to move. The sea was calling to me. "Do you mind if I open the window?"

"Go ahead, child." I could feel Esme watching me as I slowly got up again and took my time opening the window. I leaned out and took in a great gulp of cold, fresh air, filled with salt and brine. Ravens had gathered above the garden, circling and crying out. They were worried. Purdie cawed in response.

"My goodness, that bird will be the death of me." Esme had jumped at the sound. Purdie could be very loud.

"I'm sorry, shall I put her out?"

"No, no, just come and sit, I haven't quite captured either of your features yet."

I sat back down, the sea air and the call of the birds drifted into the room. Again, I looked to the painting. At my bedroom window was a woman. I thought it was myself at first, but her hair was long and loose. She wore a white nightdress. Anna was watching. How pathetic I must seem, sitting there having my likeness captured when I knew exactly what it was for. Maybe if Anna had known she would have fought; maybe she did fight. Her presence gave me strength.

Purdie suddenly hopped down from her perch on the back of the chair and up onto the table, where Esme had her paints laid out. She bit the brushes, then started picking them up and throwing them to the floor.

"Shoo." Esme wafted her hand. "Call your bird back, dear, she's causing quite a mess."

"Purdie, stop now and behave," I said, but Purdie did not stop. Instead, she knocked the cup of water onto the floor and stepped onto the paint palette. Esme looked at me with narrowed eyes. She knew this was my doing but couldn't chide me without revealing what she knew. Stalemate. I continued my charade. "Purdie, you naughty bird. I'm so sorry Esme, she can be unruly at times."

Esme continued wafting her hand in Purdie's direction, but she didn't strike her or try to get hold of her. Instead, Esme leaned away, afraid of Purdie.

I suppose someone not used to birds might be alarmed by the loud, sharp snapping of her beak, her milky black eyes and clawed talons. From a distance birds look serene, delicate even. But up close their power was surprising, their size threatening. And Purdie was large.

Esme tried to move the palette from beneath the bird's feet and Purdie bit. Only gently, but she scratched Esme's weak, papery flesh.

"Did she hurt you?" I got up to inspect Esme's hand and made a show of telling Purdie off. "We should leave the painting for today. Let's clean that hand."

Raven began snuffling from the bed. After a few moments of searching and failing to find her food supply, the snuffling turned into a wail.

Esme wrinkled her nose at the noise. "I'll come back later, when these two have stopped being so unruly." She gave a little chuckle, a weak attempt to hide her annoyance, and began collecting her paints from the table. But I wanted her gone now. I'd had enough.

A raven landed at the open window and squawked loudly into the room, making Esme drop the empty water cup she had just picked up. Purdie made some clicking sounds in response. Esme sighed and left the paints. "I'll be back for them later..." She paused, looking at Purdie and her fellow at the window. "I'd be careful of those birds around the child. They are wild animals."

I said nothing.

When Esme left, I tickled Purdie beneath her chin just the way she liked. "Clever bird." Purdie gurgled, pushed her head against my cheek and nibbled at my ear. I then settled with Raven in bed. I sighed with relief as the mattress took my weight.

It was a small victory. I had managed to get Esme out of the room for now. She would be back, but I doubted it would be today. The days were short, and the light wouldn't be any good for painting come four o' clock. I had no intention of being there when Esme returned the following day.

I longed to sleep but my mind wouldn't settle. Esme's painting was distracting me. I dragged myself back out of bed to take a look. She had made remarkable progress in such a short space of time. Already she had captured my dress and Raven on my lap. Her small features peeked through the blankets.

Purdie looked positively splendid on the back of the chair, an air of grace and mystery surrounded her. My head had been outlined but my face was blank. A white space. I swore to myself it would never be filled.

A queer feeling overcame me looking at the likeness, as if the image was stealing some precious part of me. I would never let Esme finish the painting, I was sure of that.

Over on the wall, where Esme's other work hung, there was no sign of Anna. But I closed my eyes and could feel her. I could feel all of them.

CHAPTER THIRTY-THREE

As I expected, Esme didn't return that day. After a long nap I ate my supper, brought to me by Zena. It was no longer the scarlet stew that I had been eating throughout the pregnancy. Now I was served vegetables and stock, and I could feel my muscles and bones growing stronger each day.

Then I began preparations for the journey ahead. I filled my pockets with the left-over bread and biscuits I'd been saving over the past couple of days. I wore two petticoats, a waistcoat and jacket, with my gloves and two shawls laid out ready. I wrapped Raven in her warmest blanket, another set aside for her sling. It would be cold out there, especially on the water. And then I waited. I was painfully aware that I had done this before, but I wouldn't let the fear of another failed attempt stop me. I couldn't fail this time. Raven was depending on me.

Purdie shifted uneasily. Her tail quivered in time with my heart. The fire grew small, and my confidence faded with it. Raven's hand squirmed out of her blanket. I held her tiny fingers, rubbed her palm with my thumb, and the child settled. She would need another feed soon.

A quiet knock on the door made me jump. It was time.

Mathis entered. "Are you ready?"

"Yes." I stood up, heart racing, and began putting on the extra layers and securing Raven. "Is everything ready?"

"Yes, come on."

Purdie flew to Mathis and landed on his shoulder, hunching her body down, ready to go. Mathis instinctively rubbed her chin. "We have to be vigilant; it'll be dangerous with no light to guide us. I can carry Raven if you like."

"No, I'm fine." I tightened the knot of her sling, pulling her closer to my chest. I couldn't bear the thought of her being apart from me.

We crept down the stairs. It was the first time I had been outside the bedroom since giving birth. The house felt different. A weight had descended. The walls wept with sadness. The bones of the dead brides and their children called from beneath the foundations of the house. They wanted my help. But what could I do to help those already dead? I had more to fear from the living.

We made it out of the house unseen and into the woods. The sky was clear and cold; the bare trees allowed the moonlight through. Mathis walked in front, checking there was nothing to stumble across. Purdie flew to the treetops to keep a lookout for any of the household.

We were halfway when I heard the familiar snuffling sound of my babe looking for a meal. Raven squirmed.

"I have to stop and feed her, or she'll cry."

"Alright." Mathis looked around. "Here, sit here."

He led me to a stump. I fumbled with multiple layers of clothing. Raven was growing more anxious. She would scream any second and give us away. Luckily, she found her meal before she let out a cry. But it had been a close call. My pounding heart settled into a calmer rhythm while she fed.

Mathis knelt beside us.

"We're going to be fine. Everything is ready," he said.

I nodded. There was nothing to say, all we could do was wait until Raven had fed and then push on.

The woods made their usual night-time sounds but every shuffle, every movement of a nocturnal creature, rang in my ears, amplified by fear.

"They won't notice we've gone until morning," Mathis reassured me.

My heart warmed. Not because of his words, but his need to protect us. It was comforting, even though I knew he was as scared as me. "You don't have to be so brave all the time," I said and squeezed his hand.

"What's the alternative? Collapse into a crying heap on the ground?" he joked. I laughed. The sound echoed through the trees, and I stopped quickly. "You can smile," he said, "we'll be gone soon."

"I'll smile when we're far away from here and sitting in our own home, this whole experience pushed into the realms of a bad dream."

"A nightmare," Mathis said. "Our home? Would you want me around, reminding you of all this?"

"How could I survive without you?" I said.

Mathis closed his fingers over my hand, and I listened to the sound of our breath and Raven suckling. There was nothing more to say on the matter. No plans to be made, no declarations of love; there was nothing ahead of us until we passed this moment and made our escape. The future was too uncertain to discuss it in detail. Purdie came and settled next to us.

The darkness of the woods crept closer with each moment we stalled. I willed Raven to drink up and fall into a satisfied sleep. Eventually, she did. I marvelled at her complete faith in her mother to protect her, even out here in the darkness. She had no idea how close the monsters were.

A cracking of twigs close behind startled me. "What was that?"

"A fox or a mole? Come on." Mathis took my hand and tried to pull me on, but I hesitated.

"I'm not sure. It sounded bigger." I looked into the trees. "Purdie," I whispered, and she took off, flying low through the branches. We waited, still as stone. No sound. No call from Purdie or flap of her wings. "Purdie, come back," I said to the silence. My voice trembled.

"Give her a minute, she'll be back," Mathis said.

"She's trapped," I said. "Someone has her." Panic rose, heating my body in the cool night. My breath plumed.

"No, she'll be back, just wait a moment."

But there was nothing. Something darted through the trees. "Did you see that?" I asked. "We have to hide, it's our only chance."

Mathis didn't move, he was still trying to look into the blanket of darkness.

"Come on." I tugged at him. He held my hand and led the way. We moved as fast as the darkness and the woods would let us, but it wasn't fast enough. Footsteps followed us, someone moving quickly in the darkness. Quicker than us.

Mathis' hand was torn from mine as something came at him from the side, throwing him through the air. His head hit a tree trunk, hard, and he fell, landing crumpled and motionless on the ground.

Isaiah stood before me, amber eyes blazing. I'd never seen them such a colour. "I did well, choosing you," he said. "You're strong. Powerful." He stepped towards me, and I stepped back, pulling Raven closer to my chest.

Above the treetops came the rumbling of thunder. Isaiah looked up. The moon disappeared as a mass of birds spilled into view, thousands of beating wings and screeching cries echoed through the night. Mathis groaned and put his hands to his head. He was alive. I breathed a sigh of relief.

"Yes, I did very well," Isaiah said as he watched the birds circle overhead. Mathis was getting to his feet, out of Isaiah's view. The birds could attack from above and Mathis could come from behind. Together we could overpower him.

Isaiah pulled something from his coat. "I wouldn't do anything else."

"Purdie!" She was limp in his hands. I thought she was already dead, but then the bird gave a low, defiant growl.

"I'll snap her neck."

Mathis lunged at Isaiah, but Isaiah turned and hit him in the chest with the palm of his hand, and he flew back like a rag doll.

"No!" I ran towards him. Isaiah didn't stop me. Blood soaked his shirt sleeve and dripped down the side of his face. We would find another way. I couldn't sacrifice Purdie with no guarantee of escaping.

"I'm told you called for him during childbirth." Isaiah stood over us. "You found love and now it will be taken away. I'm sorry for that."

"All your brides found love. They all had a child."

"Your purpose is of a higher calling," he said. "Now come."

I had no other choice but to follow. I helped Mathis up. He was shaking but able to walk unaided.

Purdie growled and whimpered as we made our way back to the house.

"Can I please have Purdie back?" Isaiah didn't stop, he simply let Purdie go. She flew straight to me and made herself as small as possible on top of Raven's swaddling. I had failed them both. They were relying on me to keep them safe, and now I was heading back to the house, leading them straight to the gallows. It would have been easier and far less painful for everyone if I had allowed the mob to hang me. At least it would have been only one life lost. I walked in a daze; the phantom noose choked me now, lifted me from the ground, feet kicking, lungs screaming. No escape.

Zena was waiting at the house. She ushered me towards the stairs and stayed close behind me. Isaiah gripped Mathis' collar and took him towards the kitchen.

"Where are you taking him?" No one answered me. Mathis looked back, and I knew in my heart it would be the last time I ever saw him. A fleeting glance and then he was gone, dragged down the dark corridor with Isaiah, while Zena led me upstairs. I tried not to sob. I didn't want Zena to know they had won. That I was crushed.

The half-finished painting was still there, and my blank face stared out at me. They should leave the painting as it was. What did it matter what I looked like? They only wanted my body. And Raven's, although I still wasn't sure what part she played. The thought of her life ending when it had only just begun was too difficult to imagine. I pushed the thought down. I couldn't let it happen.

The bedroom was too hot, the fire blazed, candles were lit. The windows showed my reflection, pale and shivering, small and weak. I looked like all the other brides, and I would suffer the same fate. I wanted to lie on the floor and weep, but Zena was still here, and if I did that I would never get back up.

"You need sleep, put the child down," Zena said.

"No," I answered, and climbed onto the bed with Raven still in her sling. My back ached. A groan escaped me as I let the bed take our weight. Purdie was still sitting on Raven's swaddling. I covered them both with my shawl.

"As you wish," Zena said, her stony face revealing nothing. "Drink this." She held out a cup.

"I won't take anything from you."

"It's for your benefit, not mine."

"I find that hard to believe," I said. I was so tired, but I couldn't allow myself to sleep. As soon as I was alone, I'd make a break for it, even if it was into the sea.

Anything was better than letting them have us.

Zena suddenly pinched my nose closed and I struggled. Purdie squawked and immediately went for Zena's arm, but the old woman swiped at Purdie with surprising strength, and she hit the headboard. Zena's grip was iron on my face. Purdie was injured and I was exhausted. I could hardly fight while holding Raven.

I opened my mouth, and she poured the contents of the cup into it. It was warm and spicy, like heated wine. I swallowed. It slipped down my throat, a soothing balm. My eyes grew heavy. "No, I don't want to sleep," I muttered, feeling my arm around Raven relax. "No... Raven..."

"It's for your own good," I heard Zena say as I melted into the darkness.

CHAPTER THIRTY-FOUR

"Fortune."

A rasping voice close to my ear, but I couldn't respond. My eyes wouldn't open, my mouth wouldn't speak. Cold water splashed on my face, and it felt refreshing. I wanted to lick it from my cheeks. So thirsty.

"That's it, my child, wake up," Esme said as I slowly came round. I opened my eyes a little. I could make out a shadow of Esme, but then my eyes closed again. I forced them open, but my vision was blurred. It was night-time. The room glowed orange and black in the candlelight.

"I told Zena not to give you that tonic. It would be more fun without it. 'Let the child know what's going on!' I said. But she wouldn't listen."

"What is going on?" My mind was a fog.

"This has never happened before, and there's nothing I like more than something unexpected. You well know that we get very few surprises here." Esme snorted. "It's so very dull. But this! This is exciting."

"Water." My throat was sticking, my tongue was bone dry. Esme pushed a cup into my hand, and I drank the sweet, cooling water. I passed the cup back, almost dropping it in the process.

"I think Zena may have given you too much. I did warn her."

Herbal tobacco smoke clouded my vision further as Esme puffed on her pipe.

"What's happening?" I asked. Confused and disoriented, I was unsure if this was a dream or reality. My eyes drooped but I fought to keep them open.

"Would you like me to tell you? I never get to tell my story, and it is a fantastical story. Magical."

Now I could make out the crackling of the fire, but didn't have the energy to lift my head and look towards it.

"You already know the story of how I met my husband and what a wonderful man he was, taking me in when I was almost starved to death on the streets." She paused, puffing on her pipe. "Well, as I grew, I realised that he didn't age the way other men did. His hair stayed flaxen, his face wrinkle-free, his body taut. And he was so handsome. You know I was in love with him ever since I was a child. What I didn't tell you was that man was Isaiah. Your husband. Although I'm sure you're aware now that he's not really *your* husband." She laughed and clapped her hands with excitement.

There was something else I was supposed to be doing. "Please don't tell me any more, I don't want to know how you sold your soul to the Devil."

Esme cackled at that. "Don't be so dramatic, child, the Devil has nothing to do with it. You know that better than anyone. You have a gift, too. Did you sell your soul to the Devil?" I didn't answer. "No, it wasn't anything Isaiah had done that allowed him to keep his youth. He was born that way. He comes from a long line of people like him. They are much like us, except his diet might be considered... macabre." Esme puffed on her pipe slowly, as though contemplating this thought. "Who knows the why of these things," she eventually said.

"His diet?" I asked.

"Yes, dear. The blood and flesh of others keeps Isaiah alert. Particularly their hearts. The hearts are the best part, he always says."

I felt the bile rising and Esme reached for a bowl for me to throw up in. She wiped my face, and I fell back onto the pillow. This couldn't be real. Isaiah lived on the flesh of others? Black spots formed at the corners of my vision, and I took deep breaths. I didn't want to pass out, not now, when I was finally hearing the truth. I needed to know.

"Anyway, Isaiah wanted me to be with him always and he found a way to make it happen. It was in his blood, you see. His blood kept me young, and we lived many happy years together, flitting from place to place, always at the centre of everything. Our beauty was incomparable, and when you have lived such a time you find there are many ways to create wealth. We had everything we needed. We could have survived like that forever. Until..." Esme sighed, puffed on her pipe. "I started to age. All good things come to an end." She sighed and waited a moment before continuing. "Can you imagine how difficult that was for Isaiah? He was forced to watch me waste away. *Me*. The love of his life, wasting away before his very eyes." Esme was lost in her horror story, recalling it as a glittering memory. She was a mad woman; I could see that now. And she thrived in the darkness.

"But Isaiah was still young, and as I grew older his lust found... other outlets. I may have been old, but Isaiah's blood made me strong. One night, I followed him and found he had been keeping a woman in secret. And what was worse, she had given Isaiah something I never could. She had his child." Esme lit a match and showed her face clearly to me for a moment. Her eyes glowed red in the shadows of her cheekbones. "I'm not proud of my next action, but then without it we would never have known," she philosophised. "I tied up the mother one night and waited for Isaiah to arrive, and then, before them both, I cut out the child's heart and ate it." She stopped a moment to take in my reaction, the disgust portrayed on my face produced a satisfied smile on hers. "I know, it was a little dramatic," she laughed, "but I did tend towards drama. Especially in my younger days."

"You ate a heart?" My own heart was racing now. There was something different about the room, but my mind was a murky ocean, and I couldn't quite grasp what it was.

"That was when the truly magical thing happened." Esme leaned forward and lowered her voice. "I was made young again." She tittered with glee. "Right there, before their very eyes, I was returned to my former, glorious self.

"And even more wonderful was that the woman was gifted, and that gift was passed on to me through her child. When Isaiah saw this, he immediately carved out the harlot's heart and ate it, so he too could take her gift."

"What gift?" My eyes drooped again. Esme appeared surrounded by a blue misty cloud. There was something missing.

"Her gift? Oh, that's not important."

Unconsciousness was pulling me back into the blackness.

"Are you going back to sleep, child? There's so much more I wanted to tell you. Blast Zena, she spoils everything."

Then it hit me. "Where's Raven?" I managed. "Where's my child?" I tried to move, to get out the bed, but my body would not obey, my eyes closed.

"Raven? What a pretty name."

* * *

When I opened my eyes again, Esme was humming a tune from behind her easel. A quiet "No" was all I could produce before slipping back under.

For a while, I knew not how long, I slipped between two worlds, unable to tell which was which. Dreams and reality were interchangeable. I saw Esme scuttle along the floor and up the wall like a spider, holding Raven up to the moon and then biting into the soft flesh of her chest with pike-like teeth.

Then a voice rang clear. "Now," it said. I woke with a start. This time I was truly awake. My skin was sticky with sweat, my throat and mouth felt dipped in sand, every drop of moisture gone. I clambered for the water at my bedside.

It was night. The same night or the next, I did not know. The fire was low, only one candle burned. I was alone. I wouldn't get another chance.

The house crackled with silence. Every step, every movement, was amplified by the concrete walls. An intake of breath was a rush of air, the hem of my nightdress hitting my ankles crashed like waves hitting rocks. The house knew all the secrets, and it hid them well. I begged it to hide me. I ran my fingers along the cold wall as if they might show me a glimpse of the other rooms. A gentle wisp of air at my neck made me shudder. The ghosts were alive and walking tonight, I could feel it. Their anticipation was palpable. They were watching and waiting. Useless vapour.

I headed for the kitchen. Raven would be in the dungeons.

The door inside the larder was open, no need for secrets now.

I had to protect myself. I searched the kitchen until I found a sharp knife, not too big, easy to hold. I descended the steps, knife held before me. Invisible icy fingers clawed at my skin. Goosebumps rippled along my arms and legs. But I barely acknowledged my freezing misty breath, or the fact that I had lost all feeling in my toes. The darkness was impenetrable as always, but I couldn't risk a light. I used my hands to guide the way through the dank passages. Soon, a light appeared in the distance. A beacon calling.

A single candle lit the chamber containing the gallery of brides. The corners were lost to shadow. I looked to the altar and let out a sob, quickly covering my mouth to stifle the sound. Raven's blanket lay in a heap on top of it, but she wasn't there. I was too late! Unless... unless they were completing the ceremony elsewhere. There was no blood here. Esme said she ate the child's heart. Bile rose at the thought, and I gripped the stone to steady myself.

But the absence of blood gave me a glimmer of hope.

A scratching sound inside the room started up, then ceased just as quickly. I froze, waiting for something to jump from the shadows, every muscle tensed in expectation. There it was again, louder this time. A scratch and a scuffle. It was coming from one of the tombs. I walked alongside them slowly, waiting for the sound. When the scratching came this time, it was frantic and the lid of one of the small tombs lifted for a moment. I knelt beside it, bracing myself to open it, terrified of what might be inside.

I pushed the lid back and a chaos of feathers burst from the sarcophagus. I fought to hold back a scream. But it was Purdie. The bird flapped and whined about my head, but she was struggling to stay aloft. I held out my arms and Purdie tried to perch there. "Purdie, you poor thing," I said. "What have they done to you?" I gently held her battered wing. "I'm so happy to see you." Purdie strengthened my resolve. There could still be time. Raven could still be alive.

"You'll have to wait here, Purdie," I said, placing her next to the tomb, out of sight.

I left the chamber and edged along to the next room. Their room. It was well lit; the door was open. I had no plan. I couldn't take on the three of them. My hand that held the knife shook. Isaiah would have it off me in a second. I looked inside.

Zena sat looking at something in her lap. She was alone. I breathed a sigh of relief.

I strengthened my grip on the knife and stepped inside.

CHAPTER THIRTY-FIVE

"Where is she?" I said, my voice trembling slightly.

Zena sighed, slowly looking up. In her lap was the brooch I had found in my room. "I was beautiful," she said.

"That's not you," I said, but now I noticed the similarities of the woman in miniature and the one in the huge portrait hanging on the wall. How had I not realised earlier? It mattered little now.

"Where is she?" I asked again.

I heard Raven's familiar stretching and snuffling and my whole body flooded with relief. A box lay on the table at the centre of the room. The candlelight gave the illusion of warmth, but it was ice-cold down here. Raven would be blue with it; she would get sick.

With the knife pointing at Zena, I sidestepped towards the box, not taking my eyes from the old woman.

"I won't try to stop you. You can take her," she said.

"You expect me to trust you? Don't move," I said, as Zena looked ready to stand. She stayed where she was.

"It will only make it more entertaining for her."

"She'll have to find us first," I said. I was almost at the makeshift crib now.

"She will," Zena said with certainty. "She will do anything to be young again."

"And you won't? Don't act like you aren't part of this. You've seen me as nothing but meat to be slaughtered since I arrived."

"That may feel true, but it's not." She paused. "I tried to help you."

"Help me?" My voice echoed and I looked about, afraid they were listening. I lowered my voice. "You tried to kill my child, you almost killed me in the process!"

"That may have been better for you. As soon as you arrived, I wanted you gone. I couldn't bear it, not another time. But there is no escaping this bed I've made."

"I don't believe you. Why would you want rid of me? You need me."

"No. Esme needs you. But as for me, I'm tired."

"Tired?" The knife felt incredibly heavy in my hand, my arm began to shake. "You have no idea what tired is."

She laughed lightly and I was the scolded child again. But I gripped the knife tighter.

"You have seen nothing in your short life, child. Nothing."

"I know pain. I know how it feels to lose a child. I won't lose another." I could see Raven now, her face scrunched and then relaxed. She would cry soon. I couldn't pick her up one-handed.

Zena noticed my predicament. "You can take her. Like I said, I won't stop you."

I quickly put the knife down, scooped Raven into my arms and grabbed it again. She stopped squirming, back in familiar surroundings. Zena didn't move.

"Why are you letting me take her?"

"I told you, I'm tired." Zena looked back at the brooch in her lap. "I'm ready to move on to the next stage of existence, beyond this body. I've had enough."

"You will burn in the fires of hell forever."

Zena laughed out loud, and I flinched, sure that Isaiah or Esme would come running.

"That's not how it works. You think there is a Devil waiting to punish you for your sins when you die? The Devil was created by man to keep women in their place." She smiled to herself. "I'm ready for something new, and death will bring that."

"Why didn't you send my letters, then, if you wanted me gone? Ma could've helped. She would have come, and I'd have gone with her," I said.

"I couldn't do that."

"Why not?"

"You would never have been allowed to leave with your ma. That's a fantasy, child. There are certain bonds that cannot be broken. And this I think you will understand. What would you do to save that child?"

"Anything," I said.

"The bonds of blood are strong, and I cannot betray my sister, or my husband. I will have to wait until they are ready for the next stage too."

"I don't understand. Isaiah is Esme's husband. She told me."

"He is mine too. But Esme always gets what she wants."

"You're sisters," I said. It made sense. Their deep dislike of each other, Esme's teasing, Zena's defiance. No one would stand it for all those years, unless they were family. Esme had told me a story about sisters.

"Where's Mathis?"

"Forget about him. He's dead. He was dead the moment he arrived."

A strange feeling washed over me, as if someone had removed my knees and stomach like pieces of a puzzle and all my insides were slipping out. I had feared the worst, but to hear the words aloud was too much.

I stumbled from the room. Zena didn't follow me, but I had no idea how much time I had before she alerted the others. My heart ached for Mathis, a physical throbbing in my chest that made it difficult to breathe, but I had to carry on for Raven's sake. They didn't know about the raft. I would have to manage it alone.

But I couldn't go like this, in my nightgown. We would freeze in the winter sea air before reaching the mainland.

Back upstairs, I dressed quickly while Raven slept on the bed. Purdie sat next to her, quiet and still.

"Going for a walk, dear?"

I stopped. I had not heard Esme coming. I was on the other side of the room, closer to the window than to Raven. I could make it to her first, if I was fast.

I ran for the bed, but Esme was much faster than me, far too fast for an old woman. Pain burned my scalp as she grabbed a fistful of my hair and pulled me back.

"You are the feistiest one we've ever had, be proud," she said, and then brought her foot down on mine, so hard that bones cracked. I screamed in pain and fell to the floor. Raven began to cry.

"It's alright," I said to my daughter, stifling my tears. I felt a blow to the side of my face. My mouth filled with blood, my right eye blurred and the left filled with stars. I was being dragged across the floor, away from Raven. I slumped against the cold stone beneath the windows.

"I'm afraid it's not alright. Not for you, anyway."

Esme stopped before she reached Raven, as Purdie was perched on top of her swaddling.

"Shoo, bird," Esme said. Purdie squawked, stretching her

beautiful neck, opening her beak as wide as possible to flaunt the pink inside of her mouth. She stretched out her good wing defiantly, the other sitting awkwardly at her side. I could hear other ravens calling in return. They were gathering outside.

I pulled myself up, wincing in pain as my foot took some weight. I unlocked the window and a frenzy of black feathers entered, heading straight for Esme.

She screamed as the birds attacked. They fought past her waving arms to tear at her face. They clawed her scalp and neck and pulled at her wig until it fell to the floor. She stumbled backwards, towards the door. She looked ridiculous with her wispy old hair glued to her head with beeswax, and blood sprouting over her scalp, flapping her arms wildly, dancing on the spot as the birds attacked. They were relentless. I heard laughing, and then realised it was me.

"Stop." Isaiah was at the door. "Call them off," he said. He was holding Mathis by his shirt collar. Mathis hung there, lifeless, his head facing the floor, his body stretched out behind him. Isaiah pulled him up higher and I saw Mathis' swollen face, bursting black and blue on deathly pale skin, as if all the blood had left his body.

The birds receded, flying back out the open window.

Isaiah walked in, Zena followed close behind, and he dropped Mathis by the fire. I saw his fingers curl slightly. He wasn't dead, but death was inevitable if he didn't get help soon. But still, a flicker of hope burned in my chest.

"Take the child," Isaiah said. Esme, now bloody and dishevelled, picked up Raven. Purdie had moved to the side but called out in dismay. She was screeching for me. I stood immobile while Esme walked towards the door with my babe. The pain was too deep, my body was shutting down. I couldn't fight them.

"You told me he was *your* husband," I said to Esme, and she stopped, intrigued.

"Yes."

"But he's not, he's Zena's." I spat blood on the floor. It continued to pool in my mouth. My teeth had cut deep when Esme struck me.

"He is also mine."

"He doesn't love you."

Esme laughed, but it didn't have the glee of her usual cackle.

"You told me so yourself," I said. "That story about Isaiah's first wife. You said he should have married her sister, that the sister was better suited, and she was mad with grief at not being chosen."

"I tell many stories," she said. "You have been fun, child, but it's time to end this." She made to leave but I continued, louder now, making her pause. "But that story was very close to the truth, wasn't it?" She couldn't resist the drama. "Zena is your sister, and any fool can see that Isaiah loves her more than you. I could feel their connection the moment I saw them together. I assumed it was a bond that grows between a child and their nanny when the mother is absent. But now I see the truth."

Isaiah and Zena glanced at each other. It was the smallest, but most telling, of gestures. Esme did not miss it.

"What will you do when they tire of you for good?"

She took a step towards me, anger blazing. I laughed again at how ludicrous she looked in her ostentatious gown and her powdered face streaked with blood. For a moment, I tipped into madness. I wanted to anger her so much that she would put Raven down and run at me. But then what? There were three of them and one of me.

"Enough," Isaiah said. "Take the child down."

Esme checked her anger and obeyed reluctantly, closely followed by Zena. My child was gone, and I was to face Isaiah alone.

He looked at me with something close to pride in his eyes. "You are very strong," he said. He took a step towards me.

"She has your blood in her veins," I said. "You will kill your own child."

"She's not my child, none of them are. Merely catalysts."

He took another step. Zena watched from the side.

"How long will she live?"

"She will not live."

"But if she were to live, how long?"

"Hundreds of lifetimes."

"Like you?"

"Maybe, yes."

"You are immortal?"

"Not immortal. My kind grow to their prime quickly, and then the process slows down so much it would appear immortal to humans."

"Then one day you will die. And you will suffer for all the evil you have wrought." The house was breathing again, coming alive with anticipation. Isaiah could die. The seed of an idea was beginning to form.

"And it is my heart and her heart that pass on my gift."

"It is," he said. "Be thankful that you are part of something much bigger than yourself."

He took another step closer. He was within arm's reach now. I saw the knife I'd taken from the kitchen on the floor at the end of the bed. It wasn't too far away. But Isaiah was strong, and I was broken. I could hear the birds calling outside. They circled and screeched in frustration.

Then another cry, louder than the ravens, and more powerful.

Behind Isaiah, in Esme's painting, I saw that the wives were with me. They looked from the windows of the house, some flew through the air on bird-back, others sat in the cove. Dozens of them. Encouraging me.

"Your gift will change our lives," Isaiah said. "It is wasted with you. You have no idea what we could accomplish with the power that you hold." He lifted his hand and on his thumb was a thimble, unlike any I'd seen before. The top tapered to a needle point. "This won't hurt much," Isaiah said, and he put the thimble to my throat.

"I wish I could say the same," I said. I caught the confusion in his eyes before I fell to the ground. Glass exploded into the room as the eagle flew straight through the window, her magnificent cry vibrating through the walls. Outstretched talons pierced Isaiah's chest and ripped at his throat. He fell backwards, hitting the floor with a thud, stunning him for a moment. Blood splattered the carpet and pooled in the open wound at Isaiah's neck. He hit out at the bird but the ravens were upon him, clawing and stabbing at his eyes with their powerful beaks, distracting him while the eagle tore at his flesh. Blood spread across the floor as his movements slowed and his body began to shut down.

I went for the knife, terrified that Isaiah would jump up at any moment and fight the birds off. But even more terrified of what was happening to Raven right now. Anger burned my insides. The birds screeched as I let out a guttural scream, a war-cry. They moved aside as I sat on top of Isaiah, held the knife with both hands, and stabbed him in the chest as hard as I could, careful to aim just beneath the breastbone. I yanked the knife down, exposing his innards. I reached up into his chest, found his still faintly beating heart, and yanked it free of his body. Isaiah jerked as I did so, blood spurting from his mouth.

I held it before me. My hands were painted scarlet, red rivers ran down my arms and dripped from my elbows.

I bit.

CHAPTER THIRTY-SIX

The chunk of muscle and blood slipped down my throat like warm milk, settling in my stomach. A warm glow spread from there, a healing light that rushed through my blood and bones and lifted every hair on my body. I felt everything. My skin tingled in the cold breeze coming from the window. Beneath the stench of Isaiah, I caught the familiar scent of the ocean, but now I could also smell the woods: the bark of the trees, well-hidden burrows buried deep under the snow came to me, hot and heavy, the moist earth packed and fermenting beneath, the stench of a rotting trunk. It was overwhelming.

Then I screamed as the broken bones in my foot snapped back together and the gash in my cheek began to close. I fell to the floor, dropping the heart with a wet thud. The pain in my face and head increased to an intolerable level and then slowly abated. I tentatively stood, testing my new bones. No pain.

A wave of exhilaration flushed through me, leaving me breathless. I could run forever. I could jump, climb, dance. I wanted to do everything at once.

The eagle continued to feast on Isaiah's flesh and the sound was so loud I covered my ears. I heard the flecks of blood landing on the carpet like rocks. I heard the eagle's rapid heartbeat.

"Thank you," I said. She paid me no attention, so focused was she on her meal.

Another heartbeat reached me then, this one much slower. Mathis' heart was almost done. But there was no time. I had to get to Raven. "Hold on, my love," I said.

I ran from the room. The ravens followed. They flew along the corridors and down the stairs with me, some in front, some behind. I followed Raven's cries. *There's still time*, I thought, *I can make it. I am strong. I am the wind. I am flying with the birds*.

The dungeons stank of death and decay. My stomach lurched. Every drip was a bell tolling, every spider a stomping elephant. But cutting through it all was the sweet smell of my girl and the sound of her whimpering. I needed to move faster.

I came to an abrupt stop at the open door of the brides' chamber.

Esme stood behind the altar. Raven was lying on top of it, her little body exposed and flushed red from screaming. Her tiny arms and legs kicked in protest. My instinct was to run to her, but Esme was closer, she could hurt her if I took one step.

Zena stood to the side.

The brides watched intently from their portrait prisons, their eyes lit up in the dim candlelight, their lips curled in anticipation. This was a moment they had waited a long time for. I could feel their voices whispering through the walls. *End this. End this*.

Esme smiled at me, and in one swift motion picked Raven up by her ankles. My stomach flipped. The shock of it stopped Raven's cries and she dangled there, eyes wide.

The birds cawed and flapped their wings but stayed close to me. I risked a step towards her.

"I wouldn't," Esme said, and she held up a knife in her other hand.

"It's finished, Esme. Isaiah is dead."

"I can see what you did. Clever child," Esme said. "It feels good, doesn't it? The power."

"Not good enough to hurt a child for."

"Ha! Oh it is, dear. You have no idea; you are only at the beginning. It is worth a child. Many children."

I dared not look directly at Zena, but I could see she was inching closer to Esme. I could hear her heart beating faster. Zena had said she was ready for this life to be over, and now Isaiah, her love, was gone. I prayed she was ready to act against her sister. I needed her help.

"You've lived many lifetimes, Esme. You could let Raven live."

"I'm afraid I can't. Now you have taken Isaiah from me, I need time to find another like him. Raven's heart will give me that time."

"You said Isaiah's blood gave you life?" I said, inching closer. "If you kill Raven now, you'll get a few years more. Ten? Fifteen maybe? But what if you kept her?" Esme looked to Raven, considering her. "What if her blood alone gives you back your youth, just as his did? She is his daughter. She has *his* gift as well as mine."

The knife Esme held lowered a little, her grip loosening. I wouldn't get another chance. The birds dived towards her. At the same time, Zena rushed forward and grabbed Raven as Esme lost her grip to swipe at the birds.

I leapt onto the altar and watched the frenzy of birds attacking the old woman, my heart racing. I was a wild animal. My blood burned. I wanted to tear her apart, the same way the eagle had torn at Isaiah.

I leapt again, this time throwing myself onto Esme, pushing her to the stone floor. Her head cracked against it. My strength was unexpected, exciting.

I wrestled the knife from her hand and held her down by the throat.

"Death will not be kind to you," I said, and drove the knife into her chest.

I felt a collective sigh as the blade pierced her heart. I didn't want to imagine the pain and suffering that Esme had dealt these women. Their souls would be free now. They could leave this place.

Esme tried to speak but her throat was pooling with blood. She choked on it, spitting blood across her cheek. I listened as her ragged breath became weaker.

Then all was still. The flames in her pupils died to nothing. The ravens sat around us, silent. My fingers still gripped the papery flesh of her throat.

The sound of my child's cry broke the silence.

I turned to see Raven lying on the cold ground. Zena was gone.

I picked Raven up and held her close to my chest.

She settled instantly. I lowered my face to hers, smelt her head, listened to her strong heartbeat.

"We are safe, my love," I said.

We left the chamber. The sound of wings, beating in a frenzy, filled the dank air. The ravens would feast on the old woman.

Upstairs, Mathis was where I had left him. His heart was slow, struggling to beat. His breath came in sharp movements. I put Raven on the bed and picked up Isaiah's heart, now cold, untouched by the birds. I went to him, pulled his head onto my lap, and squeezed the heart. Blood dripped onto his split lips and bruised chin. I pressed harder. It dripped into his mouth. Nothing was happening. I scraped along the flesh of the heart with my nails, breaking off tiny amounts that fell into his open mouth.

"Please drink," I urged him. "Please work."

I closed his mouth in the hope he would swallow. His heartbeat slowed further and mine raised in panic. I couldn't lose Mathis. Not now. Not when it was all done. When we were finally safe.

A small sob escaped me as the swelling on his face began to smooth out. The black and purple bruising faded. His grey skin warmed to a pale pink. He was becoming himself again. I listened as his heart beat faster, growing stronger.

He gasped, as if taking his first breath, and pulled himself from the floor.

"What is this? What's happening?" He gripped his stomach and then ran his hands over his face and through his hair. He covered his ears and almost fell to the floor again.

There was fear in his eyes.

"You're alright," I soothed. "It'll be over in a minute."

He came back to himself and looked horrified at the sight of me. "What's in your hand?"

I dropped the heart. It landed with a soft thud.

Mathis looked at Isaiah lying there, the eagle sitting on him, satisfied now with her belly full. Then the bird spread her wings and screeched. Mathis and I covered our ears. Her wingspan forced us to step back, and she flew from the room.

"You did it," Mathis said. "I knew you would."

I pulled him to me and held him for a long time.

"Where are Esme and Zena?" he asked.

"Esme is dead. She's in the chamber. Zena ran off."

"We have to find her. There's no telling what she will do."

"No, we're safe. Zena isn't a threat." Mathis looked at me questioningly. "I promise, we're safe. I'm just so tired."

In a daze, I climbed onto the bed. A great tiredness had overcome me. I held Raven, and Mathis held us both. We were safe in each other's arms.

Isaiah's body still lay on the floor. The cold winter air blew freely through the broken window, but it didn't chill me. I had a lot to learn about my new body. Everything was stained scarlet, us included. None of it mattered at that moment. Perhaps it was the transformation we had endured, or the exhaustion of fighting for our lives for days on end, but we didn't speak or question it. We slept. We slept deep, like a macabre memorial portrait consecrated in stone.

I dreamt of women and their children. Smiling and gossiping and laughing together.

They were happy.

Mathis told me later that he dreamt of Anna. She had given him the little wooden box with the ointment. They had hugged, and he said he could smell lavender in her hair.

The ravens helped us find Zena the next day. She was in the woods leaning against a tree, very cold and completely dead.

We gathered the bodies of Isaiah, Esme and Zena and burned them at the cliff edge.

Then we moved the bones of the women and their babes to the cemetery. We dug a plot for them and buried them together. It would be wrong to separate them now. Mathis planted flowers on top.

We burned the portraits of Isaiah, Esme and Zena, and anything else that was particular to them. We sealed off the dungeons for good.

* * *

The fire burned bright in the sitting room. I had found an old crib for Raven and I rocked it with my foot.

Mathis sat beside me.

"Everything is done," he said.

"Yes."

"Do you want to leave? I could take the raft to the main island, get another boat."

"How would we fare out there in the world, do you think, being the way we are now?"

Mathis looked at his hands, stretched out his fingers, as if they held an answer. "I don't know. I'm still… adjusting."

I nodded. An idea was forming.

"Would you think me mad if I wanted to stay?"

"No," Mathis said, surprisingly. There was a playful sparkle in his eyes that hadn't been there before. Hope.

"You don't have to stay," I said.

"Do you want me to stay?" He smiled at me, and it seemed he almost glowed in the firelight.

"I should like that very much," I said.

He held out his hand and I took it. It held the comfort of home, and deep desire, and uncontrollable excitement all at the same time. It would take time to learn how to manage the power and intensity of my enhanced emotions. We watched the flames dance.

"This house is large." I looked about me, at the walls and ceiling. "It could house many people," I said. "People who need a place. People like us."

"We could help them," Mathis agreed. "They wouldn't have to live in fear here. I could find them."

Purdie chattered from her place at my feet. She stayed

close to me these days. Her wing was healing, but still painful.

"Purdie agrees," I said.

It was settled, then. We had a plan. A mission.

"How long do you think we have?" Mathis asked.

I shrugged and laughed quietly. "Hundreds of lifetimes."

We watched the flames again. The enormity of this thought could turn heavy, venomous even. The power we held was corruptible; the pile of bones in the graveyard was testament to that. We were newborn babes wielding double-edged swords, a bad decision away from chopping off our own heads. We would have to tread carefully.

"So," Mathis said. He was done with contemplating eternity. "Where shall we

start?"

I smiled. "I know a lady who would love to meet her granddaughter."

Raven suckled in her sleep as if agreeing with me. One glance at her perfect little face and any dark thoughts vaporised like thin clouds on a windy day. There was only love here, and I would let that love guide me.

Acknowledgements

Thank you to my editor, Gemma Creffield, and all the amazing team at Angry Robot for taking a chance on this unknown author. Everyone is so kind and friendly and has worked so hard at every stage to get this book to be the best version of itself. The whole team has been a dream to work with!

Many thanks to my agent, Hannah Sheppard, without whom I would still be scrambling. I still can't believe you saw something in my writing after witnessing those terrible first drafts! I'll be forever grateful for all the work you have put in to make this happen.

Every writer has a tribe, and I am very lucky to have a wonderful group of friends that have seen me through the highs and lows. The Bar Babes; Emma Wilson, Kate Kenzie, Emma Jackson, Kate Baker, Julie Morris, and Sandra Forder. You ladies keep me sane! Jodie Robins, for always being there and supporting me – long live our Ghost Writing weekends! Katherine Young, who has put up with me for years yapping about big dreams. Thank you. And to all the other writers and friends who have helped me on this journey – far too many to name! I'm so grateful to you all.

Of course, I never would have achieved this without the

incredible support of my family. Your faith in me has kept me going. And special thanks to my son, Hector, who is always there with the most fantastic ideas and suggestions. I do this all for you.